Stone

Stephen White

Ewan George Productions

Every first novel is special to the author and this one is dedicated to my sons George and Ewan

10 9 8 7 6 5 4 3 2 1

Stone

Stephen White

Chapter 1

September 2018, Las Casitas, Mexico

Rosario Fernandez had awoken from a deep, peaceful sleep; it was another beautiful morning and the alarm of the cockerel had once again served its purpose. Her grandson played quietly in the room next door. Sitting on his bed, he was surrounded by his books, soft toys scattered his floor, cascading from his bed onto the colourful mat which was home to his size 12 Mickey Mouse slippers. Young Frankie was a patient young fellow of just six years old and he was looking forward to his promised day out at the beach with his grandma. His dark complexion, thick curly hair, chocolate brown eyes, cheeky dimples and husky voice made him irresistible to Rosario's friends and everyone adored the little soul.

Devoted Rosario was in her seventies but still attractive, one could tell that in her day she was easy on the eye to the local fishermen. She had been a loyal wife to her husband Pedro Fernandez for 50 years but he'd sadly passed last winter. A strong woman with firm family morals, Rosario was respected in the local village. Her dark salt and pepper coloured wavy hair and unusually big green eyes would make her stand out in a crowd. The old fishermen would still give her an admiring glance whenever she ventured down to the Marina of Las Casitas.

Rosario drew back the curtains to reveal another blistering hot summer's day and admired the beautiful views overlooking the beaches of Las Casitas. She had promised Frankie a fun trip to the beach, her most favourite place of all time. Her childhood memories consisted mostly of family days out where hours upon hours were spent on the white sands of local beaches. Rosario's family didn't have much money back in the day but quality family time was everything to the Fernandez family. As her dear old father used to say, 'love and fun needn't cost a sum' and there was not a shortage of love in this family. As she passed from her bedroom to the kitchen, she caught a glance of her father's picture on the wall, she smiled at it and continued to get things ready for the day ahead.

As she walked into the kitchen, a small voice behind her called out, "Morning grandma," she turned around to find Frankie standing at the door with his towel and bucket ready for the beach.

"Bless you, dear Frankie, you really are keen to go aren't you?"

"Si grandma," he said, with his big brown eyes peering at her. Rosario grabbed the picnic that she had prepared the previous evening and she took some cold juice from the fridge and put it in a cooler bag inside her picnic basket. She helped Frankie fasten his sandals and once they were both ready, she took him by the hand and they headed out the door.

It was a short walk to the beach, down a cobbled stone path. Traditional hanging baskets complimented the white stone walls with beautiful colours along the streets, with broken clay pots and tiny bird cages above rustic doorways. There were three skinny dogs, looking for scraps, sniffing about begging for food, standing outside a doorway as Rosario and Frankie made their way down the lane. Strays in Mexico were very common and mange was normally present in these poor unfortunate creatures. If they didn't die of starvation, it was mange or rabies which finally finished them off. "Shoo, be away with you!" Rosario stamped her feet. She was concerned for them but was also aware of the disease some carry and was very protective of young Frankie.

As Rosario and Frankie passed through the narrow streets, locals would call out 'Buenos Dias Rosario.' The old lady was a well-known face in the community. She had no need to answer everyone, just a slight nod, accompanied by her delightful, infectious smile would be enough to acknowledge the friendly locals. She clutched Frankie's hand tighter and proudly proceeded towards the golden beaches.

They crossed the road and walked down some steps onto the beach, finally settling for a cove which consisted of a small rock pool which Frankie loved. He sat with his feet buried in the sand and quietly watched as the small crabs scurried along the beach and then disappeared into the sand a few feet away. This was one of the highlights of the day for Frankie, aside from digging up half the beach with his small red plastic shovel. Frankie thought of his prized find of six months ago, he wasn't quite sure what it was but he loved it nevertheless, to him it looked like a clock but his father had told him it was a speedometer from a motorcycle. He had forgotten to show his grandmother as he had left it an old bucket just inside his shed at home with a collection of colourful rocks and shells from his previous visits to the beach. Bored with digging, he picked up his rubber ring, "not without your armbands!" his grandmother shouted.

At just six, Frankie had not taken to swimming that well which was unusual as most of the young Mexican children were confident in the water from a young age. The rubber ring, bucket and plastic shovel were too much for the young lad to carry and stubbing his toe on an object sticking out of the sand, he howled and fell to the sand but the brave young lad jumped to his feet. Rosario, not wanting to make a big deal of his fall, brushed him off and asked her grandson to go catch their dinner. "I'm going to catch a huge shark and we can cook it tonight," said the excited little lad. Rosario ruffled Frankie's hair and smiled at his naivety.

He plunged his bucket into the deep clear water and monotonously shovelled it out and watched it run back to the shoreline creating a bubbling foam. It was on his fourth trip to the water that he noticed something glistening inside the bucket, reflecting from the sweltering hot sun. It looked like gold he thought as he reached his hand into the bucket. Tightly gripping it in his hand, he wiped away the sand with his tiny fingers. Desperate to show someone his newfound treasure, he raced back up the beach to his grandmother. "Abuelita, abuelita, look what I've found!" he shouted. He came to a standstill with a small jump in the sand which kicked sand over Rosario's feet. He offered his treasure in his wet hands to his grandmother and she reached out to look. She could see it had writing on it, so she reached in her bag for her reading glasses. Putting them on, she moved it closer to her eyes. There, faintly engraved on the back, were the words 'Rachael and Stone Forever'. In an instant, Rosario was taken back over 30 years, almost like a punch in the stomach. She glanced out to sea then she stared at Frankie for a few moments and ran her fingers through his wet, salty, dark hair and gave the cute little guy a beaming smile. Frankie could sense something had touched his grandma deeply. "What's wrong grandma?" asked Frankie. The old lady had tears trickling down her warm olive skin as she looked out to sea once again. She then reached her hand out towards her anxious grandson, taking his, she pulled him towards her.

"It's ok darling, I believe a miracle has just happened! This special pendant you've found means someone very special wanted you to find this today and this means so much to grandma, more than you could ever imagine. One day I will explain everything to you but for now, just know you have made me so happy and we must keep this pendant very safe and show your mother when we get back home.

Chapter 2

32 years earlier, Summer 1986, Butterfly Beach, Santa Barbara, California

It was Friday night around 10.30pm, another warm, humid evening towards the end of the summer season. Michael Schiano brushed the grit from his leather-bound knees as he stood up by the side of the road. "Can you hear that Jimmy?" he said.

Jimmy Nash was Michael's dearest friend in the world. He was a handsome guy with dark curly hair and dark green eyes. He was much smaller than Michael but some people would mistakenly take them as brothers. He jumped off his motorcycle and positioned his ear flush to the ground pretending to witness the sound of oncoming warriors. "I think so," said Jimmy smiling.

"Did you feel the vibrations man? This is it buddy, it's now or never!" Michael shouted. The two friends were always playing practical jokes on one another. They both laughed, clearly amused by the prospect of hearing distant bikers.

It wouldn't be long before the sound of oncoming bikers would really be heard in the distance, heading towards Butterfly Beach in Santa Barbara, they were making their way to an annual race meeting called Devil's Run. The Blood Rangers and Satan's Angels were two of the most respected motorcycle gangs in the whole of California, most local folk would gather at Dawson's Point to catch a glimpse of the bikes.

This year they would witness Michael Schiano and Marco Sanchez battle it out to the top of the mountain known as Spike's Edge, aptly named due to it's sheer drop just behind the finish line. The rules were simple, the first rider to cross the rope wins. Any rider crossing the marker too fast, was likely to go over. The winner would take a cash prize and gain massive respect between fellow riders. For the last three years, Marco Sanchez had beaten Michael Schiano fair and square. Michael was a worthy leader to the Blood Rangers and the last race had been remarkably close but Sanchez just scraped in the win.

Michael was branded with the nickname Stone after he'd fallen off his bike at high speed in the last race and bounced down the tarmac for almost 100 yards. Remarkably, he walked away with minor injuries thanks to his leathers and helmet. Witnesses said Michael resembled a stone being skimmed on a lake so the name stuck with him after that and even Michael became accustomed to it after a while, often forgetting to answer to his own name.

Stone was 24 years old, he lived just outside Santa Barbara with his mother, Maria Schiano who was a war widow. Maria had moved from Ireland to California when she was just 21 and she'd fallen for a young handsome Italian guy who had just enlisted in the US Army. Maria had been a beautiful young lady in her time but sadly she was now in extremely poor health, gradually fading away with severe Multiple Sclerosis at just 50 years old. She was extremely frail with long grey scraggly hair, confined to a chair most of the time but always remained in good spirits. She had the bluest eyes and the most infectious smile which could light up a room. Most folk felt she should really be in a nursing home but Stone wouldn't have any of it and he promised Maria he would never give up on her. Although she wanted her son to be free of the burden, she was secretly grateful to him for sticking by his decision.

The Schiano family survived on a small war widow's pension and Stone's modest wage as a local mechanic. Stone never knew his father that well as he was killed in Vietnam back in 1968 when Stone was just 6 years old. Maria often told Michael how he reminded her of her dear husband Donnie. She would often reminisce and tell Michael interesting stories about him, like how they met at a local dance and ran all the way home in the rain getting soaked right through. "He took me home Mickey and took the shirt off his back and put it over my head to shelter me from the rain. Dear, dear Donnie." Maria Schiano had never stopped grieving for young Private Donnie, Michael believed part of his mother had died alongside his father in Vietnam.

Maria simply idolised her son, as Michael did his mother, it was clear to see by most of the community they had a special bond between them. Michael simply cherished his mother and wanted nothing more than to make her proud of him. Although he could do no wrong in Maria's eyes, he always felt that he'd let her down by not providing a better standard of living for her. He earned a modest wage as a local mechanic at Redwing's garage but he kind of wished he'd set his expectations higher. Michael had fallen into this line of work purely because of his infatuation with motorcycles. He wished he could afford a more comfortable life for his mother but unbeknown to him, just having him around was enough for dear Maria.

Michael knew he had to keep certain things from his mother, especially concerning his part in the Blood Rangers and the fact that tonight he was racing in a brutal tournament that carried high risks but he needed the $5000 purse so he could improve things a little at home, perhaps buy some new furniture or a better bed for his mother and a softer armchair he thought. Either way, Michael was accepting nothing less than a win tonight against Satan's Angels leader, Marco Sanchez.

The time was now 11pm and Stone was starting to feel the pressure as this was his last attempt to win back respect from all those that had doubted him. The noise of rumbling motorcycle engines had become somewhat crisp in the air now. It was a sound like nothing else to Stone and Jimmy, they would feel the hairs on the back of their necks rise as the rumble of distant engines became clearer in the air. Marco Sanchez and his crew were close to Dawson's Point, this was the usual meeting place and the starting point for Devil's Run. Stone, Jimmy and the rest of the Blood Rangers set out earlier this year as they wanted to be waiting at Dawson's Point for the rival gang, a psychological tactic which they hoped would unnerve them. For the last three years, Sanchez and his boys had been there early, as if to show no fear and their willingness to get on with the race, so Stone wanted to mix things up a little this year.

Each rider could use any machine up to 1000cc, mostly Japanese bikes, however, last year Marco Sanchez had beaten Stone on his Ducati 750, an Italian brand, bought with his financial rewards from the last few wins. Sanchez was Satan's Angels most respected leader, with three years to his belt and most thought he owned Devil's Run. This year he was expected to make this his fourth year in a row but Stone had other plans, using his loyal and faithful Honda CBR 900, still bearing the wounds from the previous year. Stone was feeling more confident this year, he was determined to win. He had been so close in the last race and if it hadn't been for his faulty brakes, he most likely would have won but that's just how it goes. This year's prize money was five thousand dollars which was raised through low key sponsors. Both Stone and Sanchez had organised the sponsors' advertisements through bike meetings and charity events the previous season.

Mandy Roberts was invited along by her boyfriend Gregg Phillips, a work buddy of Stone and Jimmy at Redwing's Garage, a local automotive service and repair centre. Gregg was a tall, thin guy with wavy, blonde hair and freckled skin. He was always such great fun to be around and everyone loved him. "Mandy, you watch this tonight, I swear you will love it baby," said Gregg in his broad South American accent.

"Really? What is Devil's Run?" asked Mandy.

"You mean you've never heard of it?"

"No, don't look at me like that Gregg, you know my parents hardly ever let me out," she giggled. Mr and Mrs Roberts were strict Catholics, they only wanted to protect their daughter from improper shenanigans in the late evenings. Although eighteen, they still expected her to respect their rules and be home before the bars closed and the streets filled with drunken yobs. Butterfly Beach had been known for local youth violence in the past and they idolised their daughter as she was their only child.

Mandy was a pretty girl with long brown hair, long legs and beautiful big brown eyes. She was slightly ditsy and said silly things but Gregg loved everything about her. "Well honey, it's like this, Devil's Run is a race between the two leaders of each crew. In tonight's race, my buddy Stone represents the Blood Rangers and he's up against Marco Sanchez, the leader of the rival gang, Satan's Angels. You see those bikes rolling in over the hill, well that's them. The guy you see over there with the flash bike and shades on is Marco Sanchez. At midnight tonight, a rope will be stretched across the road and as soon as the village church bell sounds midnight, the rope is dropped and the bikes race to the top of Spike's Edge, timed badly though or travelling too fast across the line, it's certain death! The fastest bike to cross the rope at the finish line wins the race."

"They must be crazy, why would anyone want to do that?" asked a rather confused Mandy.

"For $5000 Dollars and the respect that comes with it," answered Gregg.

Satan's Angels had started circling around the Blood Rangers, trying desperately to intimidate them but Stone just smiled at them, his eyes focused on Marco Sanchez staring through his dark glasses into his soul.

Marco was undeterred, feeling no need to rise to the cajoling and unnecessary hype.The time was now 11.30pm, with just half an hour to go before the big race.

A makeshift beer tent had been erected for the occasion and most of the bikers were hanging around, desperate to be fuelled with alcohol.

Stone always avoided booze for this kind of tournament. Previous participants had drunk for Dutch courage but Stone wanted to be sharp, alert and on top of his game to secure a win. Marco, however, was already sinking a bottle Bud in full view of everyone. "Crazy fool," said Jimmy. "Look at him, he thinks he's got this year in the bag but I know it's yours this year buddy, I can just feel it, I know you're going to win," Jimmy assured Stone.

"You bet I will, I'll kick his ass this year Jimmy, you watch me." The two friends laughed and punched each other on the shoulder in a boisterous affectionate manner. Marco looked up and caught a glance of this, he opened his throttle in a short burst and popped a wheelie in their direction, as the front wheel kissed the ground, he shouted out across the way to Stone.

"What are you looking so goddamn happy about boys? Aren't you bored with getting your arse whipped every year?"

"Whatever Marco, just get ready to race," Stone shouted back. Nothing was going to faze him tonight, he was more focused than ever. Marco muttered something under his breath and just grabbed hold of the nearest girl, pulling her towards him.

"Get your pretty little ass over here honey," he insisted. The frightened girl pulled away which angered Marco, so he dragged her back towards him.

Marco was of skinny build with a shaved head and pitted complexion, his skeleton-like features added to his rough exterior which some women found attractive, so he was never short of a girlfriend or two.

Stone was blessed with good looks, from Italian-Irish blood he was of muscular build with dark wavy hair, olive skin and blue eyes. Whilst most women found his handsome, rugged looks appealing, others would suggest he was too pretty and soft for them. Stone would never walk away from trouble but he never looked for it. He had a reputation for standing his ground, never backing down and usually coming out on top but deep inside he was a soft gentle type of guy only his mother really knew. Although never short of admirers, Stone had never found true love or been in a long-term relationship.

As the crowd became more excited and the atmosphere a little more tense, Stone checked his watch which was a battered old-time piece, left to him by his late father but it carried huge sentimental value.

The time was 11.50pm, time to get over to the starting line and get this race underway, he thought.

As Stone's bike glided through the crowds, folk cheered out, "Good luck Stone, you can do it man." Satan's Angels riders' begrudgingly moved out of his way but this still did not faze him at all. As he reached the familiar sight of the thick rope laying haphazardly across the starting line, he could feel the adrenaline rush starting to build inside, his breathing started to quicken as his thumping heart gained momentum but he tried to remain as calm as he could, he didn't want anyone to notice his increasing nerves.

Marco followed, filtering through the crowds, revving his engine in a tacky fashion to gain attention. As he pulled over alongside Stone, he glanced over and said nothing, just stared through his dark shades. One of his crew handed him a black, shiny helmet which he kissed before taking off his shades and pulling it over his head through the soft cushioned lining and adjusting his chin strap and visor. Stone had a silver helmet, with black visor, slightly grazed from last year's misfortune but it served its purpose and Stone secured it on tightly.

The two men were staring ahead, a darkened poorly lit street awaited them for the first few hundred yards of the race then they would be greeted by a sharp bend at the end of Belmont's Walk, followed by a sudden climb to Spike's Edge. For Colin Murphy and Nick Summers it was another race they would launch and as bike enthusiasts neither one belonged to any biker group, so as impartial race officials, they were always trusted. Colin took hold of the end of the rope and started to take up slack across the road, Nick did the same and before long the rope was in place, taut across the road at waist level.

It was now a few minutes before midnight and you could almost smell the tension in the air. Spectators started to gather around, others would take up residence along the road finding an ideal spot to witness the take off and see the bikes fly by. For a split second, there was silence in the crowd, everyone was feeling nervous for the riders.

Colin and Nick would now wait with their ears fully alert, the crowd were still silent with just seconds to go before the beautiful but haunting sound of the church bells. The two warriors started to count down in their heads, 5,4,3,2,1 and then they rang. Colin and Nick let go of the rope, it seemed to drop to the ground in slow motion but the riders were off. Everyone started to yell and cheer as the bikes made an almighty raw as they took off towards Belmont's Walk.

Marco, a few feet ahead, started to scream at the top of his voice, "yee haw!" Stone, close on his tail, remained focused and silent inside his helmet. The bikes ripped through Belmont's Walk and as they both started to anticipate the first bend, they adjusted themselves on their seats ready to lean. The secret was to take the bend as fast as possible and then open the throttle down the first straight, this is where riders usually lose it, by not leaning far enough over and hitting the brakes too quickly. Stone was just a few feet from Marco's back wheel before he dropped the throttle. The speedometer counted down from 90mph as he leaned hard, his knees scraped the surface of the road, his leathers grazing slightly as he pulled his faithful Honda upright before throttling up along the second straight. Marco had handled the bend remarkably well and was heading off fast, it was like a corkscrew, each bend with no barriers added to the thrill of the rider. Below, there was a drop boasting jagged rocks and there was a salty mist as the sea crashed against the shore. It happened to be a full moonlit sky, which although beautiful, gave a feeling of evil in the air and some folk believed the Devil would ride with you and interfere with the bike. Spike's Edge had a history of riders misjudging it and falling to their deaths. The name Devil's Run arrived from this myth.

As the two riders battled it out around each challenging bend, Marco would move from left to right to secure being the front runner, trying to deter Stone from passing on either side but Stone remained focused, waiting for his moment. As they approached the final bend, something inside Stone's head was nagging him, 'It's now or never man, you take him on this bend, or you lose!' He started to shout to himself as the adrenaline rush started to build higher and faster, 'No, not this time Marco, tonight is my night.'

Something snapped in his mind, he started to tighten his grip on the handlebars, twisting the throttle back as far as it would go. As the two guys' bravely approached the aptly named Death Corner, Marco caught a glance in his mirror of Stone pulling up fast behind him, 'What's that crazy fool doing?' he murmured to himself. 'You can't take me at this speed, not on Death Corner you maniac.' They were hitting close to 100 mph, this was too fast to make it around the bend in one piece.

As Marco started to release the tension on his throttle with just a few hundred yards to go, he could see Stone in his mirror closer than ever. With just seconds to go, Stone flashed by Marco at a phenomenal speed just yards before Death Corner. He dropped hard on the throttle, pumping the brakes and managed to slide turn at 70mph and somehow held it until throttling up towards Spike's Edge. Marco was furious as he knew he had to work double hard to pull this one back now. Stone just seemed to travel like a bullet, nothing was going to stop him now. He'd survived Death Corner, all he had to do now was cross the 200 yard finish line, without miscalculating it and flying off the edge. He could see Marco gaining quickly in his mirror and started to panic slightly, 'Come on man you got this,' he was telling himself. Everyone below at Dawson's Point could see the headlights of the bikes but had no idea who was who. At the finish line, the rope was waiting across the chalky track.

To witness this year's winner was Jess Cunningham who was with the Blood Rangers and Johnny Peters with Satan's Angels. Both men were peering into the darkness as they stood firm by the finish marker. Jess could just about make out a headlight in the distance and you could hear the thrashed engines being forced to their limits. Johnny joked with Jess, "Here comes Marco."

"Don't be so sure," said Jess. The two guys were just about able to decipher what colour the bike was in first line position, they both soon realised it was Stone's black and gold Honda.

Stone was just about holding it but Marco was close on his tail, with just seconds to go and both riders knew their fate should they miscalculate their speed. Stone was doing way over 100mph with just 300 yards to go and by this time Marco knew Stone was pushing to win at any cost, maybe even his life. Stone, now just a few more yards away from victory held tight on the throttle. Marco started to drop speed as he approached the danger zone but Stone was still travelling at high speed, determined to maintain just enough to hit the finish line. He shot over the marker at 120mph and then immediately dropped the throttle and hit the breaks. Marco was fighting to pull his bike to a halt, when just in front of him, Stone hit the ground and skidded towards Spike's Edge but luck was on his side as he came to an abrupt stop underneath the heavy Honda just a few feet away from the edge. He looked up to the sky, and thanked God he was still in one piece.

Jess ran over to him, he was shaking with excitement, when a voice came over the walkie talkie, "How's it going Jess?" asked Nick Summers. Jess held out his trembling hand and helped Stone to his feet, clearly shaken by the close shave he had just witnessed. He winked at Stone before holding down the trigger on the walkie talkie.

"Well Nick," he said calmly, "we have a winner guys." He deliberately paused for a second, then he yelled at the top of his voice, "Stone, Stone is this year's winner of Devil's Run!!" It fell silent down below, as if the news had taken everyone by surprise and a while to sink in, then suddenly the sound of crowds cheering, whistling, applauding could be heard at the top of Spike's Edge. The atmosphere was electric. The sound was also coming over the radio, you could almost feel the vibrations in the air.

Marco came over with his head held low, in an exceptionally soft and defeated voice he held out his hand to Stone, "Well done you crazy son of a bitch," he said, with a slight grin on his face. Stone took Marco by the hand.

"Thanks man, that means a lot buddy."

The riders brushed themselves down, checked over their bikes which were still hot from the thrashing and started to make their way down to Dawson's Point. Stone's bike was scratched up a little more and the left side indicator was smashed clean off but otherwise it was still in good shape. The exhausted warriors mounted their bikes and continued down to Dawson's Point with Jess and Johnny not far behind them. Everyone down below had formed a line to welcome the new champion. As Stone got closer, he could hear his faithful crew chanting his name, "Stone, Stone, Stone!" It was a surreal atmosphere but Stone was enjoying every single second of it. As he passed through the crowds at the end of the line, he was greeted by Colin and Nick. Stone put the bike down on its stand and walked over to a small stage which had erected in front of the beer tent. As he stepped up, Nick and Colin shook his hand and passed him a large envelope containing $5000. He turned around and everyone applauded him, including Marco, it was very admiral of him, Stone thought to himself.

Jimmy, Gregg and Mandy rushed over and hugged their friend, Mandy was beside herself with the excitement of it all.

The celebrations went on until the early hours of Saturday morning but Stone was concerned about his mother so headed home about 2am after saying goodbye to his loyal friends and supporters.

The time was nearly 2.30am when he approached his road so he was being extra careful not to disturb his neighbours and especially his dear mother, so at the top of his road he dropped the rev's on his bike and drifted down his street with the engine just ticking over. As he approached his small house, he killed the engine and wheeled the bike through the small green gate at the front of the property and parked it at the side. He tried desperately hard to keep the noise down as he made his way to the front door and gently opened it.

He was being as quiet as he could, however, it seemed the harder he tried the louder the door squeaked, so he quickly pushed the door to allow himself room to slide in and close it behind himself. Just two steps into the hallway, he heard his mother call out, "Is that you Stone?"

"Yes ma," he answered, amazed by the fact she was still awake.

"Are you ok son?" she said, in her soft voice.

"Yes, I'm fine Ma. I tried not to wake you," Stone answered.

"I couldn't rest until you were home safe honey." Stone walked into the lounge to see his mother snuggled up on her faithful rocking chair, with a blanket around her. He kissed her on the forehead and fetched her another blanket as there was a slight chill in the air. Maria would usually find the old chair more comfortable than her bed, as the cruel illness was painful on her joints.

After feeling satisfied his mother was settled, he went to bed himself to catch some well-deserved rest. Just six hours into a deep sleep, he was woken by the telephone in the lounge so he jumped to his feet and ran to answer it, almost tripping over a bundle of clothes by the side of his bed.

"Hello," Stone said in a husky sleepy voice.

"It's me, Jimmy."

"Jimmy, what time is it man?"

"It's nearly 9-30 buddy. Me and a few of the guys were wondering if you want to join us around lunchtime at Jo's diner, do you fancy it man?"

Stone paused for a second, still feeling sleepy. "Ok but I gotta go into town first to get my ma's medication, then I'll be with you."

"OK buddy, 'WOOHOO!" Jimmy shouted, before putting the phone down.

Stone took a shower, put on some clean clothes and went to see how Maria was doing.

"Hey ma," he whispered. She opened her eyes slowly. "Can I get you anything?"

"Ah no thank you," she answered in a soft timid voice. "You're a good boy Michael, a real good boy." She closed her eyes and moaned to herself slightly. Her pain would always seem to torment her more in the mornings and sleeping in a chair was not an ideal.

"Mum, I want to buy you a new bed, this can't be healthy sleeping in a chair all night." Maria told him it was ok for now and to please save his money but it was breaking the young lad's heart seeing her propped up in a chair, day in, day out.

"Hey Ma, I'm going to collect your medication later," Stone said.

"Oh, that's great Mickey, thank you," answered Maria. She had called him Mickey ever since he was a baby, he loved Mickey Mouse as a child so this name had stuck.

Maria was on various pain killers and other drugs to keep the MS under control and every month Stone would collect them from old man Johnson's drug store at Butterfly Beach.

Stone said goodbye to his mother, opened the front door and walked out onto the small stepping stones his father had laid many years back, not long after they moved into the modest little house. Leading away from the house, down the pathway was a slightly battered picket fence that his father had also made. He paused for a moment, looked up at the sky and said, "Hey pa, don't worry about a thing, I'm taking care of everything now, you'll see."

He climbed onto his bike and headed to the drug store, feeling optimistic about making things better for his mother at home.

Chapter 3

Old man Johnson had run a traditional drug store for many years and had passed it down to his son Charlie in the 60's. Charlie was a serious old man, slightly withered and quietly spoken but most of the local folk seem to respect him.

His wife, Jenny, was a nervous type of woman, never said boo to a goose, just the occasional endearment to her loyal and faithful customers. The summer staff would be grateful for the opportunity to work at Johnson's, however, they were always keen to shut up shop in the evenings to break away from the strange couple, never keen to work extra hours, just happy to get down to the beach to enjoy the long summer evenings.

This year, Charlie Johnson had hired two young girls on school leave through the summer months. Rachael Jenson, who was from a wealthy family in New York and Katie Goldberg, from a local family of Jewish descent.

The two girls were strangers at the start of the summer but since working at the drug store they had become good friends.

Rachael was a stunning looking young woman, about 5ft 7inches tall, with dark hair, olive skin and piercing green eyes like emeralds. She had a bubbly personality and a figure most girls would die for. She was well liked by the customers, especially the locals, who had really taken to her in just a few weeks. Rachael only ever spent the summer months at Butterfly Beach as this was where her parents owned their summer retreat. Christopher and Susan Jenson were strict with Rachael and she rarely left the large manor house, situated close to Butterfly Beach but as she was coming up for 19, they had finally given her permission to let her socialise a little more and her father thought working in the store would be good for her confidence, so he arranged it with the Johnson's just before the family arrived.

Katie, however, was known to most of the locals as she was raised in the area. She was short and chubby, with reddish hair, dark brown eyes and a generous nose. Unbeknown to her, most people found her delightful, she had a gentle face, with an infectious smile that would light up the faces of all those that visited the store.

The girls would often be found laughing, mainly because Charlie and Jenny could be so clumsy around the store and the girls would try very hard not to be noticed when they giggled together but it made working in the old store much more fun. The two youngsters would try to hold back their laughter until leaving the store at the end of the day then they would fall about, creasing up at all the funny things that Charlie and Jenny did throughout the day.

As Stone approached the store, Katie looked up whilst still stacking the shelves. The sound of the throaty bike would often get people's attention when pulling into town. Katie knew Stone and his mother as they were regular customers of Johnson's. She recognised the sound of his bike whenever he would pass the store and she would mutter softly to herself 'there goes Stone.'

She had a secret crush on him, as most of the local girls did but she never told a soul. Stone had parked directly outside the store, he jumped off his bike and walked through the doors, sounding the entrance bell.

Rachael was making coffee at the time for Charlie and Jenny as they were stock taking. She'd heard the bell but she knew Katie was dealing with the customers as they came in.

Katie blushed slightly as Stone looked over the counter towards her, "Hey Katie, how are you?"

Katie put down the boxes of soap she was holding and walked over to the counter,

"I'm good thanks Stone, how's it going?"

"I'm fine thanks Katie. Things are looking up actually, last night was a rush," he smiled.

"Oh yes, I heard you won, nice to see you in one piece," she laughed.

Rachael had finished her coffee and walked through the doorway where she could see Katie was behaving awkwardly, somehow timid and shy and she was anxious to see who her friend was talking to. Rachael looked over the counter and could see a tall, dark handsome guy with the cheekiest smile she had ever seen He glanced over at her and seemed to just stare at her for a while. He had no intention of coming across rude but he was speechless. As their eyes met he felt a warm sensation run through his body. He had never had this feeling around a girl and he felt instantly connected to this beautiful soul.

There was an uncomfortable silence in the store. Rachael and Stone were equally attracted to one another, it was clear to see, thought Katie which made her feel a little jealous.

"Hi, you must be new here?" said Stone. Rachael came closer to the counter, she smiled and answered.

"Yes, I'm just helping out through the holidays."

"Oh, I see, I hope Katie's looking after you," he said with a grin. Rachael laughed.

"Actually she's a terrible teacher, I still have no idea what I'm doing," she said with a wink in Katie's direction. Katie laughed in the background whilst preparing Maria's medication.

The two girls were clearly good friends, thought Stone. He really liked this beautiful girl and hoped he would see a lot more of her through the summer season.

Katie eventually came back to the front counter with Stone's completed prescription. She handed it over to him and wished Maria well. Stone smiled at both girls and thanked Katie for the medication.

"It was a pleasure to meet you Rachael," he said, as he turned towards the door.

"Nice to meet you too," she replied smiling.

Both girls watched him leave, almost in slow motion, they were both taken back by his good looks and charm.

Stone reached for the door but turned back and took a final look at the beautiful new assistant before leaving.

Both girls paused for a moment and then looked at each other and fell into fits of giggles. "Oh my God, who was that Katie?" Rachael asked excitedly.

"His name is Michael but everyone calls him Stone. I've known him most of my life, he's a great guy and lives with his poorly mother," answered Katie.

"Isn't he just so cute and so damn handsome," said Rachael. Katie laughed.

"Join the queue, he's probably the coolest guy in Butterfly Beach and very popular with most of the women."

"In California you mean," Rachael said laughing.

"Well I must say in all the time I've known him, he has never been short for words but today he was, you certainly made an impression on him," said Katie, slightly enviously.

Chapter 4

As Stone returned home, he was still smiling to himself. His encounter at the drug store with Katie and her friend had certainly stirred his mind up a little. He pulled into the side alley, jumped off his bike with a spring in his step as he walked up to the door.

When he got inside, he was whistling cheerfully along the hallway, looking forward to seeing the lads at the diner and talking to Jimmy about the beautiful girl at Johnson's.

"Hey Ma, I got your medication," he called out.

"Michael, were you whistling?" asked Maria. Stone walked into the dining room to see his mother. He was greeted by her huge smile, she was always happy to see her son but especially when he was so cheerful and upbeat. Perhaps he had a little good news she thought.

Permanently tormented by discomfort, Maria still found the strength to laugh with her son and the pair would often have wonderful moments like this where they would laugh together at the smallest things and these were treasured moments for both of them.

Stone sat down on the scruffy old floral couch opposite his ma; the faithful old couch had been there all his life. Maria would never part with it as her husband Donnie had bought it not long after they had set up home together. Maria believed in her own way that by keeping everything Donnie had loved would somehow keep him close to her.

As Stone sat back to relax on the old couch ready to explain why he was so cheerful, there was a knock at the door, it must be Jimmy he thought.

He opened the door and sure enough Jimmy was standing there with a huge grin on his face.

"Hey dude, I just went to the drug store looking for you and I overheard some hot chick talking to Mandy Roberts about you," Jimmy said.

Stone laughed, "You mean the new girl at Johnson's? What did she say Jimmy?"

"Something about a hot guy picking up his mother's medication, she must need her eyes tested," Jimmy grinned and the two friends laughed.

"Hey Jimmy, give me five minutes and I'll be with you buddy."

"Ok lover-boy," Jimmy joked. "I'll hang outside for you buddy and remember, we're all meeting at Bar Lomas tonight. I think Mandy, Katie and that girl from the drug store are going and by the way, her name is Rachael," he said smiling.

Stone closed the door and went back to his mother in the lounge. He bent down and kissed Maria on the forehead. Maria smiled and asked who it was at the door. "Oh it was only Jimmy ma. A few of the guys are getting together for lunch today and then again tonight at Bar Lomas. Would you be ok here on your own tonight if I went to join them?"

"Of course I'll be ok honey, there's some interesting stuff on the TV tonight so I'll be totally fine," said Maria.

Stone asked her if she wanted something to eat or drink but she said she would see to it. She would have good and bad days, sometimes she managed to get around the house easily but Stone had noticed she had seemed to struggle more over the past few weeks.

Stone joined Jimmy and a few of the guys for some lunch. They were laughing and joking about the previous night, mainly about the look on Marco's face when Stone was handed the prize money. After a couple of hours, he told the lads he wanted to go home and check on Maria. He insisted on paying the bill before he left as he was feeling flush from his winnings so wanted to treat his loyal friends. He agreed to meet them in Bar Lomas later that evening.

Bar Lomas was at Butterfly Beach close to the sea. They had various local bands performing including Vamps Lightning, Blizzard Nights and Dusky Manners, mostly heavy rock bands, extremely popular with the young folk. The word on the street was that most of the local youngsters on summer break would be attending tonight, so it was expected to be busy. Stone was secretly hoping Rachael would be there tonight, especially as Jimmy had mentioned it earlier. As the lads pulled up outside the bar, most of the Blood Rangers were already parked up and inside the place. Stone and Jimmy jumped off their bikes and walked over towards the rustic entrance to the bar. Vamps Lightening were blasting out their latest song, the boys were all lined up knocking back shots, the bar was soaked already in spilt beer and traces of salt and lemon.

"Hey guys, how are you?" Stone asked his half-smashed buddies.

"Man, my main Man," said a slurring Ben Abbotts with an empty shot glass still in his hand. Ben was a loyal member of the crew and he idolised Stone. The boys all exchanged man hugs whilst Ben got some more drinks in.

As the evening started to liven up, Stone couldn't help keep glancing at the entrance, hoping to see Rachael walk through the door.

Vamps Lightning started to really get the crowd going and the atmosphere in the bar was really starting to heat up. "Hey loverboy, look who's just walked in," said Jimmy. Stone looked back over to the door and could see Mandy, Katie and Rachael heading towards the bar. Just the very sight of Rachael took his breath away, she was wearing a black leather jacket, pink t-shirt, and tight blue jeans. Her hair was long and wavy and she seemed to have more make-up on than she did in the drugstore. She looked stunning he thought and it seemed a lot of the guys in the bar had noticed the three girls walk in, most of them seem to be staring at Rachael. Stone was like a rabbit in headlights, transfixed on her beautiful face.

When their eyes met, they were both equally attracted to one another, like a magnet being drawn towards a metal surface. Rachael and the girls all looked great, it was clear to see that they had dressed up for the gig and made a huge effort. Rachael raised her arm and waved at Stone to get his attention. Unbeknown to her she already had it, Stone was simply smitten by her presence. He raised his hand awkwardly and smiled. The girls walked up to the other side of the bar where some of Katie's friends were hanging out, she introduced Rachael to them all and Mandy ordered some drinks.

As the evening moved on, Stone and Jimmy started to feel a little wild, the drinks were flowing and the music seemed louder. Rachael was trying hard to think of an excuse to speak to Stone, hoping that Katie and Mandy would join the lads at the other end of the bar. As she watched the boys from a distance, the Blood Rangers were starting to get things really buzzed up. A few of the guys jumped up on to the bar and started dancing suggestively. It was like a scene from Coyote Ugly thought Rachael.

Jimmy jumped up and offered his hand out to Stone. The bar staff were used to this behaviour on gig nights and with the right crowd they could double their weekly profits, so it was always encouraged.

Mandy, Katie, and Rachael were all laughing at the boys dancing around foolishly on the bar, the music was pumping and the atmosphere was electric. Rachael had never experienced a night like this before and she could not take her eyes off Stone.

The lads were thrusting their hips back and forth, punching the air with their hands firmly around Budweiser bottles. Stone was looking for Rachael as the band finished another song but they kicked off straight-away with another one called Bang-City Cocktail which always made the crowd go wild. Stone jumped down from the bar, he was determined to talk to Rachael so he walked over to her and girls and with a new found confidence. "Hey, great to see you tonight," he said loudly over the raucous crowd.

"I'm having just the best time ever," she laughed. "It looked so much fun up there on the bar," Rachael shouted.

"It was great, you should try it," Stone said at the top of his voice.

"Oh no I couldn't, I mean I wouldn't," Rachael answered, shaking her head. With that, in a moment of pure craziness, Stone picked her up in his arms and walked towards the bar.

"Stone, put me down!" said Rachael, giggling uncontrollably.

Before she knew it, Jimmy was helping her up to the bar then Stone scrambled up. He took Rachael by both hands and pulled her close to him, putting his hands on her hips. Rachael was feeling a bit self-conscious but she soon started to sway along with him, enjoying the music and holding her arms around the guy she was clearly attracted to. "Stone, you are crazy," she said laughing.

"I sure am Rachael. So do you like it up here?" he shouted over the music.

"I never had a choice" she laughed. The band seemed to play forever and everyone was having such a great time.

The crowds were going crazy and before long the whole bar had people clambering up onto chairs and tables all doing silly ass dances. The evening was turning out to be a huge success for the owners and the punters were clearly loving it.

When the song came to an end, a new singer called Clyde Dutton took to the stage. He was a country singer and slowed the mood down a little but his timing was perfect as everyone was exhausted from dancing to the last three songs. Stone lifted Rachael down and he kissed her on the cheek. This made her blush slightly, she was so taken by him, she could not ever remember having so much fun in her lifetime. At 19, she had led a rather sheltered existence, mainly because of parents being so strict with her. She almost felt guilty for having such a good time and she knew her father would not have approved of her dancing on a bar top but for those few moments she just didn't care.

When Clyde finished his first song, he thanked everyone for coming along. "Thanks folks, thank you so much for supporting us all tonight, we certainly rocked this joint hey?" Everyone cheered and clapped to show their appreciation.

Jimmy had tried to get Stone's attention a few times whilst they were dancing but he could see in his friend's eyes that he was totally transfixed by this girl that had just walked into his life. Jimmy had never seen his friend act like this with any girl before but he could sense something magical was developing between them and this pleased him, however, he couldn't help feeling an element of jealousy towards Rachael as he was so close with Stone and didn't want things to change. Jimmy had once dated Katie Goldberg but they decided to remain friends in the end as they had known each other since they were young. In fact, Jimmy was not really the settling down type, he just liked to hang out with the guys.

Stone asked Rachael to come outside with him, he wanted to learn more about this beautiful girl and he was keen to let her know how he felt about her. He noticed the attention she was getting from all the lads in the bar and he was not going to waste any time in telling her how he felt. Rachael was keen to get to know Stone too so they headed outside. They found a bench in a quiet spot around the back of the bar and sat down to talk.

"So, Rachael, are you having a good time tonight?" Stone asked.

"Yeah, I'm having a really cool time, this place is so much fun," answered Rachael.

"I really like you Rachael." Rachael was slightly taken back by this, she felt the same but slightly embarrassed to answer so she paused for a moment.

"I like you too." They both laughed together and felt a mutual connection developing between them.

"My ma would love you," Stone said randomly.

"Ah that's a really nice thing to say, thank you."

Stone told her about his mother's condition and how he worried about her when he was out. As he'd had a few beers heading home on his bike to check on her was out of the question so he thought he'd take a walk.

"Hey, would you like to come with me?" he asked.

Rachael chuckled slightly, "You know when a guy wants to show a girl to his mother, it's normally because she is his girl."

Stone laughed, "Well ok Rachael, you fancy being my girl?" Rachael giggled, they'd both had a few drinks and found this conversation amusing. They were both a little tipsy and stumbled with their words but something magical was unfolding.

"Ok seriously, I would love to meet your mom," Rachael said happily.

"Really? Great, I promise you just a quick drop in to see how she is then we can get straight back here." Rachael stood up and reached out her hand to Stone.

"Come on let's go," she smiled. Stone jumped up and took her hand and they started walking briskly towards the main road. It was a perfect evening and what seemed like a million stars lit the sky. There was a warm welcoming breeze coming off the sea which added to the wonderful ambience of their first romantic walk together. It was not long before they approached the top of Stone's road. Rachael was looking at the small modest houses, with a sense of guilt in her heart. She was fortunate to live on a large estate in private grounds, sometimes taking it for granted but having known nothing else, she was fortunately not a materialistic girl. In her opinion, having a huge house was nowhere as important as having happiness and love between the walls of any home.

They soon approached Stone's house, "This is it," Stone said proudly as he opened the gate and they started walking up towards the door. Racheal stopped sharply and squeezed Stone's hand.

"Hey, what if your ma doesn't like me?" asked Rachael. Stone smiled at her with a cheeky grin.

"Of course she's going to like you, you're a peach," he answered. Stone squeezed her hand tightly as he opened the door. "Ma, ma, it's me Mickey."

They entered the sitting room where Maria was sitting by the piano. She looked rather startled but with a smile in her eyes, she said, "Micky, you could have warned me you were going to bring a young lady home, I would have made an effort," she winked at Rachael and gave her a warm smile.

"Sorry ma, I just wanted to see how you were doing and I wanted to introduce you to Rachael. She's here for the summer working in Johnson's drug store. We won't stop for long."

Maria could see immediately her son was smitten with this beautiful girl. She held out her hand towards Rachael. "It's a pleasure to meet you my darling, you certainly are a vision young lady," she said with a charming grin. Maria then looked up at Stone, "Well, before you leave, why not play Rachael one of your beautiful tunes on the piano," she smiled.

"Oh, ma really?" Stone answered, feeling slightly embarrassed. "I'm sure Rachael doesn't want to hear that ma," he said, almost blushing. He could see in his mother's eyes she was so proud of him and he knew that playing the piano always gave Maria great pleasure, as she herself had once played the piano herself. In fact, she had taught her son as a youngster some basic chords and popular tunes. Stone enjoyed composing his own music and Maria had found it soothing whilst he practiced in the lounge.

"Mickey, you play the piano beautifully, I would love to hear you play just one song before you leave please," Maria said, winking again at Rachael.

"Yes, please play something, I would love to hear you play," said Rachael with a grin on her face as she winked back at Maria.

"Ok, you guys win, one song then we're out of here," Stone joked. He turned and approached the piano and sat down. Rachael sat down on a chair opposite the piano by the doorway and waited in anticipation.

There was a slight pause and then Stone's fingers pressed down on the ivory keys. As he rolled his fingers over the keys, Maria shut her eyes and took a deep satisfying breath as the music flowed into her soul. Rachael was amazed at how beautifully Stone played; it was such an unusual sight to see a big guy in a leather jacket with such a tough exterior, playing a beautiful heart felt piece of music. It was a deep, quite emotional moment that drew her closer to him. She felt something in the music, like she was drifting into his soul, connecting, bonding closer to the person he was.

When he finished playing, he stood up red faced and almost too shy to speak but Rachael started to clap and Maria looked at Rachael with a look of satisfaction on her face.

Stone smiled at Rachael, "Ok ma, are you happy now, can we go?" he laughed.

"Yes, you can go now," answered Maria with a sweet smile. Stone walked over and kissed his mother on the cheek. Maria squeezed her son's arm and looked at Rachael. "You guys make a beautiful couple, you really do," she said. Both Rachael and Stone were touched by Maria's words. "Now take care you lovelies, I love you son," said Maria.

"I love you too ma, I won't be too late." Stone answered.

When they both got outside Rachael said "Oh Mickey, I love your ma and I especially loved your piano piece." Stone looked at Rachael.

"Hey, only my ma calls me Mickey," he laughed. "Thank you for coming with me, she clearly likes you."

"Ah, I hope so, she was so sweet to me."

The couple held hands all the way back to Bar Lomas, laughing and fooling around, whilst stopping occasionally for a cheeky kiss under the moonlight. They could feel the chemistry between them and could almost feel electricity running through their bodies every time their hands touched. In no time at all, they were back at the bar where they continued to enjoy the evening. Jimmy was pleased to see his buddy back and they all danced and drank away the final few hours.

When the evening ended, the bartender shouted "Time guys! It's time for all you lovely people to go home to your beds." Everyone finished their drinks and headed out of the bar. Rachael was feeling quite anxious as she'd told her parents she'd be leaving the bar at 10.30 but it was now closer to midnight.

As they all started to go their separate ways, Stone saw a black limousine race into the carpark and pull up sharply outside the entrance near where they were standing. The door flew open and a smartly dressed, middle aged man with a stern look on his face came walking purposefully towards them.

As Rachael turned towards the man, her face seemed to drop immediately. Stone noticed she had a look of fear in her eyes. "Oh no, it's my father!" Christopher Jenson was fuming, his chest was puffed out and his body language was very intimidating. At 6ft plus in solid shape with salt and pepper hair he looked distinguished and wealthy.

"What on earth do you think you're playing as a young lady?!" He shouted at Rachael.

"Daddy, please, not here," begged Rachael, with her head held low.

Jenson took no notice and just pointed at the limo. "Get in the goddamn car," he shouted. With tears in her eyes, Rachael turned to Stone.

"I'm sorry but I have to go." She turned away and slowly walked towards the car.

Stone walked up beside her and squeezed her hand. "It's ok, I'll see you soon Rachael, take care," he said, then standing back.

"No, you won't see my daughter again," said Jenson furiously. "I will not have her mixing with the likes of you," he continued.

Holding back and not wanting to make things worse for Rachael, Stone remained silent as he watched Jenson turn and get in the car next to his distressed daughter.

The black car sped off, kicking up dust from the rocky surface as it raced out of the gates towards the main road. Stone sat down on some steps leading up to the bar entrance, putting his head in his hands, he then looked up at Jimmy, "What just happened man? Why was he so goddamn pissed?" A voice from behind Stone muttered.

"Don't you know who that guy is?" Stone looked behind him to see the bar manager, Phil, locking up.

"Well I guess it was Rachael's father, I don't know anymore than that," answered Stone.

"That was Christopher Jenson, he owns most of the property in Santa Barbara. Apparently he inherited his family's oil business back in the 60's. He's a very powerful guy around these parts and someone you really don't want to piss off."

Stone looked at Jimmy and shook his head. "Trust me to fall for a girl with a father like that," he said. The two friends asked Phil if it would be ok to leave their bikes overnight and collect in the morning to which Phil happily agreed, so they walked off towards their homes, down the dusty track away from Bar Lomas.

Chapter 5

As Stone woke the following morning, he could hear Maria groaning in the lounge. The T.V was still on and it sounded like it was in between channels with a hissing sound that penetrated right through his head. "Ma, are you ok in there?" he shouted from his bedroom. Maria was not responding in her usual fashion, so Stone jumped out of bed and made his way to her. As he came down the hallway, he noticed his mother's feet just inside the doorway. His heart began racing as he quickened his step into the lounge. It seemed poor Maria had fallen out of her faithful chair and was lying face down on the floor. Stone knelt down immediately and took her hand in his. He moved his head closer to her ear. "Hey ma, can you hear me? It's me, Mickey. Ma please answer me," he said anxiously. There was no response, her hand was warm but he couldn't feel a pulse. He gently rolled her over and tried to make her comfortable on the floor and placed a cushion under her head. He could see the life draining out of her before his very eyes and with tears streaming down his face, he jumped to his feet and called 911.

He laid down beside his mother, holding her hand, until the emergency services could be heard in the street. Stone rushed to the door waving his arms and shouting. The ambulance stopped directly outside and two guys rushed up the pathway towards the house. "Please, please come quickly!" They followed Stone into the lounge and immediately started working on Maria. Stone stood back watching from the doorway, feeling totally helpless. They found a faint pulse so they immediately strapped her onto a stretcher and wheeled her into the back of the ambulance. Stone followed in shock and sat beside her, gripping her hand, with tears streaming down his face. It took just seven minutes to get out of Butterfly Beach and on to the main route to the hospital. There were huge complications with Maria's heart and although the ambulance was making good time, it was simply not fast enough and poor Maria died shortly before arriving at the hospital. The siren was still sounding as the ambulance driver screeched up outside the emergency doors. The hospital staff came running out to assist.

As the rear doors to the ambulance opened, a nurse looked in and could see Stone on his knees hugging the patient, crying uncontrollably. As they tried to pull the stretcher away from him, he knew she was gone and it was too late to save her. The medics had done all they could and there was nothing more they could do. A broken Stone sobbed like a child, his grip loosened on the stretcher rail as Maria was taken out of the ambulance.

As she was wheeled away, Stone was left feeling completely numb but he thanked the medical staff and wandered into the emergency waiting area. He sat down on a chair by the reception desk and waited for the doctor. Half an hour went by when a young doctor finally emerged from a room opposite. He explained to Stone that his mother had suffered a massive stroke and had been simply too weak to recover. He said they had done all they could for her and if he wanted to say goodbye to his mother then he could go and sit with her. The young doctor put his hand on Stone's shoulder and offered him his condolences, then turned and walked away.

Stone walked towards the private room where his mother lay, he approached the door and gripped the handle pushing it down to open the heavy door. Stone walked in slowly, his tearful green eyes focused on the hospital bed with Maria lying at rest. He walked over to the bed and pulled a chair close to it. He was still in complete shock and his heart was broken. As he reached over to kiss Maria on the forehead, he noticed she was still warm, almost as if she was just asleep. The complete silence with no trace of breathing was deeply hurtful to her devoted son. "I love you ma, I always will. Thank you for all the memories and thank you for everything you have done for me," he said softly stroking her hair. He sat there holding her hand for a while, then stood up, turned and walked towards the door. He looked back one more time and blew a kiss to his mother, then walked out.

Stone was immediately greeted by a nurse as he wandered into the corridor. As he looked into her eyes, he felt her kindness. "Hello Mr Schiano, I am so sorry for your loss. Can I get you a warm drink or something?"

"No thank you, I'm ok," Stone answered. He smiled at the friendly nurse and looked at her I.D badge, Kathryn Miller was her name. She could see the young man was clearly traumatised by the whole ordeal and she showed him over to a comfortable seating area.

"I'll be back in while Mr Schiano but if you need me, please ask at reception." Stone thanked her and she walked back over to his mother's room.

Stone laid his head back against the wall and closed his eyes and after a few moments he could hear footsteps coming towards him. He opened his eyes to see nurse Kathryn standing by him holding a white clinical looking bag. "Sorry to startle you," she said. "These are a few of your mother's personal things," she handed him the bag.

Stone reached out and gripped it tightly thanking Nurse Kathryn for everything she had done. The kind nurse wished him well and he made his way to the exit.

He walked the streets of Santa Barbara with a cigarette in his left hand and his mother's belongings in the other. In the bag, amongst other things, was his mother's wedding ring and her watch that his father had bought her overseas whilst in service. He just kept on walking, wandering in a daze. It wasn't long before he found himself back at Butterfly Beach and as he turned the corner with his house in sight, he was surprised to see Jimmy was standing outside his house. "Hey man, what's happened? Your neighbour just told me an ambulance took Maria away." Stone said nothing, the tears streaming down his face told Jimmy everything. Not knowing what to say or do, Jimmy reached out to his friend and Stone collapsed to the floor.

"What am I going to do now Jimmy? She was everything to me man, I can't believe she's gone," he said through his tears. Jimmy embraced his friend and sat alongside him on the floor with his hand on his shoulder.

"I know man, I know," Jimmy said. Searching through his leather jacket, Jimmy pulled out his cigarettes and quickly lit two, offering one to his friend. Stone accepted the cigarette with trembling hands, took a large drag and blew the smoke out slowly. Through the smokey air, Stone could see someone standing opposite them. As the smoke cleared, the two men could see it was Mandy Roberts. "Guy's are you ok? I was working at Johnson's when someone came in and said that there was an ambulance outside Maria's place. I was worried about you folks." Jimmy looked up at Mandy, shaking his head, as Stone stared at the floor. Mandy knew what he was implying. Most of the folk around Butterfly Beach knew Maria was very poorly and a worry to Michael. They respected Stone's devotion to her and the family were very well thought of. Tears filled Mandy's eyes as she looked at Stone, he was clearly heartbroken. "If there is anything I can do you, please call me," she said quietly, then stepped away. Stone lifted his head and looked at Mandy.

"Thank you, I really appreciate it."

After a little while, Jimmy helped his friend up and he then walked him to the house. He asked Stone if he wanted him to stay the evening but Stone just wanted to be alone. Jimmy understood so he hugged his friend and let him be.

Stone walked in the house and went straight to his bedroom as he could not bring himself to look in the lounge at his mother's empty chair and personal things. He laid on his bed, grabbed a pillow and buried his face deep into it and sobbed himself to sleep.

Monday morning came around quickly. He was feeling exhausted with grief, drifting in and out of consciousness allowing his brain to digest what had happened. Just as he was about to drift off to sleep again, he was woken by the loud ring of the telephone in the hallway. Stone crawled from his bed and walked down the hall to pick up the receiver. As he put it to his ear, he recognised the voice immediately, it was his boss at Redwing's garage. Billy Keegan was a tough boss but very fair at the same time and his employees respected him. Most folk found him a little brash but deep down he had a big heart and looked out for his staff. "Stone, err, I heard about Maria, she was a good lady, one of a kind, err, I'm so sorry man. Look erm, don't worry about anything, I have you covered here, take some time and if you need anything you know where I am."

"Ok thank you Billy, I appreciate it," said Stone, as he dropped the receiver onto the cradle and wallowed in his grief. Looking down towards the lounge, it was evident the room needed to be tidied; his mother's empty coffee cup laid on its side with the evidential spill clearly marking the chair before it fell to the ground. There was a blood stain highlighting where his mother had laid which clearly suggested his mother had been knocked unconscious after falling from the chair following the stroke. The realisation of how his mother must have spent her last moments was all too much for Stone and feeling nauseous he crumbled onto the floor retching.

Thoughts of guilt were starting to torment him, 'maybe I shouldn't have been so long, maybe if I hadn't been drinking I would have heard something, maybe I could have saved her, maybe, maybe,' he said to himself over and over. Different scenarios were banging through his mind, as if somehow it was his fault. He started to scream at the top of his voice, "ma, I'm sorry ma......ma.......I'm so sorry!"

Hours passed before he realised he had been just staring into oblivion, so he pulled himself together, took a shower then put on a crisp white polo shirt and jeans. He was just combing his hair when the doorbell sounded. Rachael Jenson was standing there looking extremely nervous. "Hey Stone, I heard about your ma. I'm so sorry, is there anything I can do?" asked Rachael, she was stumbling over her words and she had tears rolling down her face.

"Please come in Rachael, it's so lovely to see you," he said, with a croaky voice. Rachael followed him into the lounge. "Please have a seat, can I get you a drink?" Stone asked.

"No thank you. I just wanted to explain about the other night, when my father came to the bar but now isn't the right time." she said through her tears.

"It's fine Rachael, there's no need, honestly," Stone replied. He sat by her side and put his arm around her and pulled her close towards his chest. She felt the warmth from his body and she could sense his pain as his strong arms embraced her tightly. As she lifted her head and looked into his eyes, her cheeks were still moist from her tears. Stone lifted his hand towards her face and wiped away her tears which absorbed into his hands. Rachael held him around his waist and they both drew each other closer. As their lips met, they kissed softly, tenderly comforting each other, soothing their sadness.

They were both becoming closer by the second, a genuine, loving, caring feeling was cementing their souls. It was as if they were sealing their fate in a confusing state of joy and pain. As they eventually pulled away from one another they could hear someone outside. Rachael looked outside the window where she could see Katie Goldberg about to knock on the door. Stone jumped up to answer it, with Rachael close behind him. Katie was standing there looking worried, "Rachael, you'd better go home quickly, your father just came into the store looking for you so I told him you were at lunch," said a panicked Katie.

"Oh ok, I better go, I will call, I promise," said Rachael nervously as she ran out the house and headed back to Johnson's with Katie. Stone waved her off and thanked Katie for letting them know. He went back in the house and sat down on the edge of his bed for a while. He then paced around the old house, feeling lost and empty. He grabbed his leather jacket and helmet and walked outside. He jumped on his bike and started the engine, gathered his thoughts and moved off at a steady pace along the road. As he hit the junction to the main road, he opened the throttle and instantly gathered speed, this somehow soothed his grief for a moment, an adrenaline self medication you could say. As Stone was riding, thoughts of his mother and father were crowding his brain, he decided to head for the beach where his parents used to visit before he was born.

When Stone arrived at the beach carpark, the sun was just starting to go down behind the mountains in the distance. He took a moment and stared at the beautiful scene as if entranced by the stunning view.

He climbed off his bike, removed his helmet and wandered on to the beach. He could see children splashing around in the sea and laughing without a care in the world. He started to reminisce as he strolled along the sand, until eventually he came across the bench where his mother used to sit. He sat down and gazed out to sea longing just to hear his mother's soft voice. Stone shut his eyes and whispered in the wind, "I love you ma, I love you ma," and then he opened his eyes, took a deep breath and smiled. He sat still for a while and soaked up the warm sunshine on his face then walked slowly back to his bike, before taking a slow ride home with fond memories filling his head.

Chapter 6

Stone went back to work the following week as he decided the best way to cope with his grief was to stay busy and keep his mind occupied leading up to the funeral.

Maria had already made plans for this as she wanted a small service, with just a few simple requests; to be buried wearing a necklace her husband Donnie had given her on her 21st birthday and a photograph of her only child Michael to be placed in her hand.

The days seem to pass quickly for Stone and the time to lay dear Maria to rest had arrived. Stone, Jimmy and a few locals had gathered at the local church where Maria herself had often visited her husband's memorial stone over the years.

Stone felt satisfied his mother would have been touched by the service. It was a warm personal gathering, Stone was cried out and feeling rather numb as the priest had said his final words. Jimmy put his hand on Stone's shoulder as the guests started to leave, he gripped it firmly and remained strong for his friend. "Are you ok buddy?" Jimmy asked. Stone looked at him.

"Yeah, thanks Jimmy, I'm fine." His loyal friend had always been caring since right back to their school days. They both had mutual respect for eachother. Jimmy was clearly troubled by the loss of dear friend's mother and the effect this was having on Stone.

Once the service had finished, Stone thanked everyone for coming to pay their respects and walked back over to his mother's grave. He wanted a little time alone by the grave, so Jimmy respectfully walked away to give his friend some time.

Stone looked at the heap of earth on top of Maria's grave and then bent down and whispered, "Sleep well ma, sleep well," he stood up, wiped away his tears and headed off to the cemetery gates.

As Stone looked beyond the gates, he could see Rachael standing by a tree, with a bicycle by her side. Stone walked towards her, he was dazzled by how beautiful she looked. She was wearing a black dress, it was as if she had dressed respectfully to mark the sad occasion.

"Are you ok? I hope you don't mind me coming here?" Rachael said.

Stone immediately put Rachael at ease with a gleaming smile. "Am I pleased to see you?" he said cheerfully.

Rachael lunged forward and threw her arms around Stone. He held her tightly and she could feel his grief was still so raw.

"I wanted to see you today. I want to be with you Stone and no-one is going to stop me," she said confidently.

Stone hugged her tightly and whispered in her ear, "Rachael, I think I love you."

Rachael looked deep into his eyes, paused for a moment and said, "I love you too."

Stone was relieved as he felt he had spoken out of turn but it was the right moment. He knew it was an odd time to say it but it felt right so he just went with his heart.

Luckily, it seemed Rachael had the same feelings and the couple held hands tightly and walked towards Stone's house, just a short walk away.

Rachael had butterflies in her stomach as the couple walked along the sidewalk. She was conscious people talk and soon the word would get back to her father but she just didn't care today. She felt her hand in the hand of someone special, someone she loved, someone she longed to be with. Stone held her hand tightly most of the way home and Rachael felt protected in her lover's company, it was as if nothing could break them when they were together.

As the couple approached Stone's street, they picked up pace heading towards the front garden. They walked in through the open gate and Stone dived deep into his pockets to find the keys to the door. He opened the door quickly with Rachael close to his side, still clutching her hand, Stone nudged the door shut with his knee.

Rachael's heart was pounding; a feeling came over her like something magical was about to happen. She had not told anyone she was a virgin at 19 and vowed only to give it to a boy she loved. Stone's heart was racing too as he pressed Rachael against the wall in the hallway. In a moment of deep passion, the couple started to kiss, first gently then firmly, leading almost to a hunger for each other, a feeling neither of them had ever experienced. Stone pushed himself against Rachael's thighs and his hands gripped her firmly as he pulled her into himself. He then lifted her up and Rachael wrapped her legs around him tightly. Stone carried her into his bedroom and gently laid her on his bed. Rachael could smell the scent of his masculine cologne on his bed sheets which gave her a rush of pleasure that seemed to travel through her entire body. The couple could not help themselves, bewitched by their hunger for one another, they felt a sense of sexual healing the deeper they pushed the boundaries.

Stone removed his shirt to reveal his tanned muscular body. Rachael looked at him with pure lust in her eyes and she too, started to undress, it felt the most natural thing to do, almost as though it was meant to be.

Before long the couple were naked and entwined on the bed. Rachael groaned as Stone pushed himself against her thighs. She had been longing for this intimate moment between them for so long and it was clear both of them were taken aback by the moment. They felt like wild animals craving and lusting for one another. Thrusting against each other trying to satisfy one another, they quickly reached that moment of intense pleasure, both breathing heavy, holding each other tightly and groaning in ecstasy. They were both perspiring heavily, embarrassed as the reality of what just happened sank in.

It seemed like at least an age before either of them said a word, they just lay in the bed holding hands. A feeling of incredible guilt flooded through Rachael and she jumped up and threw her clothes back on in an instant. She said nervously, "I'd better go," and with that she walked out the door. Stone just lay numb on the bed, still trying to get his head around what had just happened as he too felt riddled with guilt as he lay there gazing at the ceiling trying to figure out the whole day's events. What with the funeral and now this. What had just happened with Rachael felt wonderful but so wrong at the same time and for a moment Stone wondered if he would ever see Rachael again. He had never felt a connection with anyone else in the past so deep, so strong, it felt different somehow, it felt meant to be, however, because of Mr Jenson's reaction to the couple dating, he was concerned about how they could ever possibly be able to be together without constantly looking over their shoulders.

Weeks went by, Stone threw himself into work and took all the over-time he could. Jimmy could see his friend was dealing with the loss of his mother in his own way and there had also been no word from Rachael since the day of the funeral so this too was clearly playing on his friend's mind, especially after their brief but amazing encounter at the house.

It was Friday evening when Stone was locking up the garage when he noticed a letter sticking out of the mailbox. It seemed it had intentionally been placed there for him to find so he walked over and pulled it out the box and for some odd reason he felt obliged to smell the envelope as it had seemed to have feminine writing on it with a scent of perfume. He recognised it immediately, it was Rachael's and clearly addressed to him, to Michael Schiano. He eagerly opened the envelope to satisfy his curiosity.

It read, '*To my dearest Stone. Sorry I haven't been in touch for a while, somehow my father found out that I met you the day of your dear mother's funeral and has forbidden me to see you but I can't stop thinking about you, especially after what happened between us. Please believe me when I tell you, I am in love with you and I desperately want to see you before I leave for New York next weekend. I really need to talk to you before I leave. Please meet me at the old boat house on Butterfly Beach on Monday evening if you can, say 7pm. I will find an excuse to tell my parents but I simply must see you, there is a lot I need to explain.*

Yours truly Rachael Jenson xx'

Stone sat down on some old tyres to digest the content of the letter. He felt relieved but at the same time disappointed that Rachael's father was so ruthless in his ways. He knew he had to see her again and felt excited about the prospect but he was saddened by the news that the family was leaving for New York the following week.

The Jenson's had their summer retreat property here in California but the family spent most of the year on the family estate just outside of Connecticut where Rachael commutes to University to study law, hoping to complete an undergraduate degree, earn a Juris Doctor diploma and pass her state's bar examination as this way she knew she could study Law anywhere in the US and be independent, finally escaping from her father's chains. It was going to be a long difficult road but she was determined to succeed.

Stone took a slow ride home with all kinds of thoughts crashing through his mind as he rode through the narrow streets leading to his house. When he pulled up at the house, Jimmy was there leaning up against his bike alongside the fence that surrounded the house.

"Hey bro, you fancy some company?" Jimmy asked. Stone was so pleased to see him that he jumped off his bike and greeted his friend with a man hug and a fist pump.

"Gee I'm glad to see you Jimmy," Stone said.

The two friends went inside the house and Jimmy made himself comfortable in the lounge while Stone made some burgers and french fries for them. He grabbed a couple of beers from the fridge and gave one to Jimmy. The two guys sat and munched their food and hardly spoke, it was clear they had both worked up an appetite after a long day.

As the friends sipped away on their bottles of beer, Stone decided to tell Jimmy about the note from Rachael and how he really felt about her and how he longed to spend time with her.

Jimmy listened intently and then spoke, 'Ok yeah, I get it Stone, you love this girl but you're forgetting one major issue here my friend. I mean this guy Jenson, he's no ordinary dude, he's probably the most powerful man in the state and if he disapproves of you, which it's clear he already does, then you got yourself a shit storm coming buddy." Jimmy had said his piece and then laid back in the chair and took a large swig of his beer.

Stone smiled at Jimmy, "I appreciate your concern buddy, I really do but there's something about her. For once in my life I've found a girl that really gets me, understands me, you know what I mean buddy?" Stone went to the fridge and pulled out another two beers, he smiled at Jimmy and said, "she makes me feel alive buddy, she wants to meet me Monday night," he handed his friend the note from Rachael. Jimmy read the note and looked up at Stone with a glint in his eye.

"Wow buddy, this chick really likes you, doesn't she?"

The two friends enjoyed each other's company and Jimmy decided to sleep over on the couch as he'd had a few too many drinks to chance riding his bike home.

Jimmy lived with his parents at Black Lake along with his two older sisters and younger brother. His parents were well respected in the community, both Stone and Jimmy's father were enlisted in the same regiment during the Vietnam conflict.

Stone and Jimmy had always had a close bond because of this and Jimmy always felt so lucky that his father had returned from war as so many did not, including Donnie Schiano. The two friends enjoyed a few more beers, they seemed to talk for hours until they both fell asleep in their chairs.

Stone woke in the early hours with a dry throat, desperate for a drink of water. He wandered into the kitchen and ran the tap to fill a glass which he gulped down in seconds. Stone wandered into his bedroom to grab a pillow and blanket for his friend.

"Jimmy, Jimmy, hey buddy," Stone whispered. Jimmy stirred and looked up at Stone.

"Wow man, I must have zonked out, what happened?" he said.

"We both fell asleep," Stone laughed. He handed his friend the blanket and pillow.

"Thanks man," said Jimmy as he moved over to the couch and settled back down mumbling, "Night man".

Stone walked back into his room, climbed into bed and drifted into a deep sleep.

Chapter 7

It was Saturday morning when Jimmy opened his eyes to feel the sunshine cascading through the curtains onto his face.

He got up and walked over to the window to draw the curtains. As he sat back down on the couch, he looked at his watch and to his amazement it was 9am so he decided to head home. He chucked on his clothes, put the empty beer bottles in the trash and made his way to the front door.

"Hey Stone, buddy, you awake?" he asked. He could hear his friend stir and reply in a tired voice. "What's up Jimmy, you ok?"

"Yeah man, I'm cool but I gotta get home".

"Ok man, thanks for last night buddy, catch up later Jimmy," Stone called from his bedroom. He heard Jimmy close the door and pull away on his bike.

Stone decided to sleep a while longer but by midday he decided to pull himself together so he jumped in the shower, got dressed and made some coffee. It happened to be a perfect day for the beach where he liked to take a swim and sunbathe on his days off, so he wasted no time in heading off on his bike towards the local beach.

When he arrived, he could see young couples holding hands and lying side by side on the sand laughing and joking. For a moment, he longed for Rachael to be with him and he felt sad that their relationship was so complicated, however, he could understand Mr. Jenson would only want the best for his daughter. Maybe in his eyes, he saw him as a downbeat mechanic with an association to a motorcycle gang which was not what he wanted for his only daughter.

As he strolled along the beach, he was hoping and praying that one day they would find a way to be together. Thoughts of the Monday evening ahead were rushing through his mind, although excited, he was feeling slightly nervous about what Rachael may have to say, especially knowing it was behind her father's back.

As the day came to an end, Stone headed back to his bike and took a slow ride home. He spent the rest of the day and most of Sunday packing away Maria's personal belongings into boxes, carefully placing them in the attic. It was Sunday afternoon when he was almost finished, just Maria's dresser was left to clear. As he opened the top drawer, he noticed a photo album resting on a pile of loose photographs so he took a deep breath, sat on the bed and opened the album.

The first few pages were photographs of his mother and father when they were dating, followed by pictures of their wedding. As Stone stared deeply at the photographs, tears ran down his cheeks as he was overcome with emotion. He glanced out of the window and up to the blue sky, "I love you ma," he whispered softly. He eventually came across his baby pictures and one caught his eye, it was of his father holding him, looking so proud and happy. It was a terrible shame, he thought to himself, that he was never able to build a relationship with his father.

After he had put away all his mother's things, he laid on her bed, shut his eyes and drifted off to sleep.

As Sunday evening drew in, he was awoken by the sound of a barking dog outside. He sat up and looked out the bedroom window to see a large, white dog. It didn't seem to be on a leash and it was barking at an elderly man as if it was troubled by the gentleman being in the street.

Stone stood up, walked over to his front door opening it quickly and asked the man if he was ok.

The man looked at him with a vacant look in his eyes, "I can't find my Sally," the man said.

The dog started to run around the elderly man, as if concerned, trying to keep him in one place.

"Is this your dog sir?" Stone asked but the elderly man just repeated.

"I can't find Sally."

Suddenly, a woman came running across the road with a very worried look on her face and looked pleadingly at Stone. "Please sir, can you help me get my father back across the street? He has dementia and I've been looking for him everywhere."

"Sure thing Mam. Do you know who the dog belongs to?" Stone asked. The woman smiled.

"yes, it's my dog. My father must've left the door open and he will always follow him to bring attention to anyone he can to alert them my father is in danger. He seems to know something isn't right with my father."

"Your father said he was looking for Sally." Stone said. The woman's face dropped; a look of sadness was apparent in her eyes.

"Oh really, he said that? Oh my, Sally was my mother and my father seems to think she is still alive. He's always asking where she is but I never expected him to leave the house and go searching for her. Come on Pa," she said.

"What's your father's name?" asked Stone.

"It's Frank" she answered, smiling.

Stone approached the gentleman, "Hey Frank, shall we get you home now buddy?" he said. Frank stared at Stone, paused for a while in a confused state of mind.

"Okay, sure, that's right, maybe Sally is at home," he said. Stone looked at the man's daughter.

"Is that your car over their Mam?" he asked.

"Yes, it is" she nodded. Both Stone and the women escorted the old man across the road to the car and the dog immediately stopped barking and climbed into the back of the car, as if it knew the drama was over.

Frank opened the car door for himself, climbed in the passenger side and secured his seatbelt. He just stared up to the sky shaking his head as his daughter climbed in beside him. "Thank you. Sorry, I didn't catch your name?" the woman asked.

"My name is Michael but most call me Stone around here." The woman gave him a huge smile of gratitude before driving off.

Stone crossed back over the road and went back into his house. He made a bite to eat, watched T.V for a while, then went back to bed with thoughts of Rachael flooding through his mind, longing for Monday evening to arrive.

Chapter 8

Monday morning soon came along and Stone's alarm was thumping through his ears. He jumped up to silence it, almost stumbling out of bed as he turned back round burying his face in the pillows.

Rachael awoke for her final shift at Johnson's drugs store. She enjoyed her time there and became very close to the locals and especially her dear friend Katie Goldberg.

She came down for breakfast to hear her father in a heated business discussion on the phone in the hallway while her mother was preparing eggs over the stove, looking deep in concentration. Rachael was feeling excited about her secret meeting with Stone that evening, she could not wait to get through the day.

After breakfast she rushed upstairs to finish getting ready and glanced in the mirror in the hallway, thinking how she should wear her hair that evening. Her father noticed her at the top of the stairs, "have a good day princess," he called out. Rachael looked round and smiled.

"Thanks Pa," she answered. Rachael then grabbed her jacket and headed back down the stairs towards the front door. "Bye mom, see you guys later and remember I'm seeing Katie tonight," she shouted.

"Ok sweetie, that's fine but don't forget we have an early start Tuesday," said Susan.

Rachael came out and walked down the large white steps of the big old house to the front yard. She noticed the gardener cutting the hedges, "Morning Rachael," he said as she approached him.

"Good morning Wesley, have a great day," she answered.

"You to mam, it sure is a beautiful day isn't it?"

"It certainly is Wesley," Rachael said cheerfully.

Wesley Taylor was a mixed-race guy in his 40's, his family had been working on the Jenson estate for decades and they were well thought of by Rachael and her family. Wesley had a great affection for Rachael as she had always given him the time of day and seemed genuinely interested in how he and his family were doing.

Stone was just leaving the house too, with thoughts of Rachael in his mind. He smiled at an elderly gentleman passing by his gate.

"Morning sir," he said politely. The man smiled and raised his hat.

"You too young man," he answered. Stone put on his helmet, climbed on his bike and headed off to work. The bike still had some fair damage from the race but mainly just scratches, nothing of too much concern. He was intending to get it patched up at the garage one weekend when it was quieter, perhaps after the summer season, when all the holiday makers had left.

The day seemed to pass quickly for both Rachael and Stone and it was not long before Stone was finishing up an exhaust change on an old Chevrolet.

As Rachael was wandering home from work, she was racking her brains what to wear for the evening and the best excuse to give her parents as to where she was actually going tonight. She had mentioned to her mother that she was seeing Katie but nothing more but suddenly she came up with the idea of telling her parents that a few of the customers at Johnson's had arranged a few drinks at a local bar to say goodbye for the season and that she was keen to attend. Mr Johnson and his wife had been extremely kind to her through the summer. She thought her father would be fine with that because he trusted Mr Johnson as they had been on hunting trips together some years back and Christopher Jenson always had a good word for old Charlie Johnson. Rachael hated lying to her parents but felt it was the only way she could get out and meet Stone.

Stone locked up the garage and headed home having similar thoughts of what to wear and feeling slightly troubled by what was so important that Rachael had to tell him.

When he arrived home, he peeled off his work clothes, threw them on the floor by the washing machine and jumped straight in the shower.

He was excited about seeing Rachael as he knew she had feelings for him and he too had feelings for her. It was as if both of them had this unbreakable connection, like nothing would ever come between them, no matter how difficult things became.

It was roughly 5.30pm when Rachael got home. She walked in the front door to find her father coming down the stairs which slightly unnerved poor Rachael as she was already anxious about meeting Stone; butterflies were an understatement, it was like she had wild birds fluttering around in her belly.

As she proceeded to the stairs, she looked her father in the eyes and with a nervous smile walked past him. Christopher smiled back, "Hi Rach, how was your day?" he asked. Rachael stopped in her tracks looking around at her father.

"It was fine pa, thank you," she answered uneasily.

"Now do not be late tonight Rachael. I understand you're seeing Katie, is that right?" he asked.

"Yes, it's just a farewell party and I won't be late pa." Rachael answered.

"Ok fine, just please remember we are leaving early for New York tomorrow morning." Rachael nodded, as she drifted into her room and closed the door.

She leaned back on the door and sighed heavily. Closing her eyes, she could feel her heart pounding as she gathered her thoughts.

Rachael had her own en-suite bathroom. The house was formerly a naval hospital back in the 1800's so Christopher's father, Frank Jenson had made some considerable major refurbishments to cater for the family's summer retreat over the course of many years.

Rachael ran a shower and started to undress but just before she entered the bathroom, she looked in the wardrobe at her casual clothes and reached in and pulled out her favourite summer dress and red shoes. The dress was a white and pink design from New York with printed flowers at the top, front and back and it showed off her summer tan and she always felt attractive in it.

She carefully laid the dress on her bed and laid the shoes at the foot of the bed and then proceeded to shower.

As the water was cascading through her hair and down her body, she enjoyed the warm relaxing water from the powerful shower jets, almost massaging her cappuccino tanned skin. She closed her eyes and ran her fingers through her hair, with thoughts of Stone flooding through her body. As jets of water teased her breasts, her hand dropped lower between her legs, she sighed and whispered his name quietly. Suddenly, she was startled by a loud bang in one of the other rooms, so she paused for a moment, feeling almost paranoid and guilty at the same time. When the noise stopped, she carried on with her shower, rubbing a scented shower cream all over her body.

After a long relaxing shower, Rachael dried herself with the pink fluffy towel from her bathroom rail and then blow dried her hair before applying her makeup. She was conscious not to over do it as Stone had always remarked on her natural beauty, so she applied some soft lipstick accompanied by some eyeliner and a dab of perfume. She glanced at the clock, it was almost 6pm. She felt the butterflies in her stomach, pressed her hand against her belly and smiling in the mirror to herself she whispered, "Stone, what have you done to me?"

By this time Stone was dressed in fitted blue jeans, a white crisp shirt and a light denim jacket. He had decided to walk to the old boat house as it was a warm evening and not far from his house.

He was sitting on the end of his bed now staring at the clock which was showing 6.15pm. He was hungry when he got home but now he had feelings of anxiety coming in to play, which completely diminished his appetite.

He stood up and took one final look at himself in the mirror and playfully said to himself, "looking good son," he giggled nervously and wandered out the door. Stone was still wondering what Rachael had to tell him that was so important; was she just going to say goodbye forever?

As he walked along the sidewalk, he took a shortcut which led down a long path heading towards the beach. He glanced at his watch which read now 6.30pm. His mother, dear Maria, had always taught him to be 15 minutes early when you have an appointment and Stone lived his life by this rule, even for dates, he always preferred to be the one that was waiting. As he walked down the steps, he could see the old boat house in the distance.

Rachael was now making her way too. She ran down the stairs and shouted out to her parents, "Bye folks, see you later, I have a key." She'd timed this perfectly so her father didn't see the effort she had made as this would only encourage doubt in his mind. Luckily for her, both her parents were in the dining room having dinner. Rachael had told them there would be food at her farewell party so they didn't suspect anything strange as she slipped out the door, they just replied casually.

"Bye Rach, don't be late, big day tomorrow."

Rachael walked along the stepping stones, leading away from the house. She soon picked up her pace when she was out of sight and made her way to the main road, sign-posted Butterfly Beach. She walked at a steady speed, realising she should make good time and should be at the boat house by 7pm.

Stone was almost there; it had turned out to be a perfect evening, the sea was calm, with gentle waves kissing the sand as they rolled in, followed by a perfect breeze that was so welcoming alongside the warm evening sunshine.

There was an old bench just outside the boathouse and Stone sat down on the rickety structure, making sure it was a clean surface as he lowered himself down.

There was no sign of Rachael but Stone was slightly relieved by this as he preferred it that way around, almost as if it were how it should be.

The young man still had butterflies in his belly as he looked far into the distance to see if he could catch a glimpse of Rachael. Unknown to him, Rachael was just approaching the boathouse from the other direction and she could see him looking in the opposite direction. A rush of butterflies fluttered around in her belly too. She was feeling extremely nervous but incredibly excited at the same time.

Stone stood up, checked his watch and then started to pace up and down nervously. Suddenly he heard a voice calling him and as he turned and looked the other way, he could see Rachael running towards him.

Her hair was flowing in the breeze, her tanned complexion looked golden in the evening sunlight and her dress was blowing around softly, revealing her beautifully shaped legs.

Stone walked towards her and as their eyes met, it was almost as though they were staring into each other's souls. Rachael looked deep into his eyes, entranced by his looks and charm. She reached out to hold his hand and Stone quickly responded. They both walked back towards the bench and sat down looking out to sea.

"You look so beautiful Rachael, I love your dress," Stone said quietly.

"Ah, why thank you kind sir, you look rather good yourself," Rachael said laughing. Stone found her adorable, her cheeky smile just melted his heart.

"So, Rachael, why did you want to meet me here?" asked Stone, as he gripped Rachael's hand more tightly, worried what her answer might be. Rachael looked deep into his eyes, lifted her arm and reached out softly to stroke the side of her lover's face. She had a deeply troubled look in her eyes, which concerned Stone and there was a long pause before she answered.

Finally, Rachael opened up, explaining why she had lied to her parents today about where she was and she also told him she and her family would be moving back to New York the following morning, which would at least allow her to finish her law degree.

Stone held on to her every word, deep in his heart he was concerned she had lied to her parents but he understood why after learning about Christopher Jenson. It was clear to see he didn't want his daughter to have any association with him.

Rachael squeezed his hand tightly, reassuring him, as she stared straight into his deep watery eyes, "the thing is Stone, once I have my law degree I intend to move back here and I will be in a stronger position to stand up to my father and make my own decisions then we can finally be together but until that time my father simply won't let me go," Rachael explained. "I love you Stone and I want a future with you. I am so sorry for the upset my father has caused you and I simply had to tell you how I feel before I leave tomorrow."

Stone took a moment to digest everything Rachael had said, as it was a lot to take in.

"I understand Rachael, I really do and I love you too. Nothing would make me happier than being with you one day." Stone said smiling.

He ran his fingers through the back of Rachael's hair and then pulled her towards him. The couple stared out to sea for a while, just as the sun started to go down.

Rachael reached into her bag and pulled out a piece of paper and handed it to Stone. "This is my address in Connecticut, you will write to me won't you?" she asked. "Of course I will," Stone answered enthusiastically.

"I couldn't leave without letting you know what was happening, or where I was going, so please promise to keep in touch won't you?"

Stone cuddled her, which reassured her that their feelings were mutual. The couple started to stroll along the beach, laughing and kissing, with lots of hugs along the way, just like how it was when they walked back to Bar Lomas, the night Rachael met dear Maria.

It wasn't long before the night started to draw in, a breeze seemed to kick up and the temperature dropped. The waves seemed to become louder as they crashed upon the sand so the lovers found refuge in an old boatshed to avoid the colder air

It was private and this was one of the reasons Rachael had suggested meeting here as she knew there was not anywhere else they could go to be alone, especially as she seemed to have eyes and ears everywhere.

Soon, the couple started to kiss and cuddle which grew more intensely and both were quickly becoming aroused, breathing heavier as the passion between them intensified.

Stone felt a sense of guilt as his eyes scanned the boatshed floor for a clean place to lay Rachael down. His imagination went into overdrive and he pictured her naked on the floor making love to him wildly but his soft decent nature got the better of him and he pulled away from Rachael. "Hey, maybe we should stop, this is no place to erm," Stone stumbled with his words but Rachael quickly responded.

"No place for what?" she muttered, "hey are you suggesting what I think you are suggesting?" Rachael laughed and smiled at Stone. "Look, I leave tomorrow and I don't know when I'm next going to see you so maybe we should say goodbye properly, if it's okay with you?" Stone laughed.

"So what's your idea of saying goodbye properly Miss Rachael Jenson?" he joked, with a cheeky grin that just melted her heart.

Unknown to the two young lovers, Charlie Johnson was about to call round and say farewell to Rachael and her family, with a basket of handy toiletries and goodies from the drug store. Obviously, Katie Goldberg knew the plan tonight and she was incredibly supportive to Rachael, especially with regards to her feelings for Stone. Rachael obviously couldn't tell Mr Johnson about her secret meeting with Stone, even though they were very keen on the Schiano family. Charlie Johnson was a firm friend of Christopher Jenson, which was one of the reasons Rachael had landed the summer job at the drugstore.

Stone and Rachael decided to take a walk back to Stone's house. It was gradually becoming colder and they hoped if they were careful, no-one would see them sneak back to the house. The sky was becoming darker so they decided it was now or never. Rachael was conscious of the time; her father had made a point of saying not to be late and this was obviously in the back of her mind. They walked at a constant steady pace, holding hands, enjoying every second of their time together.

Charlie Johnson was now entering the driveway to the Jenson estate; his headlights could be seen shining through the large windows to the front of the house.

Christopher Jenson sat up from his large green chesterfield armchair to look out the window. His wife Susan also glanced up from her chair. "Who is that Christopher, is Rachael back already?" she muttered.

"No, it looks like Charlie Johnson with some sort of parcel or basket."

As Johnson got closer to the door, it seemed to open sharply and he was greeted by Christopher. "Hello Charlie, how are you?"

"I'm good thanks, I just thought I'd call by with a few useful things for your journey, it's not much really, just a small token of my appreciation and to say thank you to Rachael for all her hard work this summer."

Jenson's eyes widened, "I'm rather confused, Rachael told us she was going to your place for a farewell party with Katie."

"Oh I see, I hope I haven't caused a problem?"

"No not at all, I'm just a little concerned but perhaps she just went to see Katie. I'll call the Goldberg's to check but thank you very much for the parcel."

"You're welcome and please thank Rachael for me, she did a great job this summer, the customers really took a shine to her," Charlie replied. He handed over the parcel filled with goodies and got on his way. Charlie Johnson had a secret hunch that maybe Rachael had gone to have a secret rendezvous with Stone as it was no secret in the store of her fondness for him.

Jenson waved him off and rushed back inside and closed the door. Susan Jenson had only heard parts of the conversation so she asked Christopher what had been said.

"It's our daughter again, it seems something isn't quite right about where she has gone tonight. I'm just about to call the Goldberg's to see if she is with Katie," he said.

Christopher placed the parcel on the floor by the door and walked over to the telephone bureau, hastily picking up the receiver, before looking up the Goldberg's telephone number.

"I'm sure there's a logical explanation Christopher, so please calm down and be pleasant to the Goldberg's dear won't you?" said Susan.

Christopher gave Susan a look that could sink a submarine as he started to dial the number. There was a short pause before the phone connected, then it started to ring. It rang at least 5 times before it was answered by Katie.

"Hello, this is Katie Goldberg, may I ask who's calling?" Katie said confidently.

"Hi Katie, this is Christopher Jenson, is Rachael with you?"

Katie's heart skipped a beat as she knew exactly why Mr Jenson was calling. She froze with the handset pressed firmly against her ear as she tried desperately to gather her thoughts for what seemed an uncomfortable amount of time. She was hoping for a comforting reply for Christopher but she hadn't one and she knew if she lied, this would cause a bigger problem, so she just said politely, "Hello Mr Jenson, no she isn't here at the moment."

"Ok Katie, listen, I need you to tell me the absolute truth, do you know where my daughter is?" Katie had been brought up in a strict Jewish community and lying was forbidden in her household. Susan walked closer to where her husband was standing, Christopher looked at her, raising his eyebrows, this gesture indicated to Susan that something was not quite right.

In a timid, soft, trembling voice Katie said, "Yes sir, I do know where she is."

"Ok Katie, thank you for being honest with me, now please just tell me where she is?" Jenson said in a louder intimidating voice.

"She has gone to say goodbye to Michael Schiano," said Katie nervously. Before she could say anymore, Jenson shouted. "That Stone guy, that damn loser again. I told her she was never to see him again!"

"Yes sir, but please let me explain. Stone is a nice guy from a decent family and she's only gone to say goodbye Mr Jenson, please see that they are doing no wrong," said dear Katie, desperately trying to defend her friends.

Susan had heard everything and she was starting to become concerned about her daughter's whereabouts but was also angry that Rachael had lied to them both.

Jenson was having none of it, "Katie, where does Stone live? I need you to tell me immediately," he said sternly. Katie started to tremble with fear, she really didn't want to betray her friends. She started to cry and Mr Goldberg had happened to overhear his daughter becoming upset on the telephone, so he took the phone from her. Katie ran off in tears along the hallway and up the stairs to her bedroom, feeling as though she had betrayed her friends.

"Hello, who is this?" said Mr Goldberg, worried why his daughter was so upset.

"Oh hello Mr Goldberg, it's Christopher Jenson. I had no intention of upsetting your daughter but you see I'm worried about Rachael. She told me she was going to be with Katie and the Johnson's tonight but it's now become clear that my daughter has lied to my wife and I and that she is actually with that no good loser who goes by the name of Stone."

"Oh I see, well as a father I understand your concern, however, please let me say Mr Jenson, I knew the Schiano family very well and I am slightly offended by you referring to Michael as a no good loser. You do realise he has just lost his mother and his father was taken in the Vietnam conflict, the family are very respected around here. Now I understand you are worried and concerned about where your daughter is but please take comfort in knowing, if she is with Michael, she will be safe," said Katie's father.

"Look ok, I appreciate you know the family, I get that but I want more for my daughter. That guy is simply not good enough for her so please Mr Goldberg I need you to tell me where he lives as I'm now fairly convinced this is where my daughter is." Jenson said.

Stone and Rachael had reached the house, they both looked behind them before entering, almost paranoid someone may see them.

Stone reached out to turn the lights on but as he did, Rachael turned it off and pulled him close to her, pressing her body tightly into his grasp, whilst kissing him passionately. This took Stone by surprise but he was feeling the passion equally so he pulled her closer and kissed her neck and lips as if he were hungry for her scent and taste.

They both moved around awkwardly in the hallway knocking things over, a wall mounted picture rocked, almost falling to the floor as Stone picked her up in his arms and walked towards the bedroom. Rachael giggled and let out a joyful scream as he dropped her on the bed, with Stone almost falling on the top of her as they continued to kiss passionately. The couple were truly in tune with one another, they both stopped for a brief moment just gazing into one another's eyes, both smiling as if their souls had become entwined and two soulmates had connected within the universe.

The young lovers had no idea that Mr Jenson was now on his way to the house.

Poor Mr Goldberg had finally caved in and given Jenson Stone's address and Jenson

was not hanging around, he was just 10 minutes away and gaining fast.

Stone and Rachael were totally mesmerized by each other, they were undressing and breathing heavy, their hearts racing and the hunger for each other was intense. It wasn't long before they were making love, the powerful connection was so electric. They were both so wrapped up in the moment, it was only a few minutes before they reached that crucial point as they were both equally turned on by each other's yearning for sexual healing, the chemistry between them was intense. They both giggled as they lay back holding hands, feeling so wrong but so right.

Then, all the sudden, they heard a car screech up outside, followed by a door slamming and heavy footsteps.

Stone jumped up immediately and glared out the window. "Oh my God, it's your father Rachael," he said, panicking.

"What, it can't be?" Rachael screeched, she tried to stand and look out the window, throwing on her clothes at the same time. She tripped on her underwear as the doorbell rang, followed by a firm constant fist knocking on the door.

"Ok, stay calm Rachael, the lights are off, we could be out, he's not to know." Stone said, surprisingly calmer now.

Rachael was now crying as she was fastening her shoes and straightening her hair. "Ok, ok" she cried.

Stone whispered, "Let's creep out the back door and head towards your house through the back roads and on the way we can figure out a story." Rachael was clearly distressed, she just kept repeating.

"How did he know? How did he know?"

Stone took her hand and led her to the kitchen where the back door was. Just before reaching for the key and opening the door, Stone whispered again, "Now listen Rachael, when I open the door we are going straight to the back of the yard and out the garage into Chestnut Grove so this way he won't see us." Rachael, still crying, just nodded with the look of fear building intensely in her eyes.

Jenson was now pacing up and down banging on the windows, shouting out. "Open up, open up, I know you're in there!" He started to disturb the neighbours and people were looking out their windows, eager to see what all the commotion was.

Stone opened the door and the two youngsters headed straight for the backyard, they moved quickly and it was not long before they were walking along Chestnut Grove in the direction of Rachael's house. Stone could feel her hand trembling as he tightened his grip to reassure her.

Christopher Jenson had finally concluded that perhaps no-one was there so he jumped back in his car and sped off in the direction of Bar Lomas as this was the last place he had found them together.

Stone and Rachael were moving fast and it was approaching 9pm, so at least she would be home in good time she thought. "Ok, now we just need to work out where you can say you were tonight. I mean, from my side, I'm happy to just come clean but I realise this is not so easy for you," said Stone. Rachael looked at him, astonished that he was prepared to take responsibility for the evening. It was her idea to meet up and she felt like she was to blame.

"No, I will have to tell them, it's just I don't understand how they knew I was with you," she said, holding the tears back.

Then all the sudden, a voice from the other side of the road shouted out, 'Rachael, Stone, it's me Katie.' Katie had been so worried about them and felt guilty that her father had given Stone's address to Christopher Jenson and she had told him where Rachael was tonight and who she was with. She soon came into view under a streetlamp and she walked quickly towards them.

Katie was panting, clearly upset. "Your father is looking for you and it's all my fault" she said. She started to sob, Stone and Rachael comforted her.

"Calm down Katie, what's wrong, why is it your fault?" asked Rachael.

"Your father phoned my house and asked where you were, I had to tell him, oh Rachael I'm so sorry, I truly am", cried Katie. Rachael hugged her.

"It's okay Katie, it's not your fault, I wouldn't expect you to lie for me. I know my father can be very persuasive when he wants to be," Rachael said.

"I simply had to come and warn you that he was looking for you, he seemed so angry."

That moment, a car came towards them with its headlights blazing and horn sounding in a constant tone. It was Jenson, he had been to Bar Lomas and with no success, decided to head home as the deadline for her return was close to 9pm and he had a hunch his daughter might try to be on time to cover up her whereabouts.

He pulled the handbrake up sharply, making an intimidating screech followed by his door swinging open violently. He marched over to the frightened youngsters and shouted. "Where on earth have you been, young lady? You lied to us, you've been with him again!" Jenson was pointing aggressively at Stone. "Why are you sneaking off with this scumbag? You have no right young lady. You are acting like a whore!" By now he was red faced and spitting with every word, almost in a rage. Stone stepped forward.

"Now hold on Mr Jenson, you can call me what you like but you have no right to call Rachael a whore!" Stone said firmly.

Jenson ignored him and grabbed Rachael's arm and pulled her aggressively towards the car. "No daddy, no, please! Stone, I love you and I'm so sorry," Rachael shouted hysterically. "Daddy, you're hurting me,' she cried as her father tried desperately to pull her towards the car.

Stone lunged at Jenson's arm that was pulling Rachael, his powerful strong grip on Jenson's arm quickly removed it from her but Jenson responded aggressively by punching Stone in the face with all his might. Stone was knocked back but not over, which caused Rachael and Katie to scream. That second, they could all see a motorcycle heading straight towards them.

It was Jimmy Nash, he happened to be in Bar Lomas when Jenson steamed in there looking for Stone, so he had decided to go and look for him.

Jimmy climbed off his bike, he could see Stone had been hit and the girls were still crying. "What the hell is going on here?" Jimmy asked.

"It's got nothing to do with you boy!" said a bright red-faced Jenson. "Now Rachael, are you going to get in the goddamn car, or am I going to drag you in it?" said her angry father. Rachael ran over to Stone and whispered in his ear.

"I'm so sorry, I love you. Write to me, please write to me," she said tearfully, hugging him one last time. She then said goodbye to Katie and Jimmy before climbing in the car.

Jenson gave them all a hateful look as he slammed her door shut and walked round to the driver side. He gave them all a final look of utter hate as he drove off at high speed towards the Jenson estate.

Once again, Stone was standing there, in shock and upset about the whole situation.

Jimmy put his arm around him and Katie patted his shoulder. "Don't worry about that jerk, karma will deal with him," said Jimmy.

"It's Rachael I'm worried about Jimmy, she leaves for New York tomorrow and this guy is ruining her life and there's nothing I can do!"

They all sat on the kerb and spoke about the evening's events and as the time was heading towards 10pm, Katie said that she better get home, she gave the guys a hug then crossed over the road towards her street. Jimmy offered Stone a ride home on the back of his bike. It was not far to walk but Stone was just hoping to get home quickly and put an end to a somewhat eventful evening. Whilst riding home with Jimmy, Stone was looking up at the stars, almost praying for a sign from Maria, as he knew she would have all the answers of what to do. He held on to his faithful friend as they pulled into his road, with thoughts of Rachael's face still fresh in his mind.

Stone's neighbour across the way was standing there watching the two lads pull the bike to a standstill outside Stone's house. Ed Miller had lived there roughly the same amount of time as the Schiano family and they were all great friends. "Say Stone, are you ok?" Ed asked. He walked over towards Stone muttering under his breath, "you had old Christopher Jenson here looking for you earlier, he seemed really pissed and looking at the state of your face, I'm guessing he found you! I presume it's to do with his daughter? Stone, of all the girls you could have chosen, you had to choose the one with an egotistical, over-protective father. You'd be better off forgetting all about her."

Stone started to feel emotional and his eyes filled with tears, "I wish I could, I really do but I love her Ed and she loves me. I can't just let her go."

Ed looked at Jimmy and they both raised their eyebrows at each other then looked at the floor, lost for words. "Well, just be careful lad, be very careful," then walked over to his house and went inside and closed the door.

Jimmy hugged Stone, "Hey man, Ed's kind of right, maybe it's time to let this thing with Rachael go. She's going back to New York tomorrow and you've got your life here man, you don't need this shit."

Stone pulled away from Jimmy, "I know you care about me Jimmy but you see buddy, I care so much about Rachael. She's 19 for God's sake and this guy is treating her like a child. If he's not careful, he's going to ruin her life and I can't just standby and let that happen Jimmy, I can't. My mother met her too Jimmy, she liked her and the last thing she saw was me being happy with Rachael so I can't let her go Jimmy." He hugged his friend goodbye, telling him he needed to go inside and clear his head. Jimmy understood and the two men started to go their separate ways. "Hey Jimmy, thanks buddy, thanks for everything," Stone shouted from his door.

"Anytime buddy," Jimmy shouted, just before whizzing off up the road on his bike.

Chapter 9

It was 7am the next morning in the Jenson house and Rachael had gone straight to her bedroom the night before. Now she laid in bed, curled into a ball, with her covers almost over her head, still upset from the previous evening. She couldn't believe how it was possible for something so perfect to go so horribly wrong. She could hear her father giving orders to Wesley downstairs, followed by footsteps approaching her door in the hallway.

Suddenly, there was a knock on her door, "Rachael, it's me, mom, can I come in?" said Susan in a soft voice.

Rachael paused for a moment before she answered, 'morning mom, yes, you can come in,' she said quietly.

Susan came in and closed the door behind her. She walked over and sat at the foot of Rachael's bed.

"Look, your father told me everything last night and I'm not going to say anymore on the matter but please, in future, don't lie to us Rachael. We were worried out of our minds when Charlie Johnson knocked on the door asking for you. This guy Stone may be good looking, cool and fun but honey, he's not the right guy for you."

Before Susan could say anymore, Rachael huffed and pulled the covers completely over her head. "Mom, please let us not talk about this anymore, I will pack my things and be ready for when we leave at 12," said Rachael abruptly from beneath her covers.

"Ok dear, we will see you downstairs. I will speak to your father and I promise we will never mention this again. You are back at University on Wednesday and after you get your law degree and meet a handsome lawyer from a worthy family, you will thank us eventually, I'm sure," said Susan. She then stood up, smiled at Rachael and walked out the door.

Rachael was angry with her mother's words so she threw back the covers and ran to the door and locked it. Back in her bed, she sobbed into her pillow, still damp from the previous night's tears.

Eventually, Rachael pulled herself together and jumped in the shower. As she closed her eyes and her mind was full of wonderful memories of making love to Stone. As the water poured down onto her soft skin, she whispered to herself, "One day, one day, no-one will stop us, we'll show them all." These words gave her hope and she smiled with a hint of deviousness aimed towards her interfering parents.

Stone was waking up just as the phone was ringing, he pushed aside the pillow that he had been clinging onto for most of the night, it was still carrying the scent of Rachael's perfume. He jumped out of bed and walked to the hallway phone, ruffling his hair and yawning as he picked up the receiver.

"Hi there Stone, it's Jimmy. I just wondered if you slept ok buddy?" His dearest friend was just checking he had not done anything crazy, what with his mother's passing and now this.

"Hey bud, yeah I'm cool, don't worry man," Stone answered confidently.

"That's cool man, listen I'll see you at work."

"No worries bro," Stone answered.

Stone had a quick shower and as he walked back into his room he looked in the mirror to see if there was any bruise or mark from Jenson's blow to his face but luckily there was hardly any damage. He threw on his work clothes and headed out the door.

Thoughts of the previous evening were haunting him but he tried desperately not to dwell on it too much although this was proving to be difficult. The first part of their evening had been so wonderful, so he just tried to focus on the good part.

As Stone came out and headed over to his motorcycle, his neighbour across the way acknowledged him with a smile and a wave before climbing into his car.

Stone waved back and turned the ignition key on his bike and proceeded out the gate and on his way to work.

It was almost 11.45am before the Jenson family were moving their final luggage to the back door. There was a tense atmosphere in the house in which you could cut with a knife. No-one was talking much and Rachael couldn't even look at her father in the eye. She was struggling to shake off the image of her father physically striking Stone in the face. The vision just kept repeating itself over and over in her mind and she was concerned that she may never forgive him. She loved her father but he had a terrible temper and he would often rough handle her when he was angry but he never hit her or physically harmed her or her mother in any way.

Jenson's real problem and downfall was that he was an overprotective father that had come from a very strict family line himself. He'd been brainwashed into the mindset of making sure your children were well educated and only mixed with wealthy people. This had been his family's way for centuries and was the only way to secure a happy life, in his opinion. He simply wanted only the very best for Rachael, making sure she did well with her career and choice of partner was of the utmost importance and failure to do so, would be a failure on his part and that wasn't going to happen on his watch.

Jenson had arranged for their chauffeur to take them to the airport and he estimated they should be in New York by at least 6pm at the latest that evening. Susan was pacing up and down talking to herself, going over everything the family had to take. Rachael had packed just one case as she was leaving most of her summer clothes behind in California. The climate in Manhattan was a lot cooler and she had a whole wardrobe of warmer clothes waiting for her in the Jenson home, aptly named Jenson Lodge. It was a grand house with 11 bedrooms and 20 acres of land just on the outskirts of Connecticut with convenient rail links to Grand Central and Boston if you so wish but most importantly, Quinnipiac University was just a bus ride for Rachael and she often caught the bus with friends.

The morning seemed to be dragging and Rachael was walking around in a daze. She was praying that in all the commotion Monday evening, Stone hadn't lost her address. She was really hoping that he would write to her.

Stone had thoughts of Rachael most of the morning whilst working underneath an old Lincoln, changing the oil. He knew that Rachael was leaving at midday and he had the crazy idea of riding down to Butterfly Beach at lunchtime so that he may catch a glimpse of her leaving. He knew for sure the only way to the main highway was straight down the old coast driveway.

"Hey Stone, can you pass me the rubber mallet please buddy?" Jimmy asked. His friend's request had snapped him away from his thoughts and he handed the mallet to Jimmy.

"Say Jimmy, can you cover me for 15 minutes so I can take an early lunch, I want to go for a quick ride to clear my head." Stone said quietly.

"Err yeah, I guess buddy. You're not going where I think you're going are you?" Jimmy asked with a concerned look on his face.

"Look Jimmy, I know this is hard to understand but I just want to catch a final glimpse of her and wave her off. I feel after last night it's the right thing to do so please buddy, try to understand."

"Yeah I get it, you're in love man but hey, buddy, be careful, this Jenson guy is a goddamn lunatic."

Stone thanked him and he removed his overalls and proceeded to wash his hands in the sink by the office entrance before he left.

He didn't spend any more time thinking about it, he jumped on his bike and headed off to Butterfly Beach.

In the Jenson household, their car had arrived out front promptly and the family all walked down the steps of the big house, making sure they had not forgotten anything.

Susan checked with Christopher that he had the passports at hand and Jenson double checked in his hand luggage before throwing it on the back seat of the car.

They all got in, Susan and Rachael in the back, with miserable old Jenson in the front. Remarkably, he had not said a word to Rachael all morning about the previous night, it was as if it had never happened. Rachael would have preferred he had said something, as this complete dismissal was just odd for her father.

Inside the car no-one spoke, not even the chauffeur said a word, apart from confirming the destination.

Stone was already at the main junction at the bottom of the hill where the main drag to Butterfly Beach started. For a moment, he wondered if Jenson's car had already gone by but he could just sense Rachael was still close. He knew Jenson had his own chauffeur, so he just had his eyes peeled for a large, flash, stretched Cadillac or something similar.

He looked as far as his eyes could see to the top of the hill when suddenly he got a glimpse of a white Lincoln coming down slowly towards the junction. It was Rachael, he just knew it, no-one else used cars like these in this small old town.

Stone started to feel anxious and awkward, almost regretting the fact that he was on full view at the junction. There was absolutely no way anyone could miss seeing him coming down the hill. As the car reached the junction, Stone's heart started to pound as he soon realised this was the car. Immediately, his eyes met with Christopher Jenson as the car started to indicate. Jenson chose to look the other way and not make a scene, hoping his daughter hadn't noticed him but Rachael had already spotted Stone so she opened her window as fast as she could. Susan soon realised what was happening and she asked their driver to speed up. As the driver's foot hit the gas, Stone blew Rachael a kiss and waved goodbye with tears forming in his eyes. Rachael pushed her head out the window as far as she could as the car started to gather speed away from the junction.

Stone continued to wave, with Rachael looking back as the car drove off into the distance. The excitement was over but Stone continued to look in the direction of the car, tears still flowing from his eyes. Would anything be the same again? He started to feel nauseous and trembly inside, a feeling he had never, ever felt in his lifetime, a feeling of complete emptiness.

In the Jenson car, it was a similar situation. Jenson had not said a word and Susan had not said anymore since her command to the driver.

But poor Rachael was heartbroken and she too had a feeling of emptiness and complete sadness. She was trying to comprehend how seeing his face made her feel so alive, so full of joy and excitement and in the next moment, a feeling of complete and utter devastation. She knew there was only one explanation, that she was truly in love with this boy and she knew that somehow, someday she would have to find a way back to him.

Stone went back to Redwing's garage where Greg Phillip's and Jimmy were standing outside having a smoke when he arrived.

He parked his bike in his usual parking spot and walked over to his pals. "So, did you see her, did you get to say goodbye?" asked Jimmy, whilst taking a drag on his cigarette.

"Yes, I saw her at the junction at Butterfly Beach at the bottom of the hill," answered Stone with sadness in his voice.

"And?" asked Greg curiously.

"Yeah, what happened man? Did that jackass Jenson say anything buddy?" Jimmy asked.

"No, nothing. Hey, if you don't mind guys, can we talk about it some other time? She's gone now and that's the end of that for now I guess," as he grabbed his overall's and proceeded to put them on. He then walked back over to the office to look at the workload sheets.

The Jenson's had a fairly drama free journey home, the plane arrived at JFK Airport on time and just as Christopher Jenson had predicted, they had arrived in good time. As they passed through the gates of Jenson Lodge it was 6.30pm which was ideal as they all had a busy evening to prepare for the following day. The family had said very little to each other on the journey home and once all the bags and luggage had been brought into the hallway, Rachael headed straight for her bedroom and closed the door where she stayed for the entire evening.

She had to be up bright and early for Uni the next morning, so she sorted her clothes out and lifted her study books from her bedside drawer.

When Stone got home that evening, he checked again that he had Rachael's address safely in his possession and decided to make a start on his first letter to her.

He pulled some writing paper from a side unit in the lounge and there conveniently happened to be some envelopes too. He wondered mindlessly how long the envelopes and paper had been there and whether or not the envelopes would still have their sticky seals.

He was not feeling that hungry but thoughts of Rachael were still crowding his mind, so he forced himself to eat some soup and a couple of slices of toast, which he struggled to finish. In his head he had so many questions for Rachael. Was she ok? Had they arrived safely? Had her father been harsh with her? How was college? But most importantly, he wanted to tell her how he felt about her, to reassure her.

Chapter 10

As the sun came up on Wednesday morning in Santa Barbara, the locals were finding it extremely quiet after the holiday season. The shops did less trade and the beach became almost empty, like a ghost town, although most folk enjoyed this period as they could finally park wherever they wanted to again.

Stone woke up relatively early and jumped straight in the shower. He had managed a start on his letter to Rachael, just a few lines, but he had intended to finish it after work.

Remarkably, he was feeling more optimistic about the situation with Rachael as he knew at some point she would leave the Jenson family and start her own life.

After rushing down some orange juice and cereal, he left the house and headed to work.

In the Jenson household things were already starting to swing back to the old stressful busy ways.

Christopher was on the phone whilst trying to also fasten his tie, Susan was making breakfast and Rachael was doing her makeup at her dressing table. Suddenly, just to add to the madness, the doorbell rang and their dog Willis started barking. Willis was a seven-year-old Golden Retriever that spent most of the time in kennels or with Wesley the gardener but all the family adored him.

Willis, please!!" Susan shouted. The excited dog sat down and panted heavily. Susan put down her plates and walked over to answer the door. When she pulled open the door, standing there was her sister-in law, Carol, with her father, Frank Jenson, who at 85 was suffering from Dementia. This seemed to develop shortly after Christopher's mother Sally had passed away a few years back. Carol was struggling to care for him alone, so she would occasionally visit her brother to share the responsibility.

Carol and Frank had also visited them whilst they were in Santa Barbara through the holiday season and now she had decided to spend a few weeks in New York with the family.

"Morning folks, sorry we're early, the roads were quiet for once. We got here in no time at all, didn't we Daddy?" Carol said to her father, whilst clinging on to him. The old man just grunted, confused by the whole episode.

"Come in, come in, lovely to see you," said Susan happily. Carol and Frank wandered in and sat down at the breakfast table. Susan continued organising breakfast whilst Carol filled them in on their journey from start to finish, Susan just nodded and smiled, unable to get a word in edgeways.

"Oh, Susan, I forgot to mention, just before we left you in Santa Barbara, daddy wandered off as I was loading the car so you can imagine how scared I was. Well, if it hadn't been for this really helpful guy getting Daddy back in the car, I don't know what I would have done," Carol said. Rachael happened to overhear her auntie as she came down the stairs.

"Morning auntie," she said breezily. So this guy, did you get his name?' she tried to ask casually.

"Oh hi sweetie, yes I think it was Michael but he said everyone calls him Stone or something" she laughed. "He was a rather handsome chap, I think you would have liked him Rachael," Carol chuckled. At that moment Christopher walked into the room and he, Susan and Rachael stared at Carol in amazement, trying to digest the words she had just spilled out. "Erm, why are you all looking at me like that?" Carol asked.

"You don't want to know Carol, you really don't." answered Christopher, shaking his head. Rachael came over and sat at the table.

'I'll explain auntie but now isn't the time, is it daddy?" said Rachael sarcastically. Christopher's body stiffened and he looked at Susan, who very quickly jumped in.

"Yes, that's right Rachael, now isn't the time and I'm sure auntie Carol and grandad Frank are gasping for a coffee right now." Rachael seemed disappointed by her mother's reaction so she shook her head in disapproval and buttered a piece of toast feeling irritated. Carol looked at Rachael and she realised she had obviously touched on a sensitive subject with the family.

"Oh I do apologise if I have touched a nerve, let's save it for another time then perhaps," said Carol, confused by her family's reaction.

Deep inside, Rachael was so happy because for the first time Stone had been recognised for his kindness in the Jenson household. Although the matter had been dismissed, it had still been said and even though her father probably hated hearing it, it was one small step in Stone's favour she thought. Rachael continued to pour everyone a cup of coffee and listen to her auntie talking about the funny things her grandfather said without knowing it himself.

Willis was snuggled up under the table close to Rachael's feet, hoping for scraps to be dropped on the floor. Rachael would often like to treat her bundle of creamy fluff, he could smell bacon and eggs on the table, hoping for a taste. Susan would always prepare a substantial breakfast for her family, especially before they went about their daily activities. In Rachael's case, it was her last term studying Law at University and she was hoping to land a work placement sometime before Christmas.

After breakfast, Rachael kissed Willis on the nose, said goodbye to everyone and walked out the door. She needed to be at the bus stop by no later than 8.30am. Her father gave her a feeble wave but Carol and Susan seemed more enthusiastic with their farewell. Quinnipiac University was on the outskirts of Connecticut, it was a huge modern building with mainly glass structure to the roof which offered a bright, fresh welcome whenever you stepped through its doors. This was Rachael's second year, so she knew what to expect this term, however, she also knew this term would be far more intense than the previous one but this didn't phase her because she was confident she would get through with sufficient grades.

Back at Redwing's garage, Stone came in bright and cheerful, which was a pleasant surprise for Greg and Jimmy as they were expecting their friend to be a little down since Rachael had left.

The guys all had a brief catch up, then jumped into their overalls and started working.

It was a busy day at Red Wing's and the boss, Billy Keegan, was due back in today after a vacation in Mexico with his wife.

Stone looked at the worksheet and the day looked full, this was unusual as things were normally quiet this time of year, but no-one was complaining as the days went more quickly.

It wasn't long before Billy arrived; he drove an old 68 Mustang which was his pride and joy with it's a unique sound. You could hear it coming a mile away.

He soon pulled up into the yard, swung his door open and walked into the workshop. Keegan was a middle-aged man in his late 40's, an ex Marine in fine shape and well respected in the area.

He said hello to Jimmy and Greg, then walked straight over to Stone. "Hey Stone, can I have a private word with you in my office?" he said.

"Yes sure Mr Keegan," Stone replied, feeling slightly concerned about what he might have to say.

"Come in, shut the door, take a seat," Billy said invitingly. Stone walked in nervously and took a seat while Billy removed his jacket and hung it over his chair behind his desk. "Hey, don't look so worried, I only want a chat, that's all. I know recently things have been tough, what with your dear mother's passing and this problem I hear you have with the Jenson family but I just want you to know if you ever need to talk about it I'm a good listener. Now I heard a rumour that Christopher Jenson took a swing at you and in my book that's not right but my advice to you son, is stay away from this guy, he has got a bad reputation round these parts and plenty of money to back him up, if you get my drift."

"Ok Billy, thanks for the advice and thank you for your concern. If I need someone to talk to in the future, I may just take you up on your offer," Stone said quietly.

"Great, I mean it Stone, anything at all and by the way call me Billy,' said Keegan with a warm smile.

"Thank you Billy, that means a lot." He stood up and the two guys shook hands firmly and as soon as Stone walked back out into the garage, the first customer was just pulling up.

The day passed quickly, mainly because of the pure volume of work, it had certainly been full on, with little breaks in between. All three of the lads were looking forward to getting home and chilling.

They wasted no time locking the place up, even Billy was not hanging about tonight.

"Goodnight boys, thanks for your hard work today, it's much appreciated," said Keegan.

"You're welcome sir," all the guys replied, before making their way home.

Stone was planning on finishing his first letter that evening and he was gradually getting his appetite back, so he decided to get some groceries at his local store on the way home.

For Rachael, it had been another regular day at Quinnipiac University, however, she paid particular attention towards her studies as this was the last term and she really wanted to pass and qualify for a placement in a law firm. She had also really enjoyed seeing her friends again. She had two best friends studying at the same college and all three girls had gone through their whole education together, from Kindergarten to University.

Nicky Chase and Debbie Orchard, also came from privileged families and they had stacks in common. Rachael had told them everything about her summer at Butterfly Beach, including everything about Stone, to which they all listened with deep interest and envy but at the same time feeling incredibly sorry for Rachael after how her family had reacted to the brief encounter, especially Christopher, as they all knew how controlling he could be.

The girls all travelled on the bus together, mostly on their way back home from University and today was no exception. They all lived just a few miles apart so they often spent weekends at the local shopping mall but Christopher Jenson had his driver take them and pick them up most of the time.

Rachael got off the bus last and as she walked towards her house, she was wondering what the atmosphere would be like this evening, especially with her father but luckily for her when she got home he was still at work. Her grandfather was asleep in the armchair in their lounge and her mother was sitting at the table with her auntie deep in conversation.

"Hi Rachael,' said Susan.

"Hi sweetie," said her cheerful auntie. Rachael waved and said hello, before heading straight to her bedroom to relax. Carol and Susan continued with their deep conversation, as Willis followed Rachael up the stairs with his tail wagging. She stroked him on the head and he followed her to her room.

Stone arrived home with his groceries, consisting of chicken, pasta and a few onions and tomatoes. He had plans to cook a substantial meal, since he had not eaten properly for the past two days and he was hoping to finish his letter to Rachael.

As he walked in the old house, it felt such a lonely place, particularly tonight. Thoughts of his mother were rushing through his mind, along with thoughts of Rachael and Jenson, banging on the window and for just a moment, he didn't want to be there.

He walked into the kitchen, put the groceries next to the cooker and took his jacket off hanging it over an old wooden chair by the back door.

He put the radio on to comfort him and he started unwrapping his chicken breast to pan fry. He put a large saucepan of water on the gas hob ready for his pasta and added some olive oil to the frying pan. His mother had trained him well, so he had become a reasonable cook in the Schiano household and he would often prepare food for Maria and himself. He found it hard just preparing for one but he knew his mother would be disappointed if he had become complacent with a poor diet.

He added the chicken to the hot pan and proceeded to chop some onions and tomatoes to add to the sizzling chicken.

The radio happened to be playing an old Elvis track 'Don't Be Cruel', which aroused his memories as his mother and father were big Presley fans. In fact, his father had seen him perform live in the early sixties and had quite an influence on the young Italian.

Stone started to sing the words, whilst adding the chopped additions to his chicken in the pan. The water was boiling now, so he added the pasta to the saucepan.

With some chopped garlic and a little seasoning, he would have a tasty meal in minutes. Stone turned the radio up, singing at the top of his voice, 'Don't be cruel, to a heart that's true, why should we be apart, I really love you baby, cross my heart.' It was as if he were singing out loud to Rachael, the words seemed so apt, so meaningful and he would be sure to mention this in his letter, he thought it would make her smile.

"Ah Rachael, her laugh, I'd love to hear her laugh," he mumbled, like a mad man to himself.

Once he was satisfied the chicken was cooked, he arranged it on a plate with the pasta, tomatoes, and onions and sat down on a stool at the kitchen bar and started to enjoy his meal.

The radio was still providing a great comfort to him and he was enjoying the tracks that were being aired. Stone was now thinking about his letter again, wondering what to say. He thought he would try to be as romantic as he could as his mother had always told him, women like their man to be romantic, so he thought he would make a special effort.

After his meal, he washed his plate and walked into the lounge to find his paper and a decent pen with plenty of ink.

He sat down at the coffee table, switched his mother's favourite lamp on and started to put pen to paper.

'Dear Rachael, I trust you had a safe journey back to New York. I hope you didn't mind me saying goodbye Tuesday afternoon but I simply had to see your face, especially after such an awful end to what started out to be such a perfect evening. I just wanted you to know you looked so beautiful Monday evening at the beach and our time together, before your father found us, was just so incredible.' Stone didn't want to go into too much detail just in case Rachael's parents got hold of the letter but he knew Rachael would know what he meant by those words.

He went on to talk about his feelings for her and signed off, 'Lots of love forever, Stone,' with a lot of kisses. He even glazed the envelope with his favourite cologne, hoping Rachael would hold the envelope close to her face and discover his scent. Stone sealed the letter and wrote the address on the envelope in bold clear letters to ensure there was no error with the post service, he then secured a first class stamp on the envelope and put it on the window seal by the front door ready to post in the morning on his way to work.

Rachael had quite an uneventful evening. She had joined her family for dinner, her father had arrived home late but managed to join them all at the table for the routine evening meal. Her poor grandfather was still sitting in the lounge with his eyes shut and Willis was back under the table hoping for scraps.

For once it was quiet at the dinner table, no-one said much to each other, including her auntie that had been very vocal up until now. It was almost like the energy had been drained from everyone and as if they all just wanted to get dinner out of the way and relax for the rest of the evening. Susan had always prepared good meals for her family and Rachael really enjoyed them and always looked forward to them. Unfortunately, the tension was still raw after their strained departure from Santa Barbara, so shortly after dinner was finished, Rachael took her plate to the sink, washed it up and asked if anyone would mind if she went to her room. Susan smiled at her daughter and said it would be fine, whilst her father was not paying attention to a word anyone was saying. He was too busy, with his nose deep in a local newspaper, whilst still slurping on a glass of white wine from a bottle he had purchased from a local vineyard near Santa Barbara.

Rachael ran up the stairs and her faithful dog followed her to her room. Thoughts of Stone flowed through her mind, hoping that she would soon receive a letter or some form of contact from him, just to know he was ok and that the way her father had acted had not frightened him away. She kept convincing herself that he would not have come to wave her off if he were not interested. She felt it was Stone's way of saying that he would not give up and that he would wait for her no matter what.

Chapter 11

Thursday morning came round fast for Stone, it was almost as if he had written his letter, shut his eyes and Groundhog Day was here again.

It was starting to feel that everyday was the same but at least when Rachael was close by, he felt something was different in his world. Even though he hadn't seen her a great deal, knowing she was just a few miles away was a comfort to him.

Stone rushed down a coffee, got dressed, grabbed his letter and made his way to work.

He posted his letter in a mailbox close to Redwing's garage, kissing it before letting it drop onto the other pile of mail. Quickly looking around to make sure no-one had seen him kiss it, he felt excited about the prospect of Rachael receiving the letter and especially excited about receiving one back.

He then made his way to the garage, where he could see Jimmy just pulling up.The two guys jumped off their bikes and fist pumped each other and laughed.

"Been a while since we did that Buddy," Jimmy said laughing.

"I know man, sure felt good didn't it?" said Stone, chuckling away.

The Blood Ranger duo walked into the garage and Greg was standing by the vending machine with what looked like a black eye.

"Hey Greg, you ok man?" Stone asked. Greg looked up.

"I've been better! I was at Bar Lomas last night having a quiet drink with Mandy when some bikers rolled up, calling themselves the Satanic Disciples. They stirred up some trouble, asking where they could find you and the Blood Rangers and that's when it all kicked off," answered Gregg.

"You know Lance Allen?" Gregg continued. Both Jimmy and Stone nodded. "Well, that idiot said that I knew where you were and when I wouldn't tell him, so he got one of his men to give me a black eye for it. He told me to tell you they were looking for you," said Gregg, who was clearly shaken up by the whole ordeal.

"I have no idea who the Satanic Disciples are and I certainly don't know why they would have a beef with us?" said Jimmy. Stone shook his head in agreement.

"Hey Gregg, I'm sorry we weren't there to back you up man. The guy who punched you, did you happen to get his name?" asked Stone, with anger in his eyes.

"Yeah, he said his name was Clarence Black and he wants to race you at Devil's Run for a 50,000 dollar prize," said Gregg nervously.

"50,000 dollars? Where has he got that amount from, it's never been that huge! Who the hell are these guys?" Just as Stone said that, about 20 bikes pulled into the carpark at Redwing's. Stone and Jimmy knew straight away who they were likely to be. Stone and Jimmy stood their ground but Gregg went into the office and closed the door, still shaken up from the previous night.

A big guy with a thick black beard and studded gloves jumped off his bike and walked over towards Stone and Jimmy with an intimidating grin on his face.

"So, which one of you is Stone?" said the thuggish looking bruiser.

Stone stepped in front of Jimmy, still pissed about Gregg's eye. "Who wants to know?"

"Ah a wise guy eh," said the big oath as he walked closer to Stone. "My name is Clarence Black and we heard this guy Stone recently won a race against Marco Sanchez, a race called Devil's Run, is that right?" asked Clarence.

"Yeah, that's right, so what," said Stone

Clarence smirked, "I take it your Stone then! Well, there was word down in Nevada there's a so-called biker gang, The Blood Rangers, riding around California kicking up a shit storm."

Stone interrupted, "Listen man, I don't know what your fucking problem is or where you're getting your information from. Yeah, we race at Devil's Run and we are the Blood Rangers but we don't cause nobody no problem and we certainly don't appreciate it when we're accused of it. We especially take offence when you hit one of our guys for no reason."

Stone had a reputation as a quiet, kind hearted guy, some might say even soft and he generally hated confrontation. It would take an awful lot to make him wild but when he lost it, boy when he lost his shit and things could get messy.

Stone could feel himself boiling up so he walked closer to Clarence looking up at the beast of a man and said, "Now this is what's going to happen, I am going to get my buddy Gregg out here, and you my friend, are going to apologise to him face to face. If you refuse, it will be a big mistake."

Stone stood his ground, intense focus on Clarence not faltering for a second.

"If it's a race you want, apologise to my buddy. Apologise and I will race you, or anyone else."

The big guy was not expecting this as normally people would be too intimidated to stand up to him. He looked back at his fellow bikers, feeling a little embarrassed and just sniggered to himself nervously.

"Ok, go get your buddy, let's do this," said Clarence.

Stone asked Jimmy to get Gregg but you could see the poor guy shaking his head through the office window. Eventually, Jimmy persuaded him to come out. He walked out behind Jimmy, with his head submissively held low, staring at the floor and stood by Stone's side.

Stone looked at Clarence, waiting for him to start talking. "I'm sorry I hit you man, it's no excuse I know but we were tired and drunk and to be honest you weren't cooperating with us, which I guess is honourable to your buddies," said a defeated sounding Clarence. Gregg looked at the guy, shrugging his shoulders and went back to looking at the chalky ground in the yard. There was an uncomfortable silence for a while and then Stone said.

'Ok, I will race you but where the heck has 50,000 dollars come from? It's never been that high!"

"Well, we live in Nevada and we hang out in Vegas so let's just say, the word got out to some big players in one of the casino's about the Blood Ranger's and a race called Devil's Run, so they sent me down to challenge you to another race but they want to sponsor it and promote it in their casino. They like the idea of raising the stakes a little and they especially got a little turned on when they heard about the possibility of one of the rider's going over the edge." Clarence spat on the floor. "Sick bastards, but hey they got the dough. Then you see, this rumour spread that the Blood Rangers were causing trouble en route from Nevada to Santa Barbara and we thought we would rise to the challenge." Clarence explained.

"Ok, well let's get one thing clear, we don't want you guys causing trouble here with any of the local folk and let me tell you another thing, this bullshit about us causing trouble is just utter crap, obviously spread around by Marco Sanchez and his crew." Any respect Stone had for Marco was now well and truly gone.

"Ok I get you, so if we can set a date for Devil's Run, we will leave tonight and put these prospect investors straight and I reckon we can raise the purse. They mentioned 50k to the winner but I reckon we can double it to 100k, trust me, these guys have got the money, how does that sound?" asked Clarence.

Stone paused for a while, staring at Clarence in the eyes. "Ok I'm in, how does a few months from now sound? Let's say November 10th," said Stone confidently. This just happened to be his mother's birthday and he knew it was a Friday.

"Ok, sounds good to me," said Clarence, who then offered his studded gloved hand for Stone to shake on it. Stone, like any warrior with honour, reached out and firmly shook his hand. Clarence looked at his guys and nodded, they all started their bikes up, it was like a sound of thunder, as they revved their machines. Clarence walked over to his bike, which was a customised Ducati, put his helmet on and started his bike. One by one, the Satanic Disciples pulled out of Redwing's garage and sped off up the street.

Jimmy looked at Stone, "What the hell just happened?"

"I don't know man but what I do know is, I'm racing again in November and if that guy is telling the truth, it could be for big bucks. To be fair, I'm doing it out of principle because he said sorry to Gregg," said Stone. Poor Gregg was back in the office sitting on the boss's chair, who luckily had not turned up yet. Stone walked into the office. "Listen man, I know you wouldn't tell them anything last night and I know that's why they spanked you, so I just want to say thanks buddy, I really appreciate it." Gregg broke into a slight smile.

"Thanks for getting that punk to apologise, I really appreciate that too." He then wandered over to the mirror in the office and looked at his eye, "what am I going to tell Mr Keegan about my eye?" he said.

"Tell him the truth buddy, he's ex-military remember, what you did was honourable and he'll love you for it" answered Stone.

Billy Keegan had heard about the biker invasion at the local shop. Word soon got around in Butterfly Beach that Gregg Phillips had been punched in the face at Bar Loma so when he arrived at work, he already expected to see a slightly troubled Gregg.

Billy walked in the garage and immediately caught sight of Gregg's eye. "Wow, buddy, that's a shiner and a half. I hope the other guy's face looks worse" said Billy, smiling.

Gregg laughed with embarrassment and just went about his work. Stone asked if he could speak with Billy in his office. The two men walked to the back of the garage, into the office and closed the door. Billy sat down in his chair and looked up at Stone.

"Hey, I didn't want to make a fuss but I heard about what happened to Gregg at Bar Lomas last night. I heard some biker dudes were looking for you."

"Well they found me and in fact, they only just left but don't worry I got them to apologise to Gregg. He wouldn't tell them where I was last night so they thumped him." said Stone.

"So why did they want you man? You're a good guy so my first thought was Jenson had arranged a little something for you but they were apparently saying something about a race for 50,000 dollars. Someone in the bar last night told Elsie Roberts in Kelly's store this morning and you know what Elsie is like, once she gets word, you can bet your bottom dollar the whole of Santa Barbara will soon know about it" said Billy with a cheeky grin on his face.

Stone smiled back at him, "It's a long Story Billy but basically, some guys in Vegas heard about Devil's Run and you probably already know, I won this summer against Marco Sanchez," Billy nodded and continued to listen, "Well Sanchez, or one of his crew have been spreading rumours about us, saying the Blood Rangers have been causing trouble along the route from Nevada to Santa Barbara. Clarence Black who rides with the Satanic Disciples got to hear about it and now these so-called big fish casino owners in Vegas want Clarence and I to race in November for 50,000 dollars. I agreed to race him and I have a slight advantage because I've ridden Devil's Run many times before. But this guy must have a reputation elsewhere, otherwise the stake wouldn't be so high." Billy took a moment to think about it and then took a sharp intake of breath.

"Well I hope you know what you are getting into Stone. You know these hoods from Vegas can be very controlling so are you sure this is nothing to do with Jenson? 50k prize money all sounds a little far fetched to me, if I am honest. Listen, I know a few people in Lake Tahoe so let me do a bit of digging, see if I can find out who these guys in Vegas are and see if they know anything about this gang the Satanic Disciples."

"Thanks Mr Keegan," said Stone. Keegan smiled.

"Hey kid, call me Billy ok."

Stone smiled, "Ok Billy, thank you, I really appreciate it." He then turned around and walked out the door.

Jimmy was waiting outside, curious to know what Billy Keegan had said. "Is everything ok Stone, what did he say?" Jimmy asked

"He just said he'd heard all about these guys rolling into town and what had happened and that they'd been looking for me. He's going to speak to some of his contacts in Lake Tahoe to see if anyone has heard about the Satanic Disciples or these guys in Vegas," said Stone.

"Oh cool, so we better get the rest of the boys in on this. It's been a while since we've all been together so I'll try to arrange a meeting at Bar Lomas Saturday night. I only wish we'd all been in here yesterday when Clarence rocked up. It would have been a different story then my friend." Jimmy said laughing.

Rachael was having another regular day at Quinnipiac until lunchtime when, suddenly, she heard a voice call her name across the crowded canteen, "Rachael, Rachael Jenson!" When Rachael looked up, she recognised an old friend that she had known a few years back. Michelle Foster was an old neighbour and school friend, right up until about two years back when her family decided to move away but she was obviously back so maybe things hadn't worked out though Rachael.

"Hey Rach, how are you doing?" She said whilst kissing her on both cheeks.

"I can't believe it Michelle, your back?" Said an equally enthusiastic Rachael.

"May I pull a chair up?" asked Michelle.

"Of course, of course," answered Rachael.

The young lady pulled a chair closer to the table and sat down. She explained that it hadn't worked out in Boston so her father's work had transferred him back to New York so it made sense for them all to move back as it was ideal being close to the University.

"My parents are allowing me to have a moving back party this Saturday, it would mean the world to me if you could come,' said Michelle.

"Oh wow, erm okay, I'll check with my family but it should be okay. Do you remember Nicky Chase and Debbie Orchard?" asked Rachael. Michelle smiled.

"Yes, of course. We all used to hang out at school, didn't we?"

"Well, they're here too, can you believe it, all of us together again so could they come Saturday too?" asked Rachael, excited by the prospect of them all being together again.

"Of course they can. If you see them today, please give them the details, the more the merrier. It's going to be such a cool party and I've invited quite a few cute guys as well Rach. Do you remember that cute guy at school, Ricky Palmer? Well, he's coming and he was asking about you and guess what, he's studying medicine, he wants to be a Doctor."

Rachael blushed and giggled slightly, "Asking about me was he? What did he say?"

"He asked if I'd seen you and whether you were coming to the party. You are so lucky Rachael, all of us girls fancied him at school but he only had eyes for you but the crazy thing was, you were never interested in him," Michelle said, shaking her head and laughing.

"As flattered as I am, my heart is with a guy I met in Santa Barbara this summer, someone so special to me.'

"Oh wow, lucky you, tell me more, what's his name, what is he studying?" asked Michelle.

"His name is Michael Schiano but he goes by the name of Stone. He's a bit older than me and not like any other guy I've known. Unfortunately, my father forbids me to see him, so it was not all sun and roses but I love him dearly and once I qualify from Law school, I intend to be with him in California," said Rachael.

"Oh, how romantic, well there's hope for me yet with Ricky Palmer," Michelle chuckled. The two girls laughed loudly and started to tuck into their lunch before it was time to go back to their classes.

Chapter 12

The rest of the week seemed to fly by. Saturday came along very quickly and Rachael had convinced her parents to allow her to go to Michelle Foster's welcome home party.

Secretly the Jenson's were hoping Rachael might meet someone else at the party, someone studying for a professional career, perhaps a Lawyer or a Doctor. Christopher Jenson was convinced that Rachael would soon forget all about Stone and move on with her life.

Rachael had invited Nicky and Debbie on Michelle's behalf, so they were all looking forward to the reunion. The girls all intended to dress to impress, as they knew that Ricky Palmer was going to be there. All their parents had hoped their daughters would meet someone like him, a handsome young man from a wealthy family, with great career prospects.

Michelle lived in a large white house with a huge conservatory, which was often used for family gatherings, especially at this time of year. The weather in Connecticut had started to chill in the evenings and the darker evenings were creeping in fast, especially towards the beginning of October. The party was set for 7pm but most of the guests were estimated to arrive around 8pm. All the girls had arranged a lift to the party but Jenson had insisted on having his daughter dropped off and collected by the family's private chauffeur. Rachael didn't mind this but sometimes she used to feel embarrassed, as if her father was trying to flaunt his wealth but those who knew Jenson knew it was mainly because he wanted to keep tabs on Rachael.

All the girls arrived at near enough the same time. Rachael was wearing a beautiful red dress with a bow in the middle and a full-length cream coat draped over her shoulders to keep off the chill. She had her hair down and she was feeling confident as she walked towards the large white house, where you could already hear the party was in full swing. Also walking towards the house were Nicky and Debbie, both looking very glamorous, thought Rachael.

"Hi ladies," said Rachael beaming.

"Hey Rach, look at you, you look amazing," said Nicky.

"Wow, I simply love your dress," Debbie agreed.

"Ah, thank you ladies, I think you both look amazing too."

The girls walked up the steps approaching the entrance to the house, when the door swung open and they were greeted by an extremely excited Michelle Foster.

"Ladies!" she shouted, with a huge grin on her face. "Come in, come in, I'm so pleased you made it."

Michelle was wearing a green emerald sequin dress with a split at the front showing her left thigh, with white high heels. She looked stunning, thought Rachael. In fact, all the girls were feeling slightly envious of the way she looked. Nicky and Debbie were both reasonably tall and skinny with little shape to their bodies, however, it was clear to see they had both made a huge effort to dress up and make the best of their looks.

Rachael was always comfortable in her own skin and her friends had joked in the past that she'd look a million dollars wearing rags. It was a very kind compliment as she could never see herself that way, in fact she was never too concerned with much makeup and flash clothes, it was only for special occasions that she would pay particular attention to her looks.

As the girls walked into the main hallway, they could hear music playing in the lounge, along with laughter and the clinking of glasses as friends were making toasts to each other enjoying the ambience of the party.

Michelle asked if she could take the girls coats and all three of the girls very obligingly removed them and handed them over. Michelle hung them on a large coat stand next to the Grandfather clock then showed them into the lounge. Debbie was the first to walk in with Nicky and Rachael in tow.

There were a lot of people standing in separate groups. The men were wearing dinner suits and the ladies were mainly in cocktail dresses. Everyone seemed to be enjoying themselves, the drinks were flowing and there was a huge buffet laid out. It was clear Michelle and her family had gone to a lot of trouble to make the evening as special as they could for their guests.

Michelle's parents were very trusting of their daughter and they had left her to organise the party and invite whoever she liked. They knew their daughter only mixed in decent circles and at 19 going on 20, she was completely capable of making sure the house was looked after and she would be considerate to the neighbours.

Rachael, Nicky and Debbie all headed over to the table where the drinks were. It was a help yourself arrangement so Rachael played bar girl, asking what the girls wanted to drink. They all agreed on white wine. After their glasses were filled, they started to mingle. Rachael was curious to see Ricky Palmer but looking around she couldn't see him, at least she certainly hadn't recognised him anyway.

Michelle came back over to the bar and told everyone that the buffet was now open. The buffet must have cost a fortune, thought Rachael, as there was absolutely everything you could imagine, from healthy salads to burger and fries.

As generous as it all was, the girls had little appetite for food right now and just wanted to get a few drinks down to help them relax.

Nicky was drinking like a fish and looking around for people she knew, when suddenly she noticed some friends from her past so she drifted off leaving Debbie and Rachael still standing rather uncomfortably on their own by the bar.

The two girls poured themselves another drink and made light conversation about University, discussing their long-term plans. Debbie surprised Rachael as her plans were to complete her studies and then go travelling around the world for a few years before settling down, however, she was adamant never to have children. She had come from a large family with young siblings and seen her parents often pulling their hair out with the stress of all the children.

Rachael just began to talk about Stone, when a tall, good looking chap with light brown hair and blue eyes approached the girls. As he got closer Rachael recognised him. It was Ricky Palmer.

"Hi Ladies, how are you doing? You may not remember me, but I remember you," he said with a cheeky grin.

"Yes, we remember you Ricky," said Debbie laughing. Ricky smiled and looked directly at Rachael.

"So, do you remember me?" he said, eager for a reaction.

Rachael was a little embarrassed as she'd remembered what Michelle had said about him always having a crush on her.

She gasped a little, almost choking on her words. "Yes of course I remember you Ricky, I think most of the girls here know exactly who you are," she said in a playful response and chuckled a little nervously.

Ricky smiled, paused for a bit and looked her deep in the eyes.

"May I say Rachael, you and Debbie look absolutely stunning tonight," rather awkwardly he continued to talk without a pause, "wasn't it just a wonderful idea of Michelle's to get us all together here tonight?"

"Yes, it's so lovely, it was a great thing to do and so nice to see everyone," Rachael answered.

Debbie seemed to jump in and grab his attention, talking about when they were kids and how he would always ride his little red pedal car up and down the street shouting "good morning" to all the neighbours. They were both giggling like school children when Rachael took a moment to reflect why she had never fallen for him. He was well mannered, good looking, well spoken with huge prospects in the medical profession and from a wealthy family she thought. Some would say the perfect catch but the more she thought about it, the more she started to realise that perhaps it was because of her family's influence. She knew her parents had almost brainwashed her into a mindset that they would only allow wealthy professional men into her life so maybe part of her had rebelled, could this be why she was so attracted to Stone. Her thoughts were broken as Madonna's latest hit started to play and everyone started dancing. The booze was free flowing and couples formed a circle in the middle of the lounge and started gyrating around. Some were mimicking moves from the movie Footloose and it was really starting to liven up. Rachael turned around to look at Debbie but she was dragging Ricky off to dance. He looked embarrassed as she pulled him into the centre of the lounge and started to perform some odd kind of sexy dance around him. He looked at Rachael and mimed the words "help me." Luckily for him the song soon came to an end, so he made a quick escape back to where Rachael was standing whilst Debbie had caught the eye of a more obliging dance partner and was now fooling around with him.

"Thanks, goodness for that," said a red-faced Ricky as he picked up his bottle of lager. He winked at Rachael, took a large slurp of his chilled Budweiser and in a flirtatious voice spoke to Rachael.

"You know Rach, I've always had a huge crush on you, since we were at school and still have." Rachael wanted the ground to swallow her up, I mean, here she was being chatted up by the best looking guy at the party, that every girl here wanted a piece of, and she just wasn't feeling it.

"Ricky, I'm flattered, really I am but you see, I'm actually seeing someone right now and it just wouldn't be right," Rachael said.

"Oh, I see, well he's one lucky guy that's all I can say Rach," said a disappointed Ricky Palmer, before staggering over to his friends on the other side of the room.

Michelle had noticed the pair talking and it was clear Ricky had been enjoying the booze through the evening. Perhaps he'd needed Dutch courage to make his pass at Rachael thought Michelle. She wandered over to join Rachael, "So, how'd you get on with Ricky? He was so excited you were coming tonight, in fact, it's the first thing he asked me when I told him about the party."

Rachael was now feeling rather guilty but she felt she just had to be honest.

"He's a great guy, he's got the whole package but he's not my type and plus I'm seeing Stone." It suddenly dawned on her how far away from her Stone really was and she missed everything about him. She became emotional in a split second and Michelle picked up on her friend's reaction.

"Oh Rach, please don't get upset, I can see this guy in California really means alot to you."

"Yes, he does, he really does, I love him Michelle."

"Let's make a toast to your man Rach, what's his name again?"

"Stone, his name is Stone," said Rachael proudly.

"Here's to Stone!" shouted both the girls. They took a large gulp of wine and then gave each other a huge hug. The party seemed to fly by and it wasn't long before Rachael's driver arrived and she found herself saying goodbye to everyone. It had been a lovely opportunity to see all her friends from school again.

Back in Santa Barbara, Stone was on his way to join all the guys at Bar Lomas. As he approached the dirt track leading towards the car park, he could hear the sound of his fellow riders in the distance. It was a sound that always made him smile as slowly, one by one, all the bikes pulled in just outside the entrance to Bar Lomas.

Parking up ahead he could see Jimmy, always eager to arrive slightly early. This was something the two guys always had in common, something that kept them close.

As Stone and Jimmy secured their bikes, the rest of the crew started to drift over. It wasn't long before the whole car park was full with Blood Ranger jackets and a mass of Japanese, Italian and American bikes.

The owners of Bar Lomas were expecting them, always grateful for the trade and happy to see the boys.

Stone walked around with Jimmy fist pumping all the loyal bandits, before walking in through the heavy wooden doors to the bar.

The staff on tonight were Terry Gamble and Sally Kent, who had been on shift the night Greg Philips got lumped.

"Where were you guys the other night when we needed you?" shouted Terry.

"I only wish we were here," replied Jimmy.

"In fact, that's kind of why we're here tonight but first off, let's all get a drink in. Say Sally, are you doing food tonight?" Stone asked.

"You bet we are, I got burgers, chicken, steak and fries."

"Ok lads, hands up for burgers and fries!" Stone shouted. Everyone put their hands in the air. "That's all of us then Sally."

He stood up and thanked everyone for coming, then started to explain why they were all there.

"Ok guys, for those of you that don't know why we are here, basically the bozo that came here the other night, kicking up a storm was a guy called Clarence Black. He was looking for me, as you may have heard, anyway he found Jimmy and I at Redwings the other morning. He said that there was a rumour going around in Vegas that the Blood Rangers were riding around town causing trouble, bragging about Devil's Run to wind up a guy called Marco Sanchez. Well, we all know this is bullshit, obviously one of Marco's boys has spread this, hence why the Satanic Disciples came looking for us. The long and short of it is guys, I put him straight and made him apologise to Gregg. What's also transpired from this is the real reason Clarence and his boys were looking for me, was to tell me that some casino owners in Vegas have heard about Devil's Run and they wanted to raise the stakes. I guess this could be a huge deal for them, depending on the interest they get from prospective investors. They want Clarence and I to race in a few months, the winner could take 50k minimum or it may be as big as 100k. I accepted the challenge, not for the cash, however, that is a bonus but out of pride and honour. Clarence apologised to Gregg so I agreed to race him. As you know, Gregg stood loyal to us all the other night, that kind of loyalty means more than any cash in my book. Now if this thing gets big publicity, as we think it will, Jimmy and I feel there won't just be one race that evening, in fact there could be a whole host of riders who'll want to ride Devil's Run so if any of you want to practice for it, now might be a good time to say. I guess Clarence and his boys will want to do a few dummy runs, so the likelihood is they will be back sooner than we think. You all know the risks and I don't want to encourage anyone to do it, I'm just saying, if you want to, the opportunity will be there, I'm sure of it."

It was a lot to take in for the guys, as up until now, the Blood Rangers had just been a bit of fun, just fellow riders that enjoyed the sense of belonging, a chance to make friends and go on summer ride outs along the coast. It had only been through the interference of other biker groups that Devil's Run was born in the first instance but this was usually an annual event that just added a little excitement to the whole biker gang culture.

Terry came over and started handing out bottles of Bud to the lads and this seemed a perfect opportunity for Stone to make a toast to the Blood Rangers.

"Here's to the Blood Rangers, may we continue to ride!" All thirty of his loyal brothers raised their bottles of beer and shouted, "To the Blood Rangers!"

Stone thanked them all for their time and Sally started bringing out their burgers and fries, which was perfect timing.

As all the lads tucked into their well stacked burgers, silence filled the room for a moment whilst everyone enjoyed the Bar Lomas homemade special.

After they all polished off their meals, the beers started to flow and they broke up into individual smaller groups. They were all discussing the prospect of riding at Devil's Run and the likelihood of earning some big bucks. Jimmy sat with Stone for the evening and the two lads enjoyed the rest of the night before heading off home around 11pm.

It had been a successful evening, thought Stone and Jimmy, not only to make amends with Bar Lomas but there was a real sense of camaraderie amongst the guys.

In Connecticut, it was the early hours of the morning when Rachael arrived home. Her faithful chauffeur opened her door and she got out feeling slightly dizzy as she walked towards her house. Rachael turned round, waved goodbye to the driver and rang the doorbell feeling a little tipsy. Christopher opened the door and Rachael just walked by him and headed for the stairs. "Excuse me young lady, don't just ignore me." said Jenson angrily. Rachael looked round at her father and said.

"I'm sorry Daddy, I feel a little lightheaded and thought it best to go straight to my room." Just as she said that Susan came out of the lounge.

"So, how did it go Rachael? I heard that nice boy Ricky Palmer was going to the party, did you see him? He's going to be a Doctor you know." Susan said cheerfully.

"Yes, I did see him Mum and he's a nice lad but he's not my type."

"Not your type?" mumbled Christopher, shaking his head in disbelief. "I suppose that loser in California is more your type, is he?" Christopher said abruptly.

Susan looked at the floor, she felt her husband had been rather harsh and she knew his words would cut deep with their daughter. Rachael turned to her father and said

"Yes daddy, if you are referring to Stone, then yes he is my type. Now if you don't mind, I'm a little tired and I would like to go to bed." Susan walked over to her husband and touched him on the shoulder so Jenson walked away in a huff. Rachael smiled at her mother and said goodnight, before climbing the stairs, with Willis eagerly following her.

Rachael walked up onto the landing and then into her bedroom, securing her lock behind her. She undressed, kissed her faithful dog on the head and jumped straight into bed. She noticed the curtains were open and she could see the moonlit sky clearly. She pulled her covers back and was just about to jump up and close them, when she noticed the stars looked so beautiful. She felt comforted by them, so she chose to climb back into bed and just stare at them. She gazed at the stars for what seemed like hours, thinking about Stone, imagining them both together in a house of their own some day and thoughts of having children with him. Dreams of a happy, loving home with a man she truly loves and a man that truly loves her back, finally, she dreamed of being free from her father's firm hold.

Chapter 13

Sunday was a very quiet day for Stone, he spent the day cleaning his bike and tidying the house as he knew his mother would always clean when she was able to and felt if she was looking down on him she would be satisfied with the upkeep of the house.

Thoughts of Rachael were constantly on his mind and he was wondering if his letter had reached her and whether she was preparing one to send back to him.

Rachael woke early Sunday morning to find rain pelting down outside. It was a kind of cosy feeling she thought, all wrapped up warm under the covers, protected from the storm brewing outside. She found the sound of the rain hitting the window relaxing and therapeutic so with no plans for the day she just rolled over into a fetal position and went back to sleep.

Awoken a few hours later by the sound of thunder crashing and lightning strikes every ten seconds was enough to make her jump up and close the curtains. How could last night be so beautiful and now we have this thought Rachael.

She glanced at a small white antique carriage clock on her Victorian dresser. It was showing midday and she thought her family may soon be checking on her, so she walked to the bathroom and took a warm shower, before jumping into some fresh clothes and venturing downstairs.

When she reached the lounge, she could see her poor grandfather sitting in an armchair just staring at the wall. She almost greeted him but soon remembered that he unfortunately had no idea who she was, so she just waved and smiled and continued walking to the kitchen. "Good afternoon," said her auntie Carol, sitting at the table. She laughed and winked at Rachael when she said it.

"Good morning auntie."

"So, did you have a good night at the party darling?" Carol asked.

"Yes, thank you, it was so lovely to see all my old school friends and neighbours from way back."

"Oh, that's good sweetie. Does you good to get out occasionally, doesn't it?" Carol said smiling. She knew her brother could be a little overprotective and strict with Rachael, so she felt it was far healthier for Rachael to get out and socialise every so often, especially as she was almost 20.

Carol made coffee and some eggs for Rachael and they both had a long chat about life in general, Rachael's University and how Carol was managing with Frank and his dementia. Every so often they would stop in their tracks, interrupted by dear old Frank as the old man would moan out, followed by a loud snore, which made Willis bark every time and Carol and Rachael would roll with laughter.

As they were still laughing, the front door opened and in walked Susan and Christopher, they had been to a morning church service and they seemed quiet as they entered the kitchen.

"Morning folks," said Carol. Christopher just rolled his eyes and went to sit next to his sleeping father in the lounge.

"Forgive him Carol, he's in one of his moods, you know what he can be like," said Susan as she started to fill the sink to finish the dishes.

"Oh let me do that mum," said Rachael wanting to let her mother know she was grateful for her input the previous evening when Christopher was shouting at her.

"Oh no, it's fine, really Rachael but thanks anyway," replied Susan, whilst continuing to scrub the plates.

"If you're sure, would you mind if I go back to my room?" asked Rachael.

"No of course I don't mind, silly. It's awful weather out there and it's a Sunday so in fact, I think we may all soon be lazing around, I mean look at grandpa, bless him," she said laughing.

With that, Rachael called Willis and headed back to her room. Willis beat her to the top and she invited him in and closed the door. He was a well-trained dog and would often just go and lay down somewhere quietly. Christopher had him trained especially hard to make him more Independent and manageable around the home. This had obviously paid off well as Willis was a truly kind dog, however, if pushed he could become a great protector.

The rest of the day seemed to pass rather quickly for Rachael and it was not long before she was back downstairs for dinner followed by University work until it was time for bed again.

Stone had given the old house the once over, cleaned his bike and even managed to cut the lawn at the back of the property. He was certainly ready for his bed that evening and after cooking himself a decent meal, he decided to have an early night.

Monday morning came round in a flash. In Connecticut, Susan was up at the crack of dawn ready to serve her family before they all went about their business. Christopher had an appointment in New York City and Rachael had another important day studying at Quinnipiac. Susan was just about to get the table set when she noticed the post had just been delivered so she went out to collect it. Whilst walking back to the house, she was scanning the envelopes. She noticed a handwritten brown envelope addressed to Rachael and she had a sneaky suspicion it was from Stone. Something smelt like men's cologne, so she guessed the envelope was scented. She put the envelope in the back pocket of her jeans and rushed into the downstairs cloakroom and locked the door and tore open the envelope. She ripped the letter from its sleeve and started to read the first few lines. Sure enough, it was most definitely from Stone. She replaced the envelope in her pocket and came out of the cloakroom just as Rachael was just passing on her way to the kitchen.

"Oh, morning Mom. Mom I just wondered, has the mail come yet?" Rachael asked.

"Erm yes honey, err, it was just a few letters for your dad and a couple of service bills, nothing interesting, said a flustered Susan, looking at the floor, unable to make eye contact with Rachael.

"Oh, ok mom but if you do receive a letter for me can you just put it on my bed please?" said a cheerful Rachael. She knew her parents, especially her father, were controlling but she felt confident they would never stoop to opening her mail. Should her parents ever question her over who the letter was from, she had her story straight in her mind and would say that Katie had promised to write.

Rachael was feeling pretty confident that at some point she would receive a letter from Stone and she decided to keep a keen eye out for the postman however, he usually came very early in the morning or later in the day whilst she was at University but even so, she would try to be the first one to get to the mailbox if she could.

As the morning rolled on, the family all sat at the table and had a hearty breakfast.

There was not much conversation at the table but Carol was always very talkative and grandpa Frank rarely said a word, bless him. It was as if he was tuned into another world, another existence. He had been a great man in his time and everyone loved him dearly.

It was not long before Rachael had finished breakfast, collated her study books and was ready to leave. She grabbed her bags and made her way to the door. She shouted out goodbye but it was only Carol that promptly replied, "Bye darling, have a wonderful day."

It was a usual start of the day for Stone, he rolled into Redwing's garage about 15 minutes early and Jimmy pulled up seconds after.

The two lads opened the main doors and drifted over to the coffee machine. "First things first man", said Jimmy. Stone laughed and nodded as Jimmy pressed the button to prepare his much needed morning coffee.

Stone was just about to put on his overalls when the office phone rang. He picked up the receiver, "Good morning, Redwing's Garage, how can we help?"

"Hey, is that you Stone?" asked a husky, excited voice.

"Yeah, speaking"

"It's Clarence Black, I know it's early but this couldn't wait. I have big news, I got two guys wanting a meeting with you and me to discuss Devil's Run."

Stone was taken back a bit, not expecting to hear from Clarence so soon.

"Hey Clarence, slow down, who are these guys and what's the hurry?"

"This thing is bigger than I first thought, we've got massive interest in it now, there's talk this could be a multi-million-pound deal," said Clarence.

"I don't understand Clarence, this was always a small-time annual event. I mean 5k was the purse this year, how could this be so big all of the sudden?"

"Man, we got some very wealthy casino owners fired up about this. There's word they want to send cameras down with a live feed on a huge screen under their own casino licence. This way people can bet on 2 racers at a time, so this would mean you and I as crew leaders race in the main event, but a further 6 races between your guys and my guys. The potential winnings per race could be huge and obviously ours has far more interest but Stone, I'm talking big bucks now estimated around 250k for each of us," said Clarence, with a huge amount of excitement in his voice.

Stone took a deep breath, "so when do these guys want a meeting?"

"Can you come to Vegas at the weekend?

"Wow, I'll see what I can do."

"We'll meet in The Tropicana Rise Hotel at around 11am Saturday. Ask for a guy called Butch Maloney."

"Ok, I'll get there somehow, let me talk with Jimmy as he may want to ride down with me." Stone put the receiver down and looked straight at Jimmy through the office glass. Jimmy could tell by the look in his friend's eyes that he obviously had some big news to discuss.

Stone walked out of the office door and straight over to Jimmy, shaking his head.

"What's wrong buddy?" asked Jimmy.

"That was Clarence Black on the phone, he wants us to meet some casino owners at the Tropicana in Vegas this Saturday to discuss Devil's Run. He's saying it's got so much interest that they're talking about millions of dollars, I mean its fucking crazy Jimmy!" said Stone, still shaking his head.

Jimmy looked at his friend in amazement and said, "I don't know if I like this Stone, it's getting out of hand. These guys in Vegas could be gangsters and they might try to get you to sign some hooky contract that ties you to them and gets you in a whole load of shit".

"I guess you could be right but I feel I need to go along Jimmy, just in case it's the real deal. I mean Clarence said we could be talking huge winnings and a further six races".

"Well, if you go, I'm coming with you man, it's a long ride and I can't let you go alone."

"I was hoping you'd say that," said Stone, smiling.

"It's about five hours straight on the bikes, so if we leave around 5.30am we should be there on time," Jimmy said.

At that moment Billy Keegan pulled into the yard. Gregg, Jimmy and Stone all started to look sharp, as the morning was passing quickly, and little had been done. Stone hadn't even looked at the worksheets because of the Clarence call.

As Billy walked in, he asked Stone to follow him into the office. Stone looked at Jimmy and raised his eyebrows as he walked closely behind Billy.

Billy opened the office door, took off his jacket and hung it up on a hook behind his desk. "Take a seat buddy," said Billy. Stone, feeling worried, pulled up a chair and gave Billy his full attention. Billy said, "Listen, I gave my buddy in Lake Tahoe a shout about this Clarence Black and his association with these Vegas big shots and turns out a guy called Butch Maloney, one of the Casino owners in Freemont Street, is getting all excited about this Devil's Run. Apparently, he's a fairly straight guy as long as you don't cross him."

"Well, I'll level with you Billy, I've just had a call from Clarence and apparently this Butch Maloney wants a meeting with me this Saturday along with Clarence. There's word they want to do a live recording to show it on their screens in their casino under their licence. It's kind of deep but there must be loopholes to allow them to take bets on their site," Stone said.

"Well, I guess I can't talk you out of it, so go along Saturday and see what their proposal is. If you're not happy, simply refuse, after all, without you, there is no race," said Billy.

"Thanks Billy, I do appreciate it, I really do. Now, let's get some work done," Stone said, smiling as he walked out the office. Billy smiled but Stone could tell he was concerned about the whole thing.

Chapter 14

In Connecticut, Rachael was halfway through her morning when she started to feel slightly nauseous during her first class. She was relieved when the first break came and she could visit the lady's room. She splashed some cold water on her face and took some deep breaths. She felt slightly giddy with a headache brewing as she walked on to her second class. It was to be a discussion about Legal Marketing and Rachael was not feeling overly excited about the prospect of sitting in the class for the next hour feeling unwell and totally bored. The speaker was a chap called Neville Jenkins, a trained Lawyer and Lecturer with years of experience but he had a very uninteresting dulcet tone about his voice and most pupils in the class would generally start falling asleep.

Rachael took a desk near the back, as she didn't feel like being the centre of attention at any point through the class. As she went to sit on a chair, she misjudged where the chair was and fell flat on her bottom. A few students sniggered but a couple of more sympathetic students quickly responded by helping her to her feet. Rachael by now was red faced, embarrassed and a little confused as to what had just happened.

She thanked the two girls that came to her aid and then successfully sat down but still felt incredibly shaken up and unwell. Rachael was trying to gather her thoughts when suddenly she felt a warm rush go straight through her body, followed by uncontrollable shaking hands. She tried to get someone's attention and found her words slurred and she was unable to focus as her vision blurred. With a failed attempt to stand, poor Rachael tripped and hit the floor awkwardly and a feeling of uncontrollable trembling gripped her body. She could see people looking down at her but she couldn't hear their voices, then she completely blacked out.

When Rachael opened her eyes, she could see a bright light shining down on her from the ceiling and she noticed a chrome shiny rail to her right and to her left she could hear a beeping noise coming from some kind of monitor. Her eyes then focused on her wrist which had a band on it with her name scribbled in black ink. She gasped and started to panic as reality was starting to materialise, like a punch in the gut when she realised she was in hospital. Thoughts were flooding through her mind like how did I get here? Why am I here? Am I dreaming? She was just about to sit up when a nurse rushed in to calm her.

"Welcome back, Miss Jenson, please don't be afraid you're in safe hands. You're in Bridgeport Hospital. You gave us all a scare, thank the lord you are awake now. Your parents are on their way, so I'm sure they will be here soon," The nurse said in a soft Jamaican accent. Rachael looked up at her name badge, it said 'Thelma Carter' and the women had a wonderfully kind smile and presence about her. Poor Rachael's last memory was falling off the chair, so she was struggling to come to terms with the loss of memory. How could this be, she thought, what had happened to her. She had so many questions but no energy to speak. The whole experience was so upsetting for poor Rachael and she started to feel frightened and anxious, tears were rolling down her cheeks and she craved to see someone she knew, anyone, just someone she trusted, someone that may be able to reassure her.

It was only minutes after nurse Thelma left the room when both Susan and Christopher rushed through the door. Susan walked straight over to Rachael's bed with teary eyes, whilst Christopher stood by her bedside not saying a word but with the look of concern in his eyes.

"Darling, baby, how are you feeling?" Susan said in an over dramatic voice. Rachael looked up at her mother and said quietly.

"Mom, what's wrong with me? I don't know how I got here. The last thing I remember was feeling unwell in one of my classes, Mom help me please," Rachael then started to sob and this was too much for Christopher. He immediately took his daughter's hand and kissed it.

"Listen darling, we'll find out what's happened to you, I promise. I've instructed the best doctors here and you are in very good hands, please don't cry darling. I know I can be a little overpowering at times but it's only because I want the best for my little girl." It was a rare occurrence for Jenson to ever show emotion or admit he was wrong but seeing his little girl in such a vulnerable state was enough to break him. Rachael looked deep into her father's eyes and she could see he was genuinely concerned. For the first time ever, he actually looked as though he was about to cry. Susan put her hand on her husband's shoulder as she could clearly see he was hurting. He stood over the bed and kissed Rachael's hand again before walking out the door. Susan knew her husband's emotions were getting too much for him and he obviously didn't want either of them to see him cry.

Susan gently brushed her daughter's hair away from her face and sat in silence for a while, waiting in anticipation for the doctor to come and have another look at Rachael.

Christopher was pacing up and down outside, near the reception desk when a Doctor approached him holding a clipboard. "Hello sir, are you Rachael Jenson's father?"

"Yes, I am," Christopher answered in a shaky voice.

"My name is Doctor Lang, I'm the head of the Neurology Department here and I'll be looking after your daughter," he said, as he offered his hand to Christopher. Dr Lang was of Chinese origin but educated in the US and he was an expert in Neurology and well respected in the profession.

Jenson shook the doctor's hand firmly. "Do you have any idea what's wrong with her Doctor?"

"Not at this stage Mr Jenson. She was admitted here following a seizure. May I ask if your daughter has a history of epilepsy?"

"No, nothing like that. She's always been healthy. I mean, she's been under a little stress lately what with one thing and another but that's it," said a puzzled Jenson.

"Ok, we'll be taking Rachael down for an MRI and CT scan shortly. It's standard procedure when anyone is admitted here after a seizure. I'll be along in a moment to speak with Rachael, so I will see you shortly Mr Jenson," he said as his beeper started going off. "please excuse me Mr Jenson, I must dash but I will be with you shortly." Dr Lang then walked off down the corridor in a hurry.

Christopher Jenson was feeling rather numb and bewildered as the news of his daughter's seizure had really troubled him.

He slowly walked back towards Rachael's room, wondering whether to tell her about the discussion he had just had with Doctor Lang.

As he entered the room, he could see Susan holding Rachael's hand, whilst trying to comfort her. Both Rachael and Susan looked at Christopher, keen to learn if he had any news. "Hey guys, how's things?" he carried a forced smile to reassure them both. Susan immediately asked if he had spoken to anyone and Rachael was looking in anticipation to see if her father had found out any news.

Jenson put on a brave confident voice as he walked closer to Rachael's bed. Looking straight into his daughter's eyes he said, "I've spoken to a Dr Lang, he's a very nice doctor darling and he's been assigned to help get to the bottom of what's going on. He will look after you and in fact he said he will be coming in shortly to talk to us." Susan looked at her husband to detect whether he was holding anything back. She knew her husband and he seemed to be showing his sensitive side a little too much for her liking as this was totally out of character for her sometimes arrogant, miserable, controlling spouse so this unsettled her.

Rachael looked at her father, with visible signs of fear in her eyes. She couldn't remember the last time her father called her darling and although it was nice, it also made her feel uncomfortable as if her father knew more than he was letting on.

Christopher walked around to the other side of her bed and sat down on a chair when nurse Thelma came in and said to Rachael, "How's my beautiful lady doing? I'm just going to take your blood pressure my darling, it's just routine, so please don't be alarmed."

The friendly nurse acknowledged Christopher and Susan with a friendly smile, wheeled her monitor over to Rachael's bed and gently took her blood pressure. "Thank you my darling, Dr Lang will be with you in just a few moments and then we can start making you all better sweetie," said the kind nurse before wandering back out the door with the monitor.

What seemed like just seconds after nurse Thelma had walked out, the doctor presented himself to the family. "Hi there Rachael, I am Dr Lang. I've already met your dad and I guess you must be Mrs Jenson?" he said, smiling at Susan. "Now Rachael, may I ask you a few questions?" Rachael nodded. "Ok, now can you remember how you were feeling when you arrived at University today?" Rachael looked at Dr Lang and said in a quiet weakened voice.

"I do remember having a headache and feeling nauseous after the first break and then feeling extremely off balance in class then the next minute, I found myself here."

"Ok thank you Rachael. You have no memories whatsoever after feeling dizzy in class?"

"No nothing, nothing at all," Rachael said emotionally. Dr Lang paused for a moment as he stroked the hairs on his goatee style beard and took a deep breath.

"Ok, may I just look in your eyes Rachael?" said the doctor, whilst pulling out an Ophthalmoscope from a small silver case. Rachael nodded and looked at her mother for reassurance. Susan smiled at her anxious daughter.

"It's fine darling, just let the doctor take a look."

Dr Lang lent over the bed and asked Rachael to close her left eye and look straight over his shoulder. Rachael did exactly what she was told, then he asked her to repeat this process with the right eye closed. Dr Lang took a little longer on this eye, he asked Rachael to look at the left corner of the room and then the right and started to make notes on his pad, which gave the impression to the Jenson's that he had found something important enough to note.

Susan looked at the doctor and asked him if everything was ok. Dr Lang explained they would need to do various tests before he could give them any answers. The doctor now looked at Susan and Christopher and explained that he would like to do a CT and MRI scan to see if he could learn more about their daughter's condition. He reassured Rachael that this was a general procedure and due to the fact she had suffered a seizure, he would like to find out more as to why this had occurred.

"I'll arrange for the scans and will get back to you as soon as I can," with that, Dr Lang made a few more notes and then left the room.

The Jenson's sat in silence for a moment, trying to compute every word Dr Lang had said, then Rachael started to cry, "I'm so scared Mom, Dad I'm scared."

"It's ok darling, it's going to be just fine. You're in the best place to get this sorted and the staff here will look after you," said Susan confidently, whilst glancing discreetly at her husband. Christopher looked at his wife and then at Rachael and this was one of the first times in his life he felt so helpless. He was so used to being in control and solving any problems the family had and if he couldn't fix it, then money generally could.

Christopher held his daughter's hand and told her he would make sure she was well again soon and back at home before she knew it.

His words gave Rachael strength as she was sure her father would not allow anything bad to happen to her. He may be difficult at times but she knew, deep down, he only ever tried to do what he thought was best for her.

The Jenson's waited patiently and it was not long at all before nurse Thelma was back.

"Ok my beautiful girl, in a few moments some very handsome men are going to wheel you down to the Neurology Department where you'll have your scans and be back up here in no time," said the cheerful nurse. The whole family nodded.

"Ok, thank you," said the Jenson's at the same time which made nurse Thelma chuckle to herself as she walked back out. Rachael asked her mother if she would come down with her for the scans.

"Of course I will darling, you try and stop me."

Christopher stood up from the chair by Rachael's side and started pacing up and down anxiously. Susan watched her husband, she could see he was struggling with this incredibly stressful situation. Christopher was feeling powerless, frustrated and helpless. Usually he could control any problem the family faced but this was totally out of his hands and he resented the fact he could not offer an immediate solution to this awful scenario the family were faced with.

He walked to the door, opened it and looked to see if he could see the porters coming to take his daughter down and sure enough two gentlemen in blue overalls were walking towards him.

"Good afternoon sir," one of the gentlemen said.

"Hello, have you come for Rachael Jenson?" Christopher asked nervously.

"Yes sir, we have," they both replied. Sure enough as nurse Thelma had said, both porters were well groomed young men and it was clear to see they took pride in their appearance and were easy on the eye.

They entered the room, "Hi, you must be Rachael. I'm Ted and this is Johnny," Johnny smiled at Rachael and acknowledged Susan. "We're going to take you down for your scan now, is that ok Rachael?" asked Johnny, "we'll look after you so you have nothing to worry about. Is mom or dad coming too?" he asked. Both gentlemen looked at Susan and Christopher for a decision. Rachael looked at Susan, then at the two porters.

"I'm good to go, my mom is coming with me. Dad, are you going to wait here?" she asked in a weakened voice. Jenson looked at his daughter.

"Yes darling, I'll wait right here. Mom will look after you and I'm sure Ted and Johnny will take good care of you," he smiled at his daughter and bent down over her bed and kissed her on the forehead. Secretly he was relieved as he was always scared of showing emotion and thought it best Rachael be with Susan at this time.

Ted and Johnny started releasing the bed, ready to be mobile for the short journey to the Neurology MRI-CT Unit.

In what seemed like seconds, the bed was mobile and ready to go. "Ok here we go Rachael. Hold on tight, Ted's a terrible driver," he winked at Rachael and she just about managed a smile. Susan stood up, kissed Christopher on the cheek and followed Rachael out the door. Christopher just stood there watching his wife and daughter drift down the corridor away from the ward and then out of sight. He walked over to the chair, sat down and put his face in his hands and sighed, it was a feeling he could not describe, one he wanted over as soon as possible. He was starting to feel guilty about how hard he had been on her recently and this made the situation a whole lot worse.

Rachael and Susan were now in the lift and the two comical porters were trying to make light of the situation to put Rachael and her mother at ease. Ted started making cracks about getting stuck in the lift for a few days and how we would try to escape through the hatch at the top. Both Susan and Rachael laughed and found the guys quite entertaining but they both were so anxious about the scans.

The lift doors opened and they were soon on the move again. After a few sharp turns and corners along the way, they finally arrived at a door with 'CT-MRI Unit' on it. Johnny pressed a bell on the door and explained that this was where he and Ted were to leave them temporarily and he explained they would be back soon to collect her and take her back to her room. They gave Rachael and Susan huge smiles and walked away. Suddenly there was a buzzer sound and the door opened with a Radiologist to greet them. She and her assistant pulled Rachael's bed through the doorway and closed the door behind them. It was a very large room and everything was spotlessly clean and white. One of the staff explained the procedure in an incredibly soft and warm voice, "My name is Jennifer, my colleague and I will be doing your scan today Rachael. It's a completely painless procedure and you can even listen to music throughout the scan if you wish." Rachael just agreed with everything Jennifer was saying. It was as if she could see her lips moving but no information was sinking in. Poor Rachael was feeling overwhelmed by the whole day's events.

"Ok Mom, if you can wait here behind the glass screen and Rachael will be just on the other side." Susan bent down and kissed Rachael on the cheek and told her she loved her. Rachael smiled.

"I love you too mom."

Jennifer looked at Susan, "I promise we'll look after her Mrs Jenson, we won't be too long." The two doctors took Rachael behind the screen and asked her if she wanted some music through the procedure as the machine could make some knocking sounds.

"Yes please," said Rachael. She was then transferred to a stretcher like contraption and asked to lay very still.

Jennifer gently adjusted Rachael's head on the thin, rubbery pillow attached to the hard bed tray and explained that throughout the whole procedure she and Rachael would be able to communicate and she would be able to see her at all times behind the glass which separated them.

Once Jennifer was satisfied Rachael was calm and settled, she left the room. Rachael waited in anticipation for something to happen, then she heard Jennifer's voice on a speaker, "Ok Rachael, in a few moments, you'll feel yourself moving backwards so I need to ask you to stay as still as you possibly can, you're in good hands. I'll play some music to take your mind off things, so feel free to shut your eyes and just relax if you can."

Rachael took a deep intake of breath and the bed tray started to move slowly backwards. She could hear the tunnel making clicking and whirring sounds, which felt very unsettling. She kept her eyes tightly closed and thoughts of Stone entered her mind. She imagined him being there, holding her hand and this was a great comfort to her. Finally, she came to a standstill and Jennifer's voice was all she could hear for a split second, "Ok now Rachael, you're doing so well. Please stay as still as you possibly can and I'll get things moving. Now, remember, please do not be alarmed by the noises you hear, we are simply taking images. Ok, here we go Rachael." There was a short pause and then the machine started making knocking sounds which was quite unpleasant but to ease the stress, music started to play. It was soothing and most welcomed by Rachael. She kept her eyes closed tightly, with thoughts of Stone walking along the beach beside her holding hands. It was almost 10 minutes into the procedure, when Jennifer called for another doctor to join her and look at the images. Rachael was unaware and dreaming about days to come with Stone in Santa Barbara. Twenty minutes into the scan, Susan could see different staff coming and going, talking between themselves quietly, which unnerved her. She kept looking at her watch, remembering what Jennifer had said about most scans only lasting 15 minutes but this was certainly well over twenty minutes now and the Radiology staff were still discussing something relatively quietly.

Jennifer spoke to Rachael through the microphone, "Ok Rachael, we're now going to slowly bring you out. The music stopped and the bed started to move forward, away from the huge tunnel of light, returning to the unsettling whirring sounds as it came to a halt. The sounds slowly diminished and the lights dimmed. Before she knew it, Jennifer was back by her side.

"Well done Rachael, you did extremely well," said the kind radiologist.

Rachael slid back over to her own bed with a few staff ready to push her out from behind the glass where Susan was waiting. Susan was so pleased the procedure was over and she was soon reunited with her daughter. Susan kissed her daughter and held her hand. Jennifer walked over to Rachael and her mother and explained that Dr Lang would come and talk to them as soon as he had looked at the results. "Was everything ok? Did you find any link to the seizure?" Susan had so many questions. Jennifer looked at the concerned mother and daughter.

"It's hospital policy that only the doctor assigned to you can discuss the results I'm afraid. Dr Lang will be along to see you in a short while, I'm sure," she answered.

"Ok, thank you," said Susan, feeling a little unnerved by Jennifer's response.

The door opened and Johnny and Ted came walking in towards Rachael and Susan. "Hi ladies, your dad will be pleased to see you back I'm sure," said Johnny. Susan and Rachael raised a smile but deep down they were both feeling rather anxious about what Dr Lang may have to say after analysing the results. There was also no mention of an MRI scan so it felt as though the radiologist had located the cause of Rachael's condition already but were unable to comment.

It was not long before Johnny and Ted safely returned Rachael back to her room, where Christopher was waiting patiently. He jumped to his feet and rushed over to see his family but allowing the two gentlemen to complete their job and get Rachael's bed back securely in position. Ted and Johnny said goodbye and walked out the room. "So, how did it go?' asked Christopher, whilst smiling at Rachael.

Susan jumped in before Rachael could answer, "Our daughter was very brave, she had to stay completely still for almost 30 minutes. Apparently the results have gone straight to Dr Lang and he'll be along shortly, they told us."

"Well done Rachael," said Jenson as he stroked her arm and smiled at her affectionately. "Did they say anything at all?" Jenson asked Susan. His wife looked pale and distant and Christopher could tell his wife was worried about the results. He got the feeling she didn't want to talk about it, so he did not push the matter just in case it unsettled his daughter.

Rachael was not saying much at all, just faint smiles from time to time and simple yes and no responses. It was clear to see the poor girl was struggling with the whole horrible situation.

As Susan was keen to give her daughter fluids, she pressed the buzzer to confirm with nurse Thelma that she was able to give her daughter a glass of water. Thelma came into the room in a flash, "Hey darling, welcome back, how can I help you?" she asked.

"May I give my daughter some water?" asked Susan.

"Yes, absolutely. Go ahead," said the kind nurse with her infectious smile. She looked at Rachael for a few seconds, "if you need anything else at all, just call me darling," Thelma said. She then turned her attention to Mr Jenson.

"Sir, may I have a quick word with you outside?" Christopher stood up.

"Yes, of course," he looked at his wife, raised his shoulders slightly and followed the nurse out of the room.

Jenson followed the nurse down the corridor to a door with 'Dr Lang' clearly written on it. "Dr Lang would like a private word with you first before he speaks to you as a family."

The nurse knocked at the door and waited for Dr Lang to invite Mr Jenson in.

"Mr Jenson, please take a seat," said the doctor. Jenson turned, closed the door and walked towards a chair beside Dr Lang's desk and sat down.

There was an uncomfortable feeling in the room, thought Jenson, as he waited for news on his daughter. Dr Lang took a deep intake of breath and then breathed out heavily. "I'm afraid Mr Jenson, I have some unsettling news for you. Your daughter's results appear to show a large tumour which is almost definitely the cause of the seizure that Rachael experienced today. Now, I know this is a shock for you so I'm sorry I can't tell anymore than that until we do a biopsy," said Dr Lang. Jenson was listening to every word that came out of the doctor's mouth, however, he was shaking his head in disbelief the whole time.

"Now because of the size of the tumour, I would like to do a biopsy as soon as I can, so that we know what we are up against." There was an uncomfortable silence in the room and Christopher Jenson was still shaking his head then he started panting and breathing heavily, holding his head in his hands. Dr Lang stood up and came over to him and put his hand on his shoulder to comfort the clearly distressed father.

"Sir, we will do everything in our power to offer Rachael the very best of care and we will do our utmost to get her well again but you I need to know what I'm dealing with to give her the best chance of recovery. I'm so surprised Rachael has not shown any symptoms until today," he said. Jenson looked at him, wide eyed and trembling.

"No, there hasn't been anything that I know of, unless of course she has been hiding it from us but I'm fairly sure that's not the case doctor."

"I promise you faithfully I will look after her as best I can. You need to be strong for Rachael and perhaps all we need to tell her at this stage is that we have found something in the scan that we would like to investigate further, by means of a small surgical procedure. Through my experience Mr Jenson, telling a young patient he or she has a large brain tumour can have devastating effects. I would like to know the results of the biopsy before we tell Rachael any more."

"Ok sure, I understand and yes, I think you're right doctor. The less we tell Rachael at this stage, the better for her. I just pray it's not serious, so that you can get her well again Dr Lang," said Jenson, clearly troubled by the whole affair. Dr Lang told Christopher he would do his very best for Rachael and that he should go back to his wife and daughter and break the news gently about the biopsy which he would like to carry out the following day.

Jenson thanked Dr Lang and walked out the door and along the corridor towards his family. His legs were heavy, his mind numb and a feeling of guilt was playing with his conscience. He had been tough on Rachael and now he has to be the bearer of worrying news. He took a deep breath and said to himself, 'be strong, be strong for her,' as he walked into Rachael's room.

"We were getting worried, you've been away for some time. Is everything ok?" asked a concerned Susan.

"I've had a discussion with Dr Lang about the scan results." Rachael sat up slightly in bed, anxious to hear her fate, whilst Susan looked with wide eyes straight at her husband. Jenson walked over to the bed, sat down beside his daughter, took her hand in his and began to talk. "Now darling, we now know why you had the seizure, Dr Lang has explained that something is showing on the scan results and he would like to run some more tests. Susan gasped at the news, whilst Racheal just lay still, holding on to every word her father said.

"So daddy, what kind of tests are we talking about?" asked Rachael in a weak, shaky voice.

"Well tomorrow, Dr Lang would like to do a small procedure, just to learn more about what's going on but don't you worry, you won't feel a thing," said her father confidently but he was dying inside, struggling with holding back the truth from his daughter.

Susan looked at her husband with tear filled eyes and squeezed her daughter's hand to comfort her.

The Jenson's sat for that evening, mostly in silence. Nurse Thelma would come in and out when necessary but most of the time the room was quiet, with a tense energy attached to it. Jenson had arranged for a guest room within the hospital for Susan and himself, as he knew Rachael would need them close by her side.

The morning came around quickly and it was not long before Dr Lang was back on the wards doing his rounds. He eventually got to Rachael's room. "Good morning Rachael, how are you feeling this morning? I am going to do your procedure today, I take it your father explained?" Rachael nodded. "Then we can get to the bottom of what's causing you these problems," he gave a soothing smile and walked out the room. It was as if he was in a hurry, he was certainly a man in demand.

Rachael looked at her parents, "I just want to go home Ma", she said nervously.

"Of course darling, we understand, but let's just get you well again and we can get you home. Christopher gripped his daughter's arm.

"We'll be right by your side all the way through this my love." Rachael smiled at him, this was a side of her father she wished she had seen earlier in her lifetime but sadly this was the first time.

The morning moved on swiftly and it was not long before nurse Thelma was back to see how Rachael was doing. She did a few necessary tests and explained that it would not be long before she would be going down to surgery for her procedure.

Moments later, Johnny and Ted were back, full of smiles, "hey beautiful, we gotta stop meeting like this," Johnny said cheekily.

"We're going for another ride around the hospital, would you like to come?" Ted said with a wink.

This gave the Jenson family a small lift as they were all feeling rather nervous. These porters were marvellous, thought Christopher, they had put a smile on his daughter's face and for him that was a good start.

Johnny and Ted got Rachael comfortable and she was ready for the journey. Susan was holding her hand and Christopher kissed his daughter's forehead and said he would wait for her, whilst Susan went down with her. "See you soon Rach, I'll be right here." Rachael smiled at her father but said nothing as the bed started to move towards the door. Susan followed and looked round at Christopher and whispered.

"See you soon." As they moved out of sight, he dropped to the chair in the empty room, put his hands on his head and started taking deep breaths. He looked up to see Rachael's jacket hanging over the other bedside chair and he walked over to it and pulled it close to his face, inhaling his daughter's scent. Returning to his seat, he embraced Rachael's jacket tightly as a teardrop rolled down his unshaven cheek. Clearly, this was having a massive effect on the usually hard nosed character, a side very few would ever witness. Rachael was now just seconds away from theatre, Johnny and Ted had been their usual humorous selves. Susan had been squeezing her daughter's hand every step of the way. They arrived at the Neurosurgery Theatre where her bed was manoeuvred into position, with Dr Lang waiting to greet them. Susan was asked to put a mask and gown on whilst the anaesthetist prepared to put Rachael under.

"Hi Rachael, please don't worry, we're going to look after you. This is Dianne, she is the anaesthetist who'll get you to sleep and you'll be back in your room before you know it," said Dr Lang reassuringly. Dianne smiled and said hello to both Rachael and her mother and very softly and professionally inserted the needle into her patient's arm.

"Ok now darling, if you can count back from ten for me." Rachael closed her eyes and was fully under by the time she got to five. Susan felt helpless, numb and emotional as she looked down at her daughter's beautiful face. One of the nurses comforted her and escorted her out of the theatre.

Susan walked with a nurse back to Rachael's room where Christopher was pacing up and down. "Susan, how is she, what happened?" he asked anxiously.

Susan walked over to him, hugged him tight and then began to sob. Christopher knew he had to be strong, so he squeezed his wife tightly and reassured her. "We will get through this darling, I promise you it will be ok," he said but deep down inside he wasn't sure. Dr Lang's words were still haunting him but it just wasn't the right time to tell Susan or anyone about Dr Lang's fears.

It was almost an hour before they heard anything when Jenson walked out to reception to find nurse Thelma. "Excuse me, erm, would you happen to have any news on my daughter Rachael Jenson? She went down to the theatre about an hour ago for a biopsy," he said to the young blonde receptionist.

"I'll see what I can find out and come and let you know as soon as I can."

Christopher walked back to the room and explained to Susan what the receptionist had said.

Susan sat back in the chair, holding her daughter's jacket for comfort. Moments later, Nurse Thelma came into the room. "Hi Mr and Mrs Jenson, I've just heard from one of Dr Lang's associate's, Rachael will be back up in about thirty minutes. The biopsy has been done but I have no further news at this stage I'm afraid." Susan smiled at Thelma as she walked out the room and looked at her husband.

"Does that seem good, I mean a basic biopsy, should it take so long? Christopher did you hear me, should it take so long?" said Susan loudly.

"Dr Lang knows what he's doing so I'm sure it will be ok. She'll be back soon and we will finally know what's going on," said Jenson.

The thirty minutes seemed like hours but sure enough as Thelma had said, Rachael back through the doors. Both Susan and Christopher jumped to their feet and rushed over to their daughter. Rachael was very drowsy and she had a bandage dressing around her head.

Johnny and Ted secured her bed back in place and left the room, surprisingly this time they were noticeably quiet. Nurse Thelma came in to check all was well and to tell the family that Dr Lang would like to see Mr Jenson in his office in the next hour to discuss the results. Susan was not paying much attention as she was stroking her daughter's arm, trying to comfort her, afraid to touch her head but talking softly close to her ear. Christopher nodded to Thelma before walking over to Susan and calmly putting his hand on her shoulder. Rachael's speech was slurred but she managed to ask if she was back in her room. "Yes, darling you are back and you'll soon wake up properly but for now just rest sweetie, we can talk later," said Susan confidently.

The family sat very quietly and after an hour had passed Christopher explained to his wife that he was going to talk to Dr Lang about the results of the biopsy. He kissed Rachael's hand and rubbed his wife's shoulder as he walked out the room. As he walked along the corridor towards the reception, his heart was breaking. He was trying to be strong for his family but inside he was dying. As he approached the reception desk, nurse Thelma jumped up. "Hi Mr Jenson, Dr Lang is ready for you, please go ahead to his office."

"Thank you, thank you," Christopher said softly. He walked up to Dr Lang's door and knocked on it with a firm meaningful fist.

"Come in," said the doctor. Christopher took a deep breath and opened the door. "Please Mr Jenson, take a seat." Christopher sat down in the chair and looked at the doctor with wide eyes, ready to his every word.

"Mr Jenson, there is no easy way of saying this but I'm afraid it's not good news. The tumour is what is known as a glioblastoma. I can try to reduce the size of the tumour. Chemotherapy and radiation treatment are options, however, patients' survival rates from this aggressive type of tumour can be rare.

Christopher looked at the doctor without saying a word, just swallowing hard and taking deep breaths, then he finally broke down. Poor Jenson was broken and he started to cry. Dr Lang stood up and walked round to comfort the big guy in any way he could, he rubbed his shoulder and promised him he would do every he could to help his daughter. After Christopher had pulled himself together, he said, "Doc, I need you to be totally honest with me, if treatment doesn't work, how long has she got?"

Dr Lang took a deep breath, "Between a year and 18 months sir."

Jenson looked up at the doctor and held onto his arm, "Dr Lang, I need you to do whatever you can to prolong my daughter's life. I have money, so if there is any treatment you know of I will pay any amount to keep my daughter alive." It was almost as if shock had switched Jenson back into his business world but unfortunately where money could normally fix everything, this was different and the fact he could not fix this was destroying him.

"Sir, I appreciate that but unfortunately the only treatment we have is chemo and radiation to shrink the tumour but as I say, we cannot completely destroy glioblastoma, sadly it always grows back at a fast rate."

"How do I tell my wife that our daughter has less than 2 years to live and what do I tell my daughter Doc?" Christopher was shaking.

"I would tell your wife privately away from Rachael today and tomorrow, we can all sit together and explain everything to your daughter. Through experience, I've found it's always best to be honest with our patients now we have the full picture. They need to know exactly what's happening to help them deal with it."

Christopher accepted what Dr Lang said and he pulled himself together, knowing he would have to be a rock now for his family. He shook the doctor's hand and walked back to the room where Rachael and Susan were now talking.

"Hey Princess, how are we doing?" asked Jenson, feeling crushed inside.

"Hi Dad, I still feel sleepy but I'm ok," said Rachael. Her words 'I'm ok' crucified poor Jenson but he smiled.

"That's great honey."

"So, what did Dr Lang have to say?" asked Susan.

"He's coming around to talk to us all tomorrow morning, so for now, let's just relax and think about what we are going to do when we get Rachael out of here." Christopher said dying inside. Susan thought that was an odd reply and she looked at her husband and frowned so whilst Rachael was not looking, he slightly shook his head and put his finger to his lips to insinuate, not now. Thankfully, Susan understood the gesture and deviated away from the subject. Strangely and luckily for Jenson, Rachael had not quizzed him about his meeting with Dr Lang. In fact, she almost looked quite content tucked up in bed talking with her mother. The day passed quickly and it was not long before they were all thinking about turning in for the night. Both Christopher and Susan kissed their daughter goodnight and went to their room.

Jenson was dreading telling his wife the news and when they got to their room Susan immediately said, "It's not good news Christopher is it?" Jenson walked over to his wife.

"Darling please sit down here on the bed." He took her hand and they both sat down. "No, it's not good news Susan, not good news at all," poor Jenson tried to be strong but he caved dramatically, bursting into tears. Susan put her arms around her husband, she had never seen this vulnerable side to him.

"What's wrong with her Christopher, I have to know?" Susan said nervously.

"She has a tumour, an aggressive incurable tumour. Susan, our baby has less than two years to live," said Jenson, collapsing on the bed in a flood of tears.

"No, no it can't be, it can't be, please God no!!" They both grabbed each other and sobbed for almost an hour until they were both cried out.

After coming to terms with the tragic news, they realised now that they had to be strong for their daughter and tomorrow when Dr Lang comes to her bedside, they needed to support Rachael in any way they could.

It was a long night and neither Susan or Christopher had slept a wink. Jenson was almost supporting a beard where he had not shaved for a few days. They both skipped breakfast and rushed to Rachael's bedside. She was sitting up eating jam on toast, looking almost well they thought. "Hi darling, how are you feeling?" said Susan.

"Apart from a sore head, I feel great," said Rachael. Christopher kissed his daughter's head and she ribbed him about his whiskers and they both laughed.

Dr Lang arrived at 10am and shut the door behind him. He had a concerned look on his face and both Susan and Christopher knew that he was probably dreading this moment too. He said good morning to everyone and sat down beside Rachael. Both Susan and Christopher held their daughter's hands.

"Rachael we have the biopsy results back so we now have the reason for your seizure. You have something called a glioblastoma which is an aggressive tumour. Although we can attack the cells around it and make attempts to shrink it, we can't completely destroy it. Now, I know this is a lot to take in for all of you but if you have any questions please just ask me and I will be completely honest with my answers," said the caring doctor.

Rachael seemed almost emotionless for a moment, she just looked at the ceiling shaking her head. After she had taken a moment for the tragic news to sink in, she looked at Dr Lang, "so, how long do I have doctor?" Dr Lang looked at her parents, took a deep breath.

"A year to 18 months," he said in a soft, troubled voice. Rachael turned her head to face the window as she felt overcome with emotion. Rachael took a deep breath, then turned back around to face Dr Lang.

"Ok doctor thank you. If I could be left with my parents now for a while that would be great." Surprised by her reaction and somewhat relieved, Dr Lang agreed and assured her he would do everything he could for her as he walked out the door with his head held low.

When the door shut, Susan broke down and Jenson kissed his daughter's hand. Rachael said, "I knew it was bad news, I was ready to hear it, I just had a feeling but let me tell you, I'm not going to give up without a fight. If I'm not in pain I want to live my last bit of time doing exactly what I want to do, for as long as I can." Christopher and Susan could not believe the strength of their daughter. They kissed her and comforted her for the rest of the day.

Chapter 15

Saturday morning came around fast for Stone. It was a big day and Jimmy had arranged to meet him on the main route junction just outside of Butterfly Beach at 5am.

Stone packed a rucksack with some snacks for the journey as it would be a 4-5 hour ride to Nevada and the meeting with Butch Maloney was at 10am at the Tropicana Rise Hotel Casino.

His loyal friend Jimmy was already at the junction when Stone rolled up. The two comrades shook hands firmly and got straight on the road.

They took a steady route through Lake Tahoe, leading through Death Valley into Nevada. After a few stops at service stations along the way, they arrived around 9.30am at their destination. It was not as grand as some of the huge hotels along the Vegas strip but apparently had an interesting history dating back to when the mob seemed to be running the electric cash machine in the desert.

The two guys climbed off their bikes and just seconds after they could hear the familiar sound of rumbling thunder coming down the Boulevard. Sure enough, it was Clarence Black with one of his crew.

The bikes pulled up next to Stone and Jimmy. Clarence was excited to see Stone again and he jumped off his bike offering his hand immediately. "Hi brother, good to see you made it," said Clarence.

"Hey big guy," Stone said casually.

Clarence then introduced them to his buddy, "Guys, this is Big Dog, he's my main man." A huge stocky guy, at least 6 ft 5 inches came walking over to meet them.

"Hey" said Big Dog. Stone and Jimmy shook the guy's hand, he had a grip that could crush skulls.

"I can see why they call you Big Dog," said Jimmy. The big guy never even cracked a smile, not a hint of emotion could be detected, he just walked back over to join Clarence. They all made their way into the hotel reception, where they were greeted by a few attractive ladies behind the desk.

"Good morning gentleman, how can we help you today?" asked one of the women.

Clarence was quick to reply, "well honey, we're here to see Butch Maloney, we have a meeting at 10am."

"Oh, ok sir, I'll just let him know you're here. Please take a seat gentleman, someone will come down to collect you shortly." said the receptionist.

Stone and Clarence paced up and down, they were showing signs of nerves and excitement thought Jimmy. The whole experience was rather surreal and slightly intimidating for the reception staff. Jimmy was calm but vigilant and Big Dog was just standing by the entrance motionless.

Suddenly they heard the lift bell ring and a smart, well groomed gentleman walked out of the lift and over towards them. "Good morning gentleman, my name's

Lance Costa, I guess you are here to see Mr Maloney?" said the smooth character.

"Yes we are," Clarence answered quickly, whilst Stone and Jimmy just nodded.

"That's great gentleman, please follow me," said Lance.

Stone, Jimmy, Clarence and Big Dog followed the guy to the lift. When inside, there was an uncomfortable silence as the lift made its way to the 3rd floor. The doors opened and Lance insisted the guys followed him. No one said a word, they just followed. When they reached room 302, Lance knocked on the door. A deep husky voice answered, "come in." Lance pushed the door open and walked into the room with Stone, Jimmy Clarence and his wing man. It was a posh, beautifully decorated room almost stuck in time, somewhere in the 1940's. In front of the window they could see an old heavy oak desk with a dark-skinned gentleman sitting behind it. Lance led them all through to a large sofa where they all sat down in front of the desk. There was an eerie pause before the gentleman spoke, probably only 10 seconds but it seemed like forever. Eventually, the guy stood up and came from behind the desk. He was a large heavily built man with dark olive skin, a defined jawline and big brown eyes, your typical gangster looking fellow. He reached out his hand and introduced himself as Butch Maloney, there was certainly a presence about the guy, that was for sure.

"Thank you for coming here today, now the reason I called this meeting was because I heard about this race called Devil's Run and if I'm honest, it's got me and a few of my associates rather excited. You see, here in Vegas everyone is looking for something new, something different, some kind of outrageous game that draws people in and encourages them to gamble and spend money. This is the city where you can arrive here poor, place a few bets and walk away rich. You see, if you guys want to make some serious doe, I can offer you an opportunity to do so, all you need to do is take part in the race. Let me explain, if we bring Devil's Run into our advertising campaign and market it the right way, I believe this thing could be potentially the biggest thing Vegas has seen for a long time. Now as a businessman obviously I want to make this exclusive to the Tropicana Rise, we can take phone bets, supported by a live TV Channel protected under my gambling licence, this will cover the races. Now I say races because just one race is not enough to capture everyone's imagination. Obviously, what is interesting here and may seem somewhat harsh, is the fact that people love danger. Man, against man, like two gladiators fighting for survival, knowing, just one wrong move could send a rider off the cliff to sudden death. You see guys, the potential winnings for each race could be as high as 250,000 dollars. I don't know what your thoughts are but if we have a series of six races on a set date and the last race will be the big one where the two biker gang leaders battle it out between themselves then that is where you Clarence and you Stone come in. Should you want to set this up, we can offer you both a down payment of 50,000 dollars up front and a further 200,000 to the winner of the race. The other participants of your crews can secure 5,000 dollars per race per win but I'll need you guys to sign a contract to offer me sole rights to Devil's Run."

Stone, Jimmy and Clarence had been listening to Butch Maloney's every word. There were a few moments of silence for all concerned.

Stone looked at Clarence, then at Jimmy then he looked at Butch, "So what are the legal implications Mr Maloney should we sign this contract, how long would we be tied into it?" Jimmy and Clarence nodded as Stone quizzed Maloney.

"I was thinking the first event would be covered to the end of the year, then depending on the success of the first race, we can review it. So, you will be contracted per race, should we run it again in your absence, that's fine but you will get first refusal. Now once the date is announced we can start taking bets, however, we cannot ever disclose the location of the event because local law enforcement may try to stop the races. The live screen film footage will only be seen by spectators in the casino. We'll need to attach cameras to your bikes and a film crew will be at the start marker and at the end by Spike's Edge. This way we can add excitement and drama to the whole race experience. Look, I appreciate this is an awful lot to take in, so my guess is you will need some time to think about but I'll need to know by the end of the week whether it's on or off, does that sound fair?" Maloney sat back in his chair and looked at the three men, waiting for a response.

Clarence said, "Well count me in, I've heard enough, I'm ready to sign."

"Ok that's great but the race will only take place if both parties are in," Butch said.

Jimmy looked at Stone and said, "Let's go away and think this through buddy, we have a few days to decide." Stone nodded and turned to Maloney. "Yes erm, if we could have a few days to think it over that would be great." Clarence was shaking his head.

"What's there to think about man, you got the chance of 50,000 up front and the opportunity to win big bucks on the day. I mean you can't earn that kind of doe working in a garage!" Stone took a deep breath and looked at Clarence, then glanced at Butch Maloney.

"So, what's to stop you using another location or offering this out to other crew, why us?"

"Well you see Stone, Devil's Run has history, it works, the location, the danger, it's perfect and to be honest, it won't work without you. Anyone that takes a punt will want to know about the riders experience and history and I can't find that anywhere else. Stone, when you beat Marco Sanchez the word got around. When I heard about it, the Blood Rangers were given a bad reputation, so when Clarence offered to find you I knew this could be the biggest new experience for my casino. Not only will I make money but we all have the opportunity to make some serious cash."

Stone replied, "Well you know the bad reputation was bullshit, just one of Marco's crew being a sore loser! We appreciate the offer but my buddy and I would like to talk privately about this and we'll get back to you Mr Maloney."

Clarence was still shaking his head when Butch Maloney stood up to shake the men's hands. Jimmy gave Butch a firm handshake, followed by Stone and finally Clarence and Big Dog. The four men walked out of the office and back towards the lift. No-one said a word as Jimmy pressed the ground floor on the control panel. When the lift doors opened, Clarence offered his hand to Stone and Jimmy. "Look guys, if you want to get this in the bag, please let Maloney know as soon as you can!"

"We will Clarence, we will," confirmed Stone.

The two friends took a slow ride back to Santa Barbara, both deep in thought for most of the ride. As they reached the halfway point, Stone signalled Jimmy and they pulled into a layby which had a diner tucked back off a dirt track. Stone was keen to hear Jimmy's thoughts on the meeting with Butch Maloney.

They got off their bikes, stretched their backs and wandered into the diner where they ordered a coffee and a couple of chilli dogs from the menu.

"So, Jimmy, what's your honest opinion about this whole thing buddy?"

"The guy seemed pretty much up front, I guess so we'd better give it some serious consideration. I mean the guy's talking about a lot of doe here, I mean what's the worst thing that can happen? We sign for one race, take the fifty gran and should we win, we get a whole bunch more."

"I just don't want to bring a problem to our town, that's my main concern Jimmy, we can't let this thing destroy our neighbourhood."

"Yeah, I guess you are right. Maybe we can get some kind of clause drawn into the contract that should any trouble be brought to Butterfly Beach, we shut it down," Jimmy said shrugging his shoulders.

"I agree man, that's a good idea," Stone said nodding. They drank their coffee and ate their chilli dogs and hit the road.

Chapter 16

Rachael woke after a lengthy sleep, it was Saturday evening and she was feeling like everything that had happened to her in the last few days was just a bad dream but waking up and seeing her parents sitting beside her in her hospital bed just savagely smashed the reality back into her mind.

She felt a sudden burst of energy rush through her body and sat up in bed.

"Mom, I want to get up and go for a walk, if I haven't got long, I'm not going to lay here and wait to die," Rachael said with a sense of new confidence and determination.

"Ok darling but let me check with the doctor," said Susan.

"No Mom, I feel ok and I'm getting up!" Rachael kicked back the covers and started to pull herself to the edge of the bed. Christopher held her arm and supported his daughter to her feet beside the bed.

Rachael walked over to the window and looked out, Susan and Christopher looked at each other and Jenson shrugged his shoulders and shook his head slightly as Susan walked over to the window to be close to her brave daughter.

Susan remembered the letter that she had hidden from Rachael and she suddenly felt incredibly guilty as she stared at her beautiful daughter gazing out of the window in her green hospital gown. She knew that it was wrong and now this awful disease has been inflicted upon her poor daughter, she felt Rachael should have the letter.

Susan knew it would be a good idea to go home and collect a few of Rachael's personal things, along with the letter, to make her feel more comfortable in her room, as she thought it may be a while before the doctors would allow her to go home. She felt she would have to discuss the letter with Christopher but felt confident he would agree under the circumstances.

Dr Lang was due to come in and have a private meeting with Rachael as she was over 18 and he felt she would perhaps like to speak to him alone, in case she had any questions or concerns that she didn't want to discuss in front of her parents.

Nurse Thelma came in to see how Rachael was, she knew Rachael's fate, however, as a religious woman she still had hope a miracle may still save the stricken youngster.

She remained her bubbly, cheerful self when she spoke, "how is my beautiful Rachael doing this morning? It's so nice to see you up and about, how do you feel?"

"I feel fine today, thank you Thelma, in fact I'd like to go for a walk and get some fresh air if I may?" Rachael said smiling.

"Ok my dear, I'll speak to Dr Lang just to confirm it's alright to do so and get straight back to you," said the nurse and she walked straight back out the door.

Susan turned to Rachael, "Darling, I'm going home shortly to see to Willis and collect a few of your things, is there anything you would like me to bring back?"

Rachael took a moment to think and then replied, "Could you bring my pink slippers and dressing gown and my Walkman, oh erm, can you also bring me back a pen, paper and some envelopes if you have some please?"

"Yes of course darling," said Susan.

The Jenson's all waited patiently for nurse Thelma to return but instead Dr Lang came through the door. "Hi there Mr Jenson, Mrs Jenson, may I have a few moments alone with Rachael? It's standard procedure, nothing to be alarmed about," he looked at his patient.

Susan looked at Christopher and said, "Okay, well perhaps whilst they talk, we could shoot home and collect those things we spoke about, does that sound ok darling?"

Christopher nodded and they both kissed Rachael's forehead gently and walked out the room.

Dr Lang closed the door behind them and walked over to Rachael. "Would you like to sit down Rachael, it might be more comfortable for you?" Rachael nodded and sat down. "Rachael, firstly I'm so pleased you feel well enough to want to go for a walk, in fact that's great news, something I want to encourage actually. You see, we find patients with your condition can feel absolutely fine through most of the illness so we encourage them to try to carry on with their lives and get some kind of normality back as soon as they can, for as long as they can. Do you have any questions? You can ask me anything that's on your mind and I promise I will be completely honest with my answers."

"Dr Lang, how long will I be able to carry on with no real side effects from the illness, how long can I just be me?"

"Well, through my experience, one can be expected to feel relatively normal for almost 6 to 9 months after diagnosis but then patients normally experience rapid weight loss, dizzy spells and moments of confusion, and finally considerable pain but we can manage this with drugs to make patients comfortable." Rachael was listening but it was still too much to take in. Dr Lang continued, "now we can try radiotherapy and chemotherapy to try to destroy the destructive cells, however, there are side effects that can make patients feel rather lousy through treatment periods, I would however, encourage you to try these treatments but only you can decide. I just want to ask you a few questions if I may, is that okay?" Rachael nodded. "Now I have to ask and I need you to be 100% honest with me too, is there any chance you could be pregnant?" Rachael paused for a few seconds, shocked by Dr Lang's question, then she immediately thought back to the first time her and Stone were intimate. She took long enough in her reply for Dr Lang to suspect there may be a possible chance.

"I did have sex with my boyfriend about 6 weeks ago, so it's possible but I am almost certain I cannot be pregnant," Racheal blushed and felt embarrassed as she answered. "Dr please, you must never breathe a word of this to my parents, I can't imagine how ashamed my father would be."

"Everything you tell me Rachael is in the strictest confidence I can assure you but we will need to do a test to be sure before we start any treatment," said the concerned doctor. He put his hand on Rachael's wrist and squeezed it gently to comfort her, "Rachael, I cannot imagine how you must be feeling right now but I promise you once we have some answers, we can start the treatment programme. I'll just get nurse Thelma to take a blood sample and we can discreetly get an answer for you, is that ok?" Racheal nodded and the Dr walked out the room. Almost immediately, nurse Thelma walked into the room and comforted Rachael with a firm hold on her shoulder.

"Hey beautiful lady, let's do a quick blood test for you." Rachael pulled back her gown sleeve and looked the other way whilst the nurse went about her business. Tears were running down Rachael's cheek. Thelma realised how distressing this must be for the poor girl so she got the test over quickly and gave her a gentle hug, "My darling, I cannot imagine how you are feeling but I promise I'll be here for you every step of the way. Now shall we go for that walk now?" Rachael wiped the tears from her face and stood up.

"Yes please Thelma, if you can come with me, I'd really like that."

"Of course, I will," first she took out her equipment along with Rachael's blood sample and she was back in an instant. "Ok my darling, do you have a coat?" asked the kind nurse.

"Yes, thank you Thelma, I will just grab it."

Nurse Thelma took her arm and they both walked out the room and along the corridor. "How are you feeling my dear? Would you like to go downstairs?" Thelma asked.

"Yes, I feel fine Thelma, yes, lets go downstairs," Rachael replied.

Arm in arm the caring nurse and her patient went down in the lift to the exit. The huge, automatic sliding doors opened and a welcoming breeze gently blew into Rachael's face. They walked outside and sat on a bench just along from the exit.

Still holding onto each other sitting side by side, neither of them said a word, they just watched people come and go through the doors. Rachael was taking large gulps of air and enjoying her first sense of freedom and normality since being admitted there. As they were enjoying the moment, along came Mr and Mrs Jenson with a small bag. "Mom, Dad," called Rachael. Susan looked over and spotted her daughter immediately.

"Hey, wow! It's so good to see you out here my darling," Susan was determined to remain strong for her daughter although inside she was crushed. She didn't want Rachael to witness that as she knew it would make her feel worse.

"Thank you Thelma for bringing her out here, would you like us to bring her in with us so you can get back to work?" asked Susan. Christopher was unusually quiet, just trying to deal with everything in his own way.

"Oh, yes that's fine, absolutely, she can come up with you guys when she's ready," said Thelma. Rachael thanked her, but she insisted it was her pleasure and she walked back through the automatic doors.

Both Christopher and Susan sat down on the bench with their daughter and they enjoyed another ten minutes of people watching before going back into the warm hospital lounge. Rachael was in between her parents as they made their way to the escalators. Both Susan and

Christopher had their arms around her as they proceeded to walk back to Rachael's room.

Susan was carrying a red travel bag in her left hand with Rachael's belongings inside, including the letter from Stone. She had discussed it with Jenson and although he was not happy about the decision, under the circumstances he could see it was the right thing to do.

Once Rachael was comfortable in bed, Susan said, "I brought the things you asked for darling and there is a letter addressed to you from Santa Barbara." Immediately, Rachael's eyes widened and a moment of excitement grabbed her body. She pulled herself upright in the bed and asked her mother to pass the envelope to her. Susan was not surprised by her daughter's response; she opened the zipper on the bag and pulled out the envelope and passed it to Rachael.

"Your dad and I can go out for a bit, give you some privacy whilst you read your letter, would you like us to do that?" said Susan as she looked at Jensen for some kind of response.

"Oh sure, erm, yes let's leave Rachael for a while," Christopher said awkwardly.

"Thank you, that would be great, if that's ok with you both?" Rachael said smiling. As her parents left the room, she wasted no time in tearing open the letter, she pulled out the paper and began to read it.

Stone's words made her smile, laugh and even cry for a brief moment. She couldn't believe this was all happening and she wondered how she was going to break the news to him, even feeling guilty and somehow unworthy of him. She was thinking perhaps the kindest thing to do for

Stone was to end their brief romance, make an excuse, so that he could get on with his life and not be burdened by her diagnosis. She loved him so much and she knew if she told him, he would try to be close to her and she knew this may bring him sadness and pain he did not deserve, so she decided she would write him a letter to say that because of the distance and the complications with her family it would be best to remember the good times and move on.

Rachael wasted no time, it would be the hardest letter she would ever have to write but she reached into the red travel bag and found the pen, paper and envelopes, and immediately started to write the letter.

When she'd finished, she addressed the envelope to Stone, sealed the letter and lay back in the bed just staring at the ceiling. When her parents came back into the room, she explained to them her decision and both Susan and Jenson agreed it was probably the right thing to do. They took the envelope and assured Rachael they would post it the first opportunity they had.

Chapter 17

On Monday morning, Stone heard the post van pull away outside, so he wandered out to the mailbox. As he reached in, he could see a hand written envelope with a New York Postmark on it. He rushed back inside, curious to see who the letter was from, praying it was his dear Rachael. He sat on a chair in the lounge and opened the letter in a hurry. As he pulled the letter out, his eyes were immediately searching in anticipation to confirm who the letter was from, he looked at the last words written, and it said From Rachael Jenson.

He then started to read from the top of the letter, his heart sank as his eyes worked their way through the words. He felt a rush of nausea as the letter of rejection registered in his mind. Such a cold, matter of fact letter cut him deeply and he felt completely heart broken. As he sat back in the chair to reflect, he could not help feeling this was Jenson's doing and he felt so disappointed Rachael had finally accepted her father's decision but being the kind of guy Stone was, he knew he would have to respect Rachael's decision and move on with his life.

Stone threw the letter in the bin, took a deep breath and continued getting ready for another stint at Redwing's garage.

When he arrived at work, he told Jimmy and Gregg, and they both sympathised with their buddy and supported him through the day.

As they walked out at the end of the shift Jimmy said, "So, buddy have you decided what to say to Butch Maloney?"

"Yeah, I want in Jimmy, especially now. I'm ready for a battle so I'll call him tomorrow morning,"

"Way to go bro," Jimmy said whilst fist pumping Stone. "Speak tomorrow buddy."

"Will do man," said Stone, as he made a swift pull away on his bike.

Stone took a slow ride home, thoughts of Rachael rushing through his mind. It was as if he could sense something didn't fit, something just wasn't right about the whole thing. The connection he had with Rachael was so strong, he felt the words in the letter were not her true feelings.

When he arrived home, he got straight on the phone to Butch Maloney.

It took a while to get connected but finally he got through to Maloney's secretary and explained he needed to speak with Butch as soon as possible.

"May I take your number sir and I'll pass your message on to Mr Maloney, he will no doubt get back to you in due course," said Maloney's secretary.

Stone gave his telephone number and put the receiver down.

He felt frustrated, disappointed, the whole day had been nothing but aggravation. In fact, he was so hurt over Rachael he had lost his appetite so he went to the fridge to grab a couple of beers, and sat down in the lounge waiting for the call from Butch Maloney.

Stone glanced at his mother's small carriage clock on the mantelpiece. It was just about to chime on the hour, when the phone rang. Stone jumped, the combination of the clock and the phone ringing had startled him as he was deep in thought. He lifted the receiver to hear Butch Maloney on the other end. "Stone, is that you?"

"Yeah, it's me Mr Maloney, thank you for returning my call,"

"So, what's it gonna be big guy, are you in?" Butch said confidently.

"Yeah, I'm in sir,"

"Great, then I'll get the papers drawn up and I'll get one of my guys to drive down to Butterfly Beach to save you coming up, how does that sound?"

Stone paused for a moment to gather his thoughts, "Ok great, I will be at Redwing's garage tomorrow until 5pm if you want to send someone down."

"No problem. Hey, I hear your real name is Schiano, so you have Italian blood, right?"

"Yeah, that's right sir, my father's side is from Sicily," Stone replied.

"I can see we're going to get on just fine, I have Sicilian roots too. I've been thinking, this whole thing can't happen without you and I know Devil's Run means a lot to you and your crew, so I'm willing to throw in a few grand to everyone of your riders that compete, and an extra 5k down payment for you but don't mention it to Clarence okay?"

"Oh really, that's very decent of you Mr Maloney, thank you," said Stone

"Hey forget about it, tomorrow I will send a guy called Vince Alito to Redwing's by 5pm, is that okay?" asked Maloney.

"Yes that's fine Mr Maloney, I'll expect him tomorrow," answered Stone.

"Ok caio," said Mr Maloney and his receiver was put down.

Stone got straight on the phone to Jimmy. It was as though his friend was standing right by the phone, picking the phone up as soon as it rang. "Hi Stone, is that you buddy?"

"Yeah it's me bud, I just had a conversation with Maloney, he's sending a guy down to Redwing's tomorrow with the contract and a further 5k down payment for my race."

Jimmy took a moment to digest the information. "Ok erm, well I suppose it will save us driving down to Nevada again and it's a generous amount of money he's offering but I'm slightly concerned why he's so keen to get this deal completed so fast."

"I think it's just in case we change our minds but we should really have a meeting with the rest of the guys and see who wants in because it won't be long before Clarence and his mob come down to start practicing the route to Spike's Edge and we need to warn our boys Jimmy," said Stone.

Jimmy agreed and they both decided to meet with the rest of the crew straight after the contract was signed the following evening.

Stone was still heartbroken over Rachael's letter but now he decided the best way to get over her was to throw all his attention into this race and make sure Blood Rangers came out on top.

The following morning came round amazingly fast, Stone had been trying to put Rachael out of his mind but it was not easy as he really loved her and letting her go was very painful. He grabbed a piece of toast and a coffee before heading off to Redwing's for another shift. At lunchtime, he thought it best to inform Billy Keegan what was happening so he knocked on Billy's door. "Come in," said Keegan.

"Hi Billy, can we talk, or is now not a good time?"

"It's fine, sit down, what's up?"

"Well, I just thought I'd better bring you up to date with the meeting I had in Vegas with Butch Maloney. I won't bore you with the details but we've agreed a deal. I don't have a date yet but Devil's Run is looking to be big in Vegas via video link and the long and short of it is they're sending a guy to meet me after work tonight, to sign a contract." Billy inhaled a deep breath and blew out through his lips.

"Ok, do you want me to speak to my guy in Lake Tahoe before you sign anything?"

"No, it's fine, Jimmy and I have decided we want in. They've promised me 50k up front and a further 200k if I win and to be honest Billy, I need this. I've struggled since losing my ma, I never knew my dad and now Rachael Jenson's ended things and she's the only girl I ever really loved, so I need a distraction, otherwise I'm going to go crazy Billy."

"Ok man I get it, sorry about Rachael but maybe that's a blessing, I mean what with her father and all," said Billy.

"I don't know Billy but I just wanted to tell you, as the guy is coming here at 5pm when we lock up,"

"Ok listen, I tell you what, bring the guy into my office and I'll stick around too. It won't hurt having a little support around and if you like I'm happy to sign as a witness for the contract so they know you ain't no jackass, willing to sign your life away,"

"Thanks Billy, I appreciate it, thank you," Stone said as he stood up and shook Billy's hand.

"No problem, now get out there and have something to eat before I kick your ass," Billy said laughing.

Stone smiled and nodded, then shut the office door behind him. He sat down with Gregg and Jimmy and they all had a good chat over lunch. The afternoon passed quickly and dead on 5pm a black limo with blacked out windows pulled into the yard.

The door opened and a tall guy in black suit emerged from the car, he was wearing dark glasses and he looked like something from the Godfather. He walked over to where the guys were standing and introduced himself. In a deep Italian accent, he said, "Hi, I've come to meet Michael Schiano."

"That's me, please follow me into the office," Stone said calmly.

The huge guy looked behind him, paused for a moment, then proceeded towards the office. When they reached the door, Billy opened it and escorted the large mysterious guy into the office. "Please sit down, make yourself comfortable," said Billy. The big guy sat down in the office chair and placed a large briefcase on the table. Stone and Jimmy came in and closed the door with Gregg Philips looking through the glass.

The big guy spoke again. "My name is Vince Alito, Butch Maloney has sent me to get Mr Schiano to sign a contract for Devil's Run," he then went silent and took off his dark glasses to reveal big brown emotionless eyes, dead eyes like a shark.

"Okay, that's right we were expecting you, may I have a look at the contract?" said Stone.

The man reached into his briefcase and handed the contract to Stone.

Stone looked at it and although in small print it was easy to read. He could see it was for just one event, however, all gambling rights were strictly governed by Butch Maloney's casino affairs and should further races take place, he would have to be notified and given sole rights to video coverage and be entitled to any revenue made from such an event. The fees were included, the prize money and down payment.

Stone asked Mr Alito if Jimmy and Billy could also just have a brief look at the document, but he felt confident it was a reasonable offer. Mr Alito just nodded, so Billy and Jimmy looked over it. They both scanned over the document and Billy asked if he could sign as witness after a few quick questions. "Ok Vince, I'm a businessman and have friends in Lake Tahoe that know some of your associates, now can I confirm that this event will never bring trouble to this neighbourhood and can I confirm that Michael Schiano and his crew will always have free will to commit to any further event. For example if they decide to never race again after this event then they have that choice?" Vince Alito stared at Billy with his intimidating eyes.

"I am not a legal representative, I am purely here to see that Michael Schiano signs the contract." The big guy went quiet again. This annoyed Billy, he looked at Stone and told him to get Butch Maloney on the phone. Stone did what he said, picked up the phone and dialled his number and passed the phone to Billy. Butch answered straight away, as if he was expecting the call.

"Hi Mr Maloney, my name is Billy Keegan, I'm the owner here at Redwing's garage and your guy Vince Alito is here with a document for Michael Schiano to sign. Michael has asked me to look over the contract and as a close friend to Michael, I want to just clarify a few things."

"Yes of course, I have no problem with that Mr Keegan," said Maloney.

Billy was pleased by Butch Maloney's response and pressed record on his telephone system. He confirmed that Michael and his crew were free to pick and choose future events and he also confirmed no trouble would ever be brought to Butterfly Beach. In fact Butch Maloney had been fully cooperative so Stone went ahead and signed the contract with Billy Kegan as a witness whilst Butch was still on the phone. Butch then asked if he could speak to his guy Vince. They both spoke Italian, so it was not easy to tell what they were saying, however, the conversation was still being recorded so that gave them peace of mind. Vince put the phone down and pulled from his briefcase a large brown envelope and gave it to Stone.

"Here's the 55k from Mr Maloney and I am now going to leave you gentleman," said the big guy as he stood up and walked out. Stone thanked Billy for everything, Billy laughed.

"I found that all rather exciting guys, didn't you? Like a scene from the Godfather," Jimmy and Stone laughed, as Billy ejected the tape from his telephone recorder and put it in his safe. All three men shook hands and walked out and locked up the premises.

Stone was still clutching the brown envelope as the men walked towards the parking area, he undid his jacket and put the envelope in his inside pocket. "Hey Jimmy, meet me at mine in half an hour if you can buddy, just before we go meet the guys," said Stone.

"Will do buddy," said Jimmy. Billy pulled out the yard, beeped his horn and headed home.

Stone gave Jimmy a nod and pulled away, "see you soon buddy," Jimmy said as he pulled out onto the road behind him.

Chapter 18

It was Tuesday morning when Doctor Lang came into Rachael's room, holding a clipboard.

Christopher and Susan were sitting by her side and greeted the doctor. "Good morning all, I just wondered if I could speak for a moment in private with Rachael, would that be okay?"

Christopher looked a little taken back by the doctor's request but both Susan and he respected his request and agreed. "Ok darling, dad and I will go for a coffee and be back soon." Rachael nodded, smiled and looked intently at Dr Lang.

As her parents left the room, Dr Lang shut the door behind them and walked back towards Rachael's bed.

"Ok Rachael, I have the results here from your pregnancy test and I can confirm you are pregnant. The blood results are showing detectable levels of HCG, this indicates you're around 6 weeks pregnant, would this seem right?" Rachael gasped, she instantly filled up with tears and began to cry. Dr Lang put his hand on her wrist and gave it a reassuring squeeze. "I can't imagine how you must be feeling, what with your diagnosis and now this but we will support any decision you make," said Dr Lang.

Rachael put her head back on the pillow, shaking it in denial but she knew this had to be from the first time she and Stone had been intimate, shortly after his mother's funeral.

"What happens now Doctor? I can't let my parents know this, it will finish my father and my mother will be so disappointed in me. Doctor, please ensure me this news is strictly confidential, I need to know that," Rachael said, still weeping in between her words.

"Yes of course Rachael, this is why I asked to see you alone but you see, my main concern is the treatment I wanted to offer you, should not be carried out on a pregnant woman," replied Dr Lang.

"Look Doctor, tell me straight, am I likely to live long enough to give birth to this baby, I mean if I'm going to die, I will at least live on in my child,"

"Yes, it's possible, however, my advice would be to terminate the pregnancy and get moving on with chemo and radiotherapy to at least fight the Cancer and prolong your life as long as we can," Dr Lang replied.

Rachael sat up in bed with a sense of determination and strength in her eyes, she looked at the doctor and said, "I'm not silly, I know this treatment is intense and it could even kill me before the Cancer but if I manage the pain and live long enough to deliver this baby, that's my way of winning, I know it sounds crazy but it's what I want. Can you help me?"

Dr Lang paused for a moment then sighed and put his hand on his head and pulled his fingers through his hair.

"Ok if you wish, I can support you with pain killers for as long as it takes, we can write up a diet plan which can make a difference but you need to speak to your parents."

Unknown to Rachael, Christopher was already asking questions at the reception desk. He had asked nurse Thelma why Dr Lang was having private consultations with his daughter. Thelma explained that due to Rachael's age, she was entitled to patient confidentiality but explained this is common where young patients don't want their parents to be traumatised by further discussions on their condition. Christopher and Susan had thought this typical of their unselfish daughter and waited patiently for Dr Lang to come out.

Rachael told Dr Lang that she would explain to her parents that the private consultations were to discuss treatments and spare them the gory details. She would tell her parents when it felt right, she knew now would be the wrong time and too much for them to digest. The doctor respected her decision and then carried out a brief examination which he found encouraging. Rachael was in no pain whatsoever, her balance and reflexes were normal, her appetite was good and he explained that as the illness takes hold she may start to get frequent headaches with dizzy spells and tiredness but he was pleased so far how she had recovered from the seizure.

After a reassuring handshake, Dr Lang left the room. Christopher and Susan smiled at him as he passed by reception, he acknowledged them with a slight nod and a nervous smile as he proceeded along the corridor.

Christopher and Susan walked back in the room to see their daughter sitting up in bed. Rachael was determined not to show her feelings and said, "Well, the doctor says I'm doing well under the circumstances, my balance and reflexes are normal, I'm in no pain and feel hungry, what more could a girl want?" she laughed nervously.

"Well my dear it's great to see you in such high spirits. Did Doctor Lang have much to say?" said Susan.

"He just did a brief examination and talked to me about treatments but if you don't mind, I'd rather not talk about them right now," Rachael replied.

Christopher and Susan agreed and just took comfort in seeing her looking bright.

As the evening progressed, the family watched TV together whilst eating snacks and dosing in between. When Susan and Christopher left Rachael for the evening, she finally had some time to reflect on the day's events.

She cried for a bit but strangely she felt a weird sense of excitement to think she was carrying Stone's child. She thought about the letter she had sent, praying he was ok but now wondering whether he should know the truth, the possibility of a child would change everything. If only I could spend my last moments with him, she thought. She even had an odd visualisation of the three of them together, her Stone and the baby. This thought brought great pleasure to Rachael but she knew her father would most likely put a stop to it.

She lay awake most of the night, dreaming of running away somewhere with Stone to live out her final moments with the love of her life but then feeling riddled with guilt over the prospect of telling him she was pregnant and dying, I mean how do you tell someone that, she thought.

One thing she knew for sure was that her overprotective parents would just want to terminate the pregnancy and get her hooked up on a chemo line to keep her alive for as long as they could. Although she knew they loved her, she just knew there was no way they would accept her wishes of spending it with Stone, refusing treatment and having a baby before she checked out of this life but this was her life, however short it may be, she was going to do what she wanted to do, for the little time she had left on this earth.

She decided to write a letter to her dear friend Katie Goldberg, telling her everything that had happened since she had been back in Connecticut. Then asking her to explain to Stone her reasons for calling it off. She also decided to write another note for Stone and put it inside Katie's envelope so that her parents didn't notice. In it she suggested they run away somewhere far away, to be alone and god willing, have the baby. Rachael realised this would be an awful lot of news for Stone to take in but she felt he loved her and would want to know. She had no doubt whatsoever of her feelings for him so she addressed the envelope to Katie and put Stone's letter inside with instructions to pass it on to him. Rachael put the letter on her bedside cabinet and finally went to sleep.

The following morning Rachael was awoken by nurse Thelma. "Good morning beautiful, may I just take your blood pressure?" Rachael sat up in bed and noticed the sun was shining through the window. She looked at the envelope on the bedside cabinet remembering her words to Stone and Katie.

As Thelma was taking her blood pressure, Christopher and Susan came in the door.

"Good morning Rachael, how are you feeling?" said Jenson.

"I feel okay Dad thanks," Rachael replied. Susan sat down by her side and held her hand whilst Thelma went about her business.

"Okay that's good, your blood pressure is normal my darling, I will quickly get out your way before the breakfast trolley comes round," said Thelma cheerfully. She smiled at Rachael's parents and walked out with her equipment.

"Oh mom, before I forget, can you post this letter to Katie Goldberg, I promised I would write her, just wish I had better news," said Rachael.

"Oh ok, yes of course we will post it, there's a mailbox near the exit, next time we go down we will post it for you darling," said Susan, completely unaware of the envelope's contents.

"Katie may want to visit once she hears what's happened. In fact, I guess sooner or later you will have visitors from all over, many of your friends at College have already been trying to find out how you are," said Jenson.

It was around 9am when the breakfast trolley came around. Rachael had a round of toast and jam, some orange juice and a coffee. She was in good spirits and her parents could see she seemed more upbeat than the previous days.

"I might take a shower and walk the envelope down to the mailbox myself, if anyone wants to come with me?" said Rachael.

"If you feel up to it my darling, then yes, let's all take a walk downstairs," Susan replied. She looked at her husband, nodded and smiled, as if satisfied with her daughter's positive attitude.

Rachael had a shower, put some clean clothes on, pulled her dressing gown around her shoulders and slipped her feet into her pink fluffy slippers.

With her parents in tow, the family walked to the escalators, Rachael had a firm grip on the envelope as they came out on the ground floor. They walked into the small hospital store and purchased a first-class stamp, guaranteed next day delivery.

Rachael put the envelope in the mailbox outside the store and as her fingers let the envelope slip away on top of the heap of mail, she knew it was too late now to change her mind. She took a few seconds staring at the mailbox, imagining the pain this letter would cause but she felt it was the right decision.

It was a sunny day, so the family walked outside to sit on the bench just outside the exit. The Jenson's sat there for a while, enjoying watching the world go by but after a while they all got a bit fed up with the automatic doors opening and shutting every few seconds.

When they got back upstairs, Rachael asked Nurse Thelma if she would be so kind to get another chair put in her room as she did not feel like sitting in bed all day. Nurse Thelma dealt with Rachael's request immediately as she could understand her frustration. This was great thought Rachael, if I can gradually build myself up to get out of here, then I will at least have normality back in my life again, no matter how long I have left. The family sat and enjoyed a few TV shows together, then the lunch trolley came around and they all had a bite to eat. Christopher and Susan were desperate to know when Rachael's treatment would start but they were hesitant to ask her right now as she seemed so at peace with everything for a moment.

The day was flying by and it was not long before another day had ended. Christopher and Susan kissed their daughter goodnight and it was not long before they were all in their beds. Susan had been slightly concerned that the family were still yet to discuss treatment options for Rachael and she felt that she would need to discuss it with Rachael sooner rather than later.

Chapter 19

In Santa Barbara, Stone had split the 55k with Jimmy and the meeting with the Blood Rangers crew had gone extremely well. At least six of the crew were keen to race at the event and make some quick cash, so it was looking like a win, win situation for everyone right now.

It was lunchtime when Katie Goldberg called home for lunch, whilst doing some extra shifts at Johnson's drug store.

She grabbed the mail on the way in and her eyes scanned through the envelopes, noticing a letter addressed to herself as she was walking along the pathway to the door.

She put her parents' mail on the hallway table and went to her bedroom to open her letter. She guessed it was from Rachael as it had the New York postmark on it.

When she opened the letter, she pulled out two pieces of paper, one addressed to her and one to Stone.

She started to read the one addressed to her, and seconds into it, she was heartbroken.

Rachael had explained that she had suffered a seizure at University mid-class a week ago and been rushed to hospital in Connecticut. After investigation she had been informed by doctors that the cause of the seizure was due to a large brain tumour and that her condition was terminal. She had 18 months to live at the longest, furthermore she was pregnant and needed to know that

Katie would swear to keep this to herself and not tell a soul. Katie guessed the letter to Stone was likely to be carrying the same awful news.

Poor Katie put her hand on her head and started to weep over the news of her dear friend. She was to respect Racheal's wishes and not tell a soul, but she knew she had to get the other letter to Stone.

She had lost her appetite for lunch so decided to spend the rest of her lunch break cycling over to Redwing's Garage to give Stone his letter.

She wasted no time at all, the letter had to reach Stone as soon as possible.

As she pulled into Redwing's, Stone was standing by his bike, drinking a can of coke.

"Hi Katie, what are you doing here?" Stone said smiling. Katie immediately jumped off her bike and ran over to her friend. Her voice was weak and shaky as she told Stone that Rachael had sent her letter with a note for him. Stone could see how distressed poor Katie was. She handed over the note, turned her back with tears running down her face and cycled off without saying anymore. "Katie, Katie, what's wrong?" Stone shouted after her.

Stone teared open the small pink envelope, desperate to see what it said. He sat down on a small wall by his bike and started to read.

As he eagerly read through the note, he felt an instant flow of nausea rush through his stomach. Rachael had explained in her previous letter about her reasons for calling it off and this was typical of the unselfish beautiful soul she was. Although happy she had confirmed her love for him, he found the news unbearable, 'Why, why her?'

he thought as his eyes filled with tears. He continued to read with a broken heart as she mentioned the pregnancy and her wish to spend her final moments somewhere far away, where her father cannot control her and make decisions for her precious time left.

Although he understood and respected her wishes, he also felt totally responsible for allowing her to become pregnant. Racheal had taken it upon herself to say that although in normal circumstances being pregnant would not be ideal, it was now giving her the motivation to stay alive and give birth to the child. She kept apologising all the way through the letter but Stone felt there was absolutely no reason to ever apologise, he loved her so much and just wanted to help her in any way he could. As he finished the letter, Jimmy came over. "Are you ok buddy?"

Stone just handed him the note, his silence and glassy eyes told Jimmy something was desperately wrong. Stone walked back in the workshop towards Billy's office whilst Jimmy read the letter.

After he'd finished reading, he came in and consoled his friend with a hug.

Billy noticed through the office window that something was up. He came to the door and asked the two lads if everything was okay. Stone looked at Billy but could not find the words, so he just handed Billy the letter.

He asked Stone into the office and closed the door, "Sit down son," he said.

Stone sat down quietly and his boss started to read the letter. Billy was shaking his head most of the way through the letter, he could not believe the sad news.

After he finished the note, he walked around to Stone and squeezed his shoulder. Rachael had explained the illness was terminal and that treatment would only prolong her agony so she felt by running away and spending her last moments with Stone, with the possibility of a baby, part of her would live on. It all seemed crazy but when you looked at all the facts, you could understand her thought process, thought Billy.

"Stone, look if you really love this girl, maybe I can help. I have some friends in Mexico with an apartment in the mountains, close to the sea. No-one would find you there. It's an unfair set of circumstances buddy but I can see why she wants to get away. Her father will likely control her final time left and he will fight to terminate the pregnancy if it means Rachael would live longer".

"I'm gonna contact Butch Maloney and bring this race forward and I'm gonna win that 200k for Rachael and our baby then we can get away," said a determined Stone. "Billy, if you can get me the details for your friends in Mexico, I will be eternally grateful." Billy agreed to help and he suggested Stone should call Butch sooner rather than later and handed him the telephone on the desk and walked out the office.

Stone had Butch Maloney's number in his jacket pocket and wasted no time in ringing him. Butch answered the phone straight away. "Hi Mr Maloney, it's Stone, look erm, something has come up, I need this race as fast as we can get it on."

"Wow! Ok, the earliest I can probably do is a fortnight's time. I know Clarence and his guys are planning on coming down next week to practice the run but I'm still waiting for a film crew to confirm they can televise the race live. We've started marketing the event and the interest is just as I expected. Listen, leave it with me but I reckon two weeks max," said Maloney. 'Ok, please try to get back to me with a date as soon as you can, thank you," Stone replied.

Butch Malonely agreed and Stone took a deep breath in and out and walked into the workshop. Billy asked him how the call went and Stone told him Butch said he would be getting back to him soon but it was looking likely for a fortnight's time.

"That's great, well that's a start buddy," said Billy as he walked back into his office and sat down.

Stone walked over to Jimmy, "sorry I didn't run it by you man but I called Butch Maloney to try get this race on as quickly as we can because I'm going to need the cash to get away with Rachael."

"Yeah I guessed that bro. I'll be sorry to see you go but I understand. I know you love Rachael." Stone nodded, "Yes I do Jimmy, I really do and this all seems like a bad dream right now but I just know I need to be with her, especially as she doesn't have much time."

In Stone's heart he was relieved she still wanted to be with him and that her previous letter was not her true feelings but at the same time, he felt saddened by the card his poor Rachael had been dealt.

The letter explained that all further contact should be passed through Katie Goldberg to safeguard her father finding out.

When Stone got home, he immediately started to write Rachael a letter. He told her he was working on a plan to get her out of the hospital and had found somewhere far away where they could hide out. He also explained he needed two weeks to get everything organised. He didn't want her to know about the race in case this added to her already high stress levels.

Stone wasted no time in running the letter over to Katie. When he got to her door, she opened it before he knocked as she had been expecting him. He handed her the letter and the two friends hugged. Stone walked away without saying a further word. They both knew what they had to do for Rachael now.

Katie had also written a letter to Rachael, reassuring her that she would do all she could for her.

She put Stone's letter inside her envelope and walked it over to the post box at the end of the street. She prayed the letter would reach her friend in good time.

Chapter 20

It was Thursday morning around 8.30 when Rachael had a visit from Dr Lang, "Rachael, I'm sorry to disturb you but I just need to be clear on your decision. Are you sure you still want to go ahead with your pregnancy and forego any treatment. If you are, your parents should be told about your reasons for refusing treatment as your father will soon be asking questions."

"Yes, I most definitely want to continue with my pregnancy but I just need to know that there is a good chance I will be able to carry the baby as near to full term as possible?"

"It has been known for cancer patients to have normal pregnancies, however, there are always risks. In some instances even women having chemotherapy can still produce a healthy child, but we obviously don't encourage it."

"That's all I want to know Dr Lang, thank you. Oh, another thing Dr Lang, I do appreciate your position and I will speak to my parents but under no circumstances can they know I am pregnant."

Dr Lang looked at her with a broken smile, "Rachael, it's your decision but I strongly advise that you tell them."

With that, he checked the small wound on her head from the biopsy and both Christopher and Susan walked in. "Hi honey, hi doc," said Susan. Dr Lang acknowledged them and walked out the door.

Susan was holding an envelope, "Here you go, you have a letter from Katie I think, well it's from Santa Barbara, she certainly wasted no time responding to your letter did she?" Susan smiled.

Rachael was secretly so excited about the fast response. She was hoping there was a letter from Stone too. She put it in her bedside cabinet and said to her parents she would read it later.

"Look guys, I need to talk to you. I've had a discussion with Dr Lang I've decided not to go through with chemo or radiotherapy. I know my fate, so why put myself through further pain. I feel well at the moment, so my wish is to get out of here and carry on as normal a life as I can and just be me again.

Christopher and Susan were visibly upset by Rachael's decision as they were hoping having treatment might prolong their daughter's life and the chance of new medicines may come along. Jenson was even considering hiring specialist scientists to see if they could come up with a new breakthrough if he funded it.

Rachael explained it would still be possible to live at least a year to 18 months without traditional methods. "Look, mom, dad, this is what I want so please respect my wishes."

There was an uncomfortable silence in the room then Susan lent over the bed and hugged her daughter tightly.

"If this is what you want, dad and I will respect your decision."

Christopher stood up and walked out the room overcome with emotion and he didn't want Rachael to see him cry. Susan made her excuses to go and check on her husband. As soon as Susan walked out, Rachael wasted no time in reaching for Katie's letter. She opened it as fast as she could, looking for any news she could find from Stone. There were two letters, she recognised Stone's handwriting immediately and started to read it.

'To my darling Rachael, I cannot not tell you how sorry I am to hear your news and although I'm relieved you still love me, I am heartbroken you have been through such hell. I should have been more responsible the day you came into my bed, please forgive me. If you want to have this baby then I will do all I can to support you but my love, the thought of losing you is a pain I cannot describe. You mentioned you want to get away so all I need is a fortnight to get everything organised, I hope that is ok! I've got some unfinished business to take care of first but after that I'll be making plans for us in Mexico. My boss Billy Keegan has connections there so we'll have somewhere to stay. You will need your passport to cross the border so I hope this doesn't cause you problems but if you communicate through Katie, she will feed any news back to me and I'll get everything ready for two weeks' time. Let's make a date and I will come and get you. All my love forever Stone xx'.

Rachael put the letter back in the envelope just as her parents came back into the room. She knew her passport was in her college bag which was hanging up in her locker at the other side of the room. She waited until her parents went for a coffee and climbed out of bed to check it was still there, concerned her mother may have taken it home. Luckily for Rachael her bag was still there with her passport safely tucked inside.

That evening Rachael read Katie's letter and she wasted no time replying to both Katie and Stone. She had suggested she make her escape on Thursday, two weeks to the day. She also confirmed she had her passport and was excited about Mexico. She asked Stone to be outside the hospital exit at 8.30am before her parents arrived. This would be perfect as she would tell the nurses she was just getting some fresh air and meeting her parents.

Rachael had a few stamps left in her bedside cabinet but she felt her parents may think it's odd to post another letter so quickly, so she asked nurse Thelma if she would post it for her. The friendly nurse was only too happy to help Rachael.

Stone had been waiting for Katie to get in touch with news from Rachael. He was just about to take a shower when the doorbell rang. Katie was standing there holding a letter. He invited her in and she followed him to the lounge where they both sat down. She passed Stone the letter and he immediately started to read it.

Rachael had said she felt so bad putting this all on them but felt she had nowhere else to turn. The thought of living her last moments happily were keeping her strong. She had explained that her parents would simply never respect her final wishes to be with Stone and have the baby but this was her life and time to choose her final destiny.

Katie could see the emotion in Stone's eyes as he put the letter on the coffee table beside him.

"Katie, I guess you know what Rachael wants?" Katie nodded. "You see, when we run away, Jenson will try to track us down and he'll start by questioning you no doubt, so you may want to think about that prospect Katie just to be prepared dear friend. I don't know if you've heard anything but in less than two weeks, there's going to be some activity here, a few races at Dawson's Point," said Stone.

"What, Devil's Run?" Katie said surprised.

"Yes but this time it's a much bigger deal. I'm gonna race Clarence Black for big bucks which will be enough to take care of Rachael when we get away. I have to win the race before we go Katie but Rachael can't find out because it will only worry her," said Stone.

"Oh my God, do you have to do this Stone?" asked Katie with a concerned look on her face.

I've signed a contract with some big people in Vegas and a casino is sponsoring the event this time, in fact in a few days, there'll be a lot of commotion here as Clarence and his crew will be practicing the route."

"Oh wow, I didn't know anything about this but whatever you do Stone, please take care, Rachael needs you more than ever now," pleaded Katie.

"I will Katie, I promise but I simply need this cash to give us a way out."

"Ok, I understand, I'll write back to Rachael confirming the details."

The two friends hugged, and Katie left the house feeling she was at least helping her friend in her time of need.

Stone had a shower, got ready and took a ride out to meet Jimmy and the rest of the crew. They spent the day practicing the route up to Spike's Edge. Stone showed the riders some useful tactics and helpful tips on leaning around the awkward bends. When they arrived at Spike's Edge, Stone explained the dangers of crossing the rope at high speeds, suggesting if they got a fair lead on their opponents then they could brake hard before crossing the rope. He made it clear that this was a matter of life or death and winning a few thousand was not worth dying for. The Blood Rangers were confident in each other's abilities and were looking forward to the event.

Chapter 21

It was Monday morning when Rachael was given a letter from nurse Thelma.

"Someone's popular here," she said smiling.

"Thank you, Thelma," said Rachael and jumping out of bed, she took the letter into the bathroom and closed the door. Quickly opening the envelope, she pulled out Katie's response. She explained that Stone would be outside on the date arranged and he would be in a silver RV so that she could travel more comfortably.

Rachael felt excited and scared at the same time. She knew this was the only way forward but she couldn't help worrying about her parents. She decided she would leave a note on her bedside cabinet explaining everything, although she had no intention of telling them about pregnancy. Deep in her heart, she knew her parents would take the baby away from Stone and control it's life, as they had done hers and she didn't want this for their child.

That evening she started to write a letter to her parents, it was the hardest letter she had ever written but she was still determined to run away with Stone.

Once she felt sure she had written everything she wanted them to know, she sealed the envelope and put it under some clothes in her bag.

Time soon passed by in the hospital and Rachael was slowly but surely getting ready to make her move. Dr Lang had done his daily checks and Christopher and Susan were looking to bring her home anytime now. Rachael had been on a strict, healthy diet and she was taking high doses of vitamins to boost her low immunity levels.

Luckily, she had not had any serious headaches, dizziness, or nausea so she was feeling surprisingly positive about the time she had left.

Back in Butterfly Beach, things were really cooking up. The race date was approaching fast so Clarence and his boys had been practicing the route for Devil's Run and Butch Maloney had also been down to visit Butterfly Beach.

The event was booked, brought forward as discussed and things were really starting to heat up. Stone had been asked to pose with Clarence for a few promotional posters and film promotions as there was huge interest in Vegas.

The race was set for the coming Saturday, so Stone was spending time working on his bike; new tyres and a full service on the engine.

Stone knew he had to win the race and that he had a slight advantage over Clarence as he had beat Marco Sanchez in the summer but word on the street was that his opponent was a very experienced rider, and he had plenty of guts and a fast bike.

The race was to be filmed live, two cameras to be set up. One at the start and one at the finish line on Spike's Edge. Individual cameras were to be fitted to the bikes to give viewers the maximum thrill factor and ensure there was no foul play or cheating.

Stone knew he had to secure the money, at least 250k was up for grabs and this would offer Rachael and himself a solid start in Mexico, so he simply had to win.

Saturday came around and the bikers met near the church at Dawson's Point. Butch Maloney had instructed his team to keep a low profile, so if locals asked or the Police questioned them, they were to say they were filming promotional advertisements. Little did everyone know that by midnight a live coverage of the race would be shown on huge screens inside Butch Maloney's casino, including a pay view channel for guests in the hotel to watch in the comfort of their own rooms. Large amounts of money was expected to be made at the Tropicana establishment, not only by Butch Maloney but anyone placing bets on the winners.

Stone and Jimmy were making final adjustments to their bikes. Jimmy had decided to race as well but he wasn't too bothered about winning, he just felt like he wanted to take part. He wasn't sure who his opponent would be, however, he had heard a rumour it might be Big Dog, which was slightly unnerving.

Riders were expected to be at the starting point by 9pm at the latest, so at 8.30 Stone, Jimmy and the boys made their way to Dawson's Point.

When they rolled in, there were hundreds of bikes starting to gather. Katie was standing behind Gregg Phillips in the crowd and she rushed over to hug Stone. She knew how much was riding on this for him and the importance of winning the prize money. Jimmy was likely to be up for the first race, so the tension was high, Katie hugged him and wished him luck too.

Clarence and his crew were already there, they were surprisingly a little less intimidating than before as Butch Maloney had warned them not to create any trouble.

All those taking part were to report to a temporary portacabin and give their names. Stone and Jimmy walked inside where there was a woman sitting behind a desk, booking the riders in. Jimmy approached the desk.

"Name please?" she said.

"Hi there, my name's Nash, Jimmy Nash," he answered.

"Next," said the woman. Stone approached the desk, he looked at the women, she was dressed very formally in a blazer style jacket with a name badge, Karen Stiller, with Tropicana Sunrise clearly printed at the top. "Name please?" she repeated.

"Michael Schiano, or you may just have me down as Stone." The women looked up at him, "Ah, so you're Stone? Please sign here sir, you're in the final race with Clarence but I guess you know that?" smiled the woman.

"Yes, Mam," answered Stone. Karen Stiller handed over a piece of paper with the race itinerary on it and then he walked outside to join Jimmy. They both looked at the itinerary which had the rider's names, along with each of their opponents, the time of the event and the basic rules. First up was Jimmy and Big Dog so Stone put his arm around his buddy and whispered words of encouragement in his ear. Stone and Jimmy fist pumped then moved Jimmy's bike over to the start line. Big Dog was already there, revving his bike, focused on the road ahead. Both riders pulled down their visors and rolled their bikes up against the rope on the floor, which was then raised by two of Butch Maloney's fancy girls, obviously sent down from the casino.

The glamourous girls were wearing tight shorts and pink T-Shirts with Tropicana printed all over them, clearly to promote Maloney.

The T.V cameras were rolling and there was a huge digital countdown clock placed by the line.

As it counted down 10,9,8,7.......... the rope was dropped as the riders opened up their clutch and launched off as fast as they could.

Jimmy was leading up to the first bend then Big Dog took him on the straight. Both riders seemed to be giving it their all and the crowd were going wild, the atmosphere was electric. There were large P.A speakers blasting heavy rock music to thrill spectators. In Vegas, Butch Maloney was watching the race unfold on his huge screen at the Tropicana. The atmosphere was so exhilarating, the bike cameras gave a shaky, distorted view of everything the riders could see and this added to the excitement of the whole experience.

Halfway up the mountain road, Jimmy was now slipping behind. Big Dog was obviously a confident rider as he leaned low around the bends, hardly touching his brakes. The music down below was so loud, both riders could hear it. Big Dog seemed to relax a little on the straight, so Jimmy decided to throttle up fast and make some ground up. His loyal Yamaha FZR was performing well and with a spike of energy, Jimmy pulled close behind the big guy, who was thrashing his Suzuki GSX. Big Dog could see Jimmy on his tail and started to zig zag to avoid being overtaken so this made it almost impossible for Jimmy to pass him. Just ahead was a sharp bend but Big Dog was strong on bends, rarely breaking, just leaning hard with his knees scraping the road. Jimmy felt he could probably take him as soon as they came out of the bend so he kicked down through the gears, dipped the clutch for a quick burst and was back on with a chance to take Big Dog. Jimmy went for it, he started to pass Big Dog when suddenly his front wheel hit a large rock and his bike just couldn't recover. Poor Jimmy hit the ground and rolled over the edge and down the bank. Luckily it wasn't a huge drop but enough to do damage. Jimmy's bike came crashing over behind him, bouncing on the rocks, smashing into pieces. Down below Stone sensed something bad had happened as the guys watching the T.V monitors were shouting out obscenities and holding their hands over their mouths. Stone ran over to one of the monitors, one of the bike cameras was down. "Excuse me guys, what's happened?" asked a worried Stone. One of the Engineers looked up.

"Looks like one of the bike's is down," he answered. Stone had a feeling it was Jimmy and he just stared at the other monitors hoping and praying it was not his friend.

Back at the scene, Jimmy was conscious and checking himself over. He managed to stand up, luckily no bones were broken it seemed. He looked at the wreckage of his bike and started to climb his way back up to the road. As he almost reached the top, Big Dog was standing there, he reached out his hand and pulled Jimmy back up onto the roadside. "Are you ok man? Shit, I thought you were history!" said the big guy.

"I'm okay but my bike isn't," laughed Jimmy. Big Dog gave Jimmy fist bump.

"Respect brother," he said. Although Big Dog had officially won the race, he seemed more concerned about his opponent's wellbeing which showed Jimmy this huge guy had a big heart. Big Dog gave Jimmy a lift back down to Dawson's Point where, waiting in anticipation for some news, was Stone. As Big Dog's bike rolled down to the portacabin, Stone could see his friend was on the back of the bike so he rushed over. "Holy shit buddy, you had me worried for a while there, are you ok?" asked Stone.

"I'm cool, I hit a rock and slid over the bank,"

"Thank God you're ok brother," said Stone. Jimmy seemed surprisingly ok as he walked over to the side-line and sat on the grass. Big Dog was enjoying the rush, his crew were cheering his name and the race was generating a massive surge of interest at Butch Maloney's casino, with bets going through the roof.

As the late evening moved on, the races were now in full swing. A few wins to the Blood Rangers and a few to the Satanic Disciples and luckily there were no further crashes and everyone was enjoying the atmosphere.

It was nearly time for the big race so Stone pulled his bike close to the line, the church clock chime was now just ten minutes away from midnight. This was the big event that everyone was waiting for, the last race of the evening. The hype and tension attached to this finale was very high and it felt as though the music and crowd had just disappeared. There was almost no breeze in the air, with an eerie, uncomfortable silence all of the sudden. Everyone seemed to just focus on Stone and Clarence now, just staring at the two finalists as if bewitched by every movement they made. Jimmy and Katie made their way through the crowd and they rushed over and hugged Stone. "You got this brother," said Jimmy.

"Thanks buddy." Stone then looked at Katie, he could see she was very emotional.

"Do it for Rachael," she said before standing back out of the way of the bikes. Stone nodded, he was touched by her words.

The riders moved over to the starting line, Clarence pulled up beside Stone, he looked at him and smiled before pulling down his visor. Stone acknowledged him and remaining calm, he pulled down his visor and gripped his handlebars.

This was the big one, Vegas was silent, everyone was feeling anxious just staring up at the screens waiting for the crucial moment the bell chimed midnight and the bikes launched off into the unknown.

Stone's heart was now pumping fast, the adrenaline rush was indescribable. The two women lifted the rope, it was just a moment of seconds now. The church bell chimed, the rope dropped to the floor and they were off. The music started up again and the crowds started cheering. The noise was so much louder than the previous races, everyone was amazed the police had not shown up to investigate. Perhaps Butch Maloney had some influence down here too, thought Jimmy.

Stone and Clarence were side by side up to the first bend, they were both full throttle on the straight, the bikes were pushed to the limits. This was a totally different race to the previous one as the stakes were so much higher. Both Stone and Clarence were desperate to win, the risk of injury or death were highly likely should a rider lose concentration for just a split second.

Clarence was starting to lead as they approached the first difficult bend, he was leaning hard but this didn't phase Stone as he kept tight on his tail, waiting for an opportunity to pass him. Their bikes were being stretched to their limits as they were changing up and down through the gears. Spike's Edge was getting closer and closer, just a few more bends to tackle, then a straight home run to the finish line. The whole experience was bringing back memories of his race with Marco Sanchez in the summer and thoughts of his dear mother were entering his mind. Stone was experiencing an adrenaline rush, breathing heavy as thoughts of Rachael were going through his mind. He knew he had to take a risk on the last bend before the straight run to the finish line. This would mean leaning low, scraping his knees on the tarmac, without braking whatsoever. As the last bend came up, he was so close behind Clarence, his front wheel was almost touching. It was now or never so he opened the throttle, lent hard and passed Clarence on the inside. With just a straight road now leading up to Spike's Edge, he felt hopeful but of course it was each rider for himself now and anything could happen.

Stone gave it everything, flat out as fast as his machine would carry him but Clarence was still tight behind him, clearly eager to pass him.

They both raced side by side, with just a few hundred yards before the cliff edge. Suddenly, Clarence's handlebars hit the mountain rock on the inside ledge, causing him to collide with Stone.

Both riders instantly dropped their bikes with just yards before the finish line. Stone was thrown against the tarmac hard and Clarence bounced off the inside mountain edge, their bikes scraping along the road with sparks flying all over the place. Down at Dawson's Point and in Vegas, everyone seemed to feel the impact as the bikes' cameras captured everything. Both riders knew the rules, the first bike to cross the line wins the race, no matter what. Stone slid along the tarmac at high speed until he eventually stopped. He sat up quickly then managed to get to his feet. Thankfully, his leathers and faithful helmet had saved him once again. He looked around at Clarence who was trying to stand up and retrieve his bike, he was limping, clearly hurt by the fall.

Both men knew they had just one option, they would have to try to drag their broken bikes across the line. Remarkably Stone had no serious injuries at all, he tried to stand his bike up but it was severely damaged, the front buckled, unable to turn. Clarence's bike was still running, he tried to pick it up but he was clearly hurt badly, moaning in agony as he tried to level the bike.

Stone started to drag his bike, with all the strength left in his body towards the line. The crowds in Vegas and down below at Dawson's Point were going wild.

Stone and Clarence, like two warriors, continued to fight for the win. Stone's bike was just inches in front of Clarence's as it crossed the line. Clarence accepted defeat, he dropped his bike then fell to the ground clearly in pain.

Stone comforted him, he was bleeding badly from the head, looking concussed and confused.

Although Stone was obviously relieved he had won the money, he was now concerned about Clarence. It was their bikers code, respect your fellow riders, stand shoulder to shoulder in times of need. Luckily Butch had organised a medical team to be on-site, so it was not long before they were up at Spike's Edge seeing to Clarence. Stone was given a lift down to Dawson's Point and when he reached the bottom, he was greeted by Vince Alito.

"Congratulations Stone," he said, then handed him a cheque for 200k. The crowd cheered as Stone made his way over to Jimmy and Katie. His friends threw their arms around him as they knew how important it was for him to win. "Are you okay, do you have any injuries buddy?" asked Jimmy.

"I'm fine bud, just a few scratches," Stone replied.

It wasn't long before the film crew started packing things away and the crowds started to disperse. The whole event had gone incredibly well, Clarence's injuries were not life threatening and although disappointed, he still had his 50k down payment.

Butch Maloney was thrilled by the success of Devil's Run and although concerned for Clarence, the crash had added to the sheer excitement from everyone who had placed bets. Devil's Run featuring at the Tropicana Casino was a huge revenue maker for the casino and proved to be extremely popular with the punters.

Stone was desperate to get to Rachael now, he couldn't wait for Thursday to come round but he had a lot to get organised. He had planned to collect Billy Keegan's RV

Tuesday morning as it was a long drive to Connecticut, at least 38 hours, plus he had to pay his cheque into the bank and retrieve his damaged bike. He had a trailer to collect the bike and he felt once in Mexico, he may be able to get it repaired in a workshop somewhere.

Chapter 22

It was Wednesday night in Connecticut and Rachael was laying in bed with her parents sitting by her side.

She felt very emotional as she knew this may be the last time she would ever see her parents but she knew that leaving was the right thing to do. Her parents would try to control the small time she had left and Rachael was not going to allow this to happen. She knew her parents loved her very much but she felt smothered by their strict hold over her and this could not continue.

As they said goodnight and left her room that evening, Rachael hugged them tight and told them she loved them. They turned around just as they walked out of the door and smiled. Rachael felt guilty as she waved goodbye to them, wondering if this were the last time she would ever see them.

As soon as they were out of sight, she packed her bag and made sure she had her letter to leave for her parents.

Once she was satisfied that everything for the morning was organised, she climbed in bed to get some rest although the excitement of seeing Stone in the morning made sleep difficult.

Stone was well into his journey by now, the RV was running like a dream and his faithful bike was on a trailer behind.

He had planned one more stop Wednesday night then the last part of the journey early Thursday morning.

After a disturbed sleep, Rachael woke around 7am. She got up and took a shower then put some clothes on and even took time to apply some makeup for the first time since she'd been there. She wanted to look the best she could for Stone and to feel like Rachael again.

It was 8.00am when Rachael decided to leave her room. She grabbed her bag and left her letter to her parents on her bedside cabinet. When she approached reception, nurse Thelma was just coming on shift. "Hey beautiful, you're looking great this morning, off anywhere nice?" said Thelma, smiling.

"Morning Thelma, I'm just going to get some fresh air before my parents arrive," she said quickly, pressing the button for the lift. Her heart was pounding, she was full of mixed emotions, guilt, betrayal, excitement, nerves, the works.

As the doors opened, the feeling of freedom gripped her imagination. This is it, this is my life now, my time to be Rachael.

She was early but her anxious eyes started to scan the car park for the silver RV. She couldn't see it and started to panic, then suddenly she heard a voice.

"Rachael, Rachael," she turned around and Stone was standing there, he was wearing a denim jacket, white T-shirt and faded blue Jeans. She had almost forgotten how handsome he was. His smile was like medicine, like a soothing welcoming breeze she had pined for.

He reached out and wrapped his arms around her. Rachael was overcome with emotion and started to cry. "Please, please get me out of here Stone," she sobbed.

Stone escorted her to the side of the hospital, purposely out of the way a bit so as not to be seen by anyone. He opened the passenger door and Rachael climbed in. Stone jumped in the other side and he gave her hand a reassuring squeeze before starting the engine. As they pulled away from the hospital, Rachael looked at Stone, she could not believe they were finally together.

Billy Keegan had been incredibly helpful to Stone, he had given him contact details for some friends he knew in Las Casitas, Mexico. Rosario and Pedro Fernandez were the owners of a small guest house next to their property. Billy Keegan and his wife Ellen had been guests at the beautiful farmhouse for the last 10 years. The Fernandez family had always made them welcome and over the years they had become close friends. They had a son of just six years old called Enrique, after experiencing some fertility complications they had almost given up, when they were blessed in their later years with little Enrique.

Billy had told Rosario and Pedro all about Stone and Rachael and they were willing to let them have the farmhouse for as long as they wanted at a reduced rental cost. There was a hospital close by for emergencies and due to Rachael's condition Rosario was willing to do all she could to help, should the couple, God willing, go the full term with their baby.

With a long trip ahead of them, Stone had decided to break up the journey with at least two overnight stops at drive-in hostels. With a full tank of gas and fifty thousand in the glove compartment, Stone felt comfortable they had more than enough cash to get them to Mexico and pay at least six months rent up front when they arrived.

Meanwhile, back in Connecticut at the Bridgeport Hospital the Jenson's had arrived and after finding no sign of Rachael in her room, just the note on the cabinet, they started to panic. As Susan started to read it, she gasped and immediately became tearful. Christopher grabbed the note from his distraught wife and read it through. He punched the wall with his fist, screwed up the note and threw it at the window, watching it bounce off and hit the floor.

Christopher comforted his wife with a hug, he could feel her body trembling as she sobbed into his arms.

Thelma came into the room to see if everything was ok and she could see the couple were clearly distressed and asked them what was wrong. "It's Rachael, she's run away," said Susan tearfully.

Christopher explained angrily that Rachael had decided to spend the last time she had left with a guy she met over the holiday season in California. She had said that due to her terminal condition, she had wanted to live her last days out close to a beach but has not said where.

Thelma was shocked, although she had found Rachael slightly odd this morning, she hadn't thought much of it.

Dr Lang was called into the room shortly after. The Jenson's had many questions about her condition to which Dr Lang answered honestly and professionally but with no word of the pregnancy. He had explained that the best scenario mortality rate for Rachael would be between a year to eighteen months, however, towards the end she would most likely be unable to walk.

The Jenson's thanked all the staff for what they had done, collected a few things Rachael had left behind and made their way home. Christopher felt confident their daughter would be in touch at some point in the coming weeks and at least for now, that is all they could hope for.

It had been a long few days driving for Stone but now the young lovers were approaching the Mexican border and the whole situation was really starting to sink in.

The RV was ideal for them because whenever they got tired they would pull over, crawl in the back and cuddle up together on the small cosy bed, listening to the birds singing. Stone had been so gentle with Rachael, she still had small patch of shaven hair just above her right ear bearing the biopsy scar which she would try to hide with her hand every time Stone got close but he would gently pull her hand away and kiss her head softly, telling her how beautiful she was.

Being with him made her feel strong and determined to last long enough to have the baby. Luckily at the moment she felt relatively well, with hardly any symptoms at all just feeling more tired than usual on occasions but thankfully that was all. As they got closer to border control, Stone reached into the glove compartment for his passport. Rachael pulled hers out of her bag as they approached the barriers and handed it to Stone.

A stocky built Mexican guy in a smart uniform approached the window. "Passports please," he said, almost emotionless. Stone handed them over through the window. The man looked at them for a few uncomfortable seconds then looked at Stone and Rachael and in a deep Mexican accent, said, "what's the purpose of your visit?"

Stone said, without hesitation, "we're going to stay with some friends in Las Casitas."

"Las Casitas ah, nice, okay thank you," said the Mexican as he handed Stone the passports back through the window.

"Thank you, sir," Stone smiled and drove through the barrier. Just a few hundred yards up the road, Stone turned to Rachael and said, "this is it, we made it baby." Rachael could not be happier at that moment, she could not feel more alive and for a brief moment she had forgotten about her illness.

For the rest of the journey they played songs on the radio and enjoyed the scenery of Las Casitas. The sun was pounding down on them, accompanied by blue skies and ocean views, it was like driving into paradise.

When they arrived at the Fernandez property, it was amazingly beautiful. There was a stunning traditional courtyard, with a few chickens walking around and a large German Shepherd laying on the steps to the main house, completely undeterred by the visitors, just basking in the warm sunshine.

As Stone brought the RV to a standstill just outside the main house, a beautiful middle-aged woman came out to greet them. She was holding the hand of a small boy with black hair and big brown eyes. "Hello, you must be Stone and Rachael?" the woman said, smiling. "My name is Rosario Fernandez and this is my son Enrique."

Stone and Rachael opened their doors, climbed out and walked over to the welcoming lady and her son. "Yes, I'm Michael and this is my girlfriend Rachael."

"It's so lovely to meet you both," Rosario said. The large dog decided to come over and greet them, his tail was wagging and he was clearly a gentle giant. Rachael immediately took a liking to the dog and stroked his head gently. She then shook hands with Rosario and said hello to young Enrique. The place had such a peaceful, happy atmosphere to it and Rachael was so happy Stone had contacted the Fernandes family.

"My husband will be out shortly to show you where you're staying," said Rosario.

Billy had told the Fernandes family everything, so the lovely lady came over to Rachael and gave her a hug. "My darling, if you need anything whilst you are here, please just let me know and I will do my best to get it for you."

Enrique started to talk Spanish to the dog, it was adorable to watch such a small boy play with the giant dog.

Rosario's husband arrived from the back of the house. He was a handsome, typical looking Mexican guy, with salt and pepper hair, a thick moustache and a warm, kind face.

"Hi guys, I'm Pedro, pleased to meet you," he said, with a husky Spanish accent. He shook Stone's hand and kissed Rachael on each cheek, in the traditional manner. "Welcome to Las Casitas, I will show you your place, please follow me," he said.

Stone grabbed a bag in each hand and they followed Pedro to the back of the big house, where there was a smaller property, laid back across the courtyard. It was a cottage style farmhouse painted white with beautiful flowers in hanging baskets on each side of the door.

Pedro opened the door and like the gentleman, he asked Rachael to go in first followed by Stone then himself. Rachael was mesmerised by the place; it was simply perfect she thought. With a small, traditional open plan kitchen, log beamed ceilings and fireplace, it was so cosy. Upstairs consisted of a double bedroom with an adjoining bathroom, just ideal for the young couple's situation. Both Stone and Rachael were very happy with the place. Stone handed Pedro six months rent, cash up front, as the couple were turning down holiday bookings to cater for the couple in need and Stone wanted to show Pedro they were grateful and serious about being around for as long as possible.

"Gracias Senor," said Pedro, shaking Stone's hand firmly. Stone went to get the rest of their bags and Pedro gave them some privacy.

Rachael sat on the sofa in the lounge looking out the patio doors at the back of the room. It was a beautiful view, with the sun kissing the distant mountain tops and a clear view of the sea. As Stone came back in with the last of the bags, he shut the door behind him and sat beside Rachael. "Do you like it baby?" he said.

"I love it, it's perfect babe," said Rachael, smiling. Stone reached out and cuddled her, his arms embraced her tightly and she burrowed her face into his neck.

"I wouldn't mind a siesta," she said with a cheeky grin.

"What a great idea," Stone agreed, smiling.

They walked up the stairs, pulled the curtains, undressed and got in the bed. Rachael snuggled up to Stone and before long the tired couple had fallen asleep.

They were awoken by a knock on the door, Stone looked at the clock on the wall it was 7pm. He put on his t-shirt and Jeans and walked downstairs to see who it was.

Rosario was standing there with a tray of food and wine. "I'm sorry to disturb you but Pedro and I thought you might like some homemade food," she offered the tray to Stone.

"Oh wow, thank you so much Rosario, please thank Pedro for us too," Stone said. Rosario smiled,

"You are most welcome, see you both tomorrow," the lovely woman said. She turned and walked away and Stone closed the door.

Rachael had dressed and walked down the stairs, as Stone placed the tray on the kitchen top. "Look baby, Rosario and Pedro have done us some traditional Mexican food." There was chicken enchilada, tacos stacked with beef and cheese, a plate of fresh salad and a bottle of red wine.

"How sweet of them," said Rachael.

They were both hungry and wasted no time tucking in. Rachael found a corkscrew and two wine glasses in one of the kitchen cupboards. There was a large oak table in the kitchen area with four chairs, perfect for mealtimes, thought Stone as he poured the wine. "Erm, something is missing," said Stone. He got up from the table and opened a few drawers, clearly looking for something. "Bingo!" he said laughing. Rachael could see he had a candle and matches in his hand. He placed the candle in a silver holder already on the table and lit it. "Ah, something else still missing," he said looking around. Rachael found him amusing, the thought of him trying to bring some romance to the table was making her feel so happy inside. What with all that was going on in her mind, these moments made her feel invincible, as if everything was just perfect.

Stone noticed a radio on the shelf, he turned it on and twisted the dial on the tuner until he found the right song to match the mood. A soft piece of salsa music was playing so he turned the volume up slightly then sat at the table. "Now this is much better, he laughed." Rachael was touched by this gesture, she looked at him with a smile.

"I love you Michael Schiano."

"And I love you Rachael Jenson," said Stone. They both laughed and continued eating the lovely food and drinking the wine.

Once they had eaten, they just sat at the table, gazing into one another's eyes over the candlelight, holding hands across the table and talking about everything that had happened to them through the summer. Stone got emotional talking about his mother and Rachael obviously got upset talking about the last few weeks in the hospital. "Stone, why did this have to happen? Why did I have to get sick?" she cried. Stone comforted her and squeezed her hand tightly.

"Darling, I wish I had the answers but I'm afraid I don't. All I can say is that I will do all I can to make the time we have left as special and comfortable for you as I can and when God wants you to join him, I pray my mother will be at heaven's door to meet you and look after you and when God calls for me and I catch the train to heaven, I pray you will be at heaven's door to meet me." As he finished talking his eyes filled with tears and Rachael squeezed his hand.

"Baby, I'll be there for you," she said "but promise you'll try to get a late train." They comforted each other for the rest of the evening before heading to bed.

In the morning, they woke up to the sun cascading through the gap in the curtains and the sound of a cockerel in full voice which made Stone chuckle, "Ok Mr Cockerel, we can hear you," said Stone. Rachael sat up in the bed and stretched her arms.

"Morning handsome," she said, smiling. "So, we have Mr Cockerel every morning, do we?" Stone turned and looked at her and he raised his eyebrows up and down in a suggestive manner.

"You certainly can have Mr Cockerel if you'd like mam," he said laughing.

Rachael swung her arm onto his chest, "hey cheeky guy, I meant the bird outside." Stone found this hilarious and the cute couple laughed until their faces hurt. After they had breakfast, they both decided to go exploring but first Stone took his bike off the trailer and pulled it over to the garage at the side of the property. Rachael noticed it was damaged quite badly. "What happened to your bike, Stone?"

"Oh, I took a little tumble, it's nothing I can't fix," Stone said, playing it down.

They walked a couple of miles up the hillside where they came across a beautiful tree, all on its own at the top of the hillside, almost as if it were looking over the edge at stunning views below. It was such a beautiful spot, the birds were singing and there wasn't a cloud in the sky.

"Stone, can we just sit under the tree for a while and take in the views?"

"Yes, of course baby," he said, whilst taking off his jacket and laying it at the bottom of the tree for Rachael to sit on. Rachael was wearing a beautiful red and white summer dress and Stone didn't want it to get ruined. The couple sat down, holding hands they took in the beautiful sites below.

They sat in silence for a few moments then Rachael said, "Stone, I love this tree, let's call it the Love Tree."

Stone pulled out a small Swiss army knife from his pocket and began to carve their initials into the soft bark. "Where did you get that little knife'?" Rachael chuckled.

"Oh, it was my father's, I carry it with me everywhere. It comes in handy, especially for things like this." He carved RJ & MS 87 inside a love heart. "Ok, it's official, this is our tree and we shall name it The Love Tree." said Stone. Rachael leaned over and kissed him on the cheek,

"I love you Mr Schiano and I love our tree," she said laughing. They both stood up, had a final look over the hills into the distance and then started to walk back to the farmhouse.

Chapter 23

Back in Connecticut, Christopher Jenson had made a series of calls to try and trace where the couple had gone. As expected, he started with Katie Goldberg then Jimmy Nash and finally, Billy Keegan at Redwing's.

They all remained loyal and said they knew nothing but should hear anything they would be in touch. In fact, Billy had said, "Look Mr Jenson, he was here one day, gone next, that's all I can tell you." Jimmy had basically said the same, however, one of the neighbours had informed Mr Jenson about the race that took place a week ago or so. Jenson was not going to let up until he found Rachael.

Weeks turned into months, their time in Las Casitas was passing very quickly. The couple had become incredibly close to the Fernandes family. They had barbecues together, visits to the beach and weekend markets and on some occasions, even to church. The couple had also become fond of the little lad, Enrique and Stone would often play football with him in the courtyard. They also enjoyed evenings in the town square, dancing, listening to live music and singing at the top of their voices. It was an enjoyable existence. If only they could have more time, thought Rosario. She could see Rachael's belly was growing by the day and she was secretly worried about her underlying illness. She prayed to God in the local church that this young girl would live long enough to see her baby born.

Jimmy and Billy had travelled up together to collect the RV so Pedro and Rosario put them up overnight and they all had a wonderful evening down at the beach front. Jimmy was so pleased to see Stone and Rachael together enjoying the time they had left. Before he left, he made Stone promise to call him if he needed anything, as he knew at some point he may need him more than ever. Stone and Rachael thanked Billy for everything he had organised for them and Billy was just so happy it was all working out.

Stone had managed to find a garage and get the bike fixed up so he took Rachael out for rides up to their Love Tree for picnics and down along the beachfront. She absolutely loved their rides out.

Rachael had been keeping a diary of her pregnancy but Rosario had suggested she go with her into town to see if there was any chance she could see a doctor, just to perhaps carry out a scan and check all was well with the baby.

Rosario was well connected in the area and there was a medical centre in town where she had a close friend called Angelina Garcia who happened to be a midwife there.

Over dinner one evening, Stone agreed this would be a good idea, so the couple decided to see Miss Garcia.

So, on Monday morning after young Enrique had gone off to school, they all drove to the Medical Centre. Rosario had explained on the phone to her friend what the couple's situation was and that her medical records were held in Connecticut.

Somehow, Angelina had contacted Dr Lang's office in confidence and Rachael's notes were faxed over.

Angelina was waiting in reception to greet them all when they arrived. She had a warm friendly smile and Rachael felt instantly at ease.

Rosario was invited into the examination room by the couple whilst Angelina organised the ultrasound.

Everyone waited in anticipation whilst Angelina began to look at the baby's progress on the monitor. She carried out a thorough examination of the baby and assured the couple everything she could see on the monitor was looking perfect, however, she did think a C-Section would be safer as she felt a natural birth could cause Rachael to have another seizure or worse and felt it would be a good idea for her to see a doctor.

After the scan, they were introduced to Doctor Vincent who understood Rachael's illness. He asked Rachael lots of questions to see if she was showing any signs of confusion, dizziness or nausea, as these were common symptoms of her illness. Remarkably, she had none of them but she did explain to the doctor that she got tired very easily and he said that was expected with the pregnancy.

Dr Vincent said he'd like to see them every week leading up to the birth to check on to Rachael and make sure the baby was doing ok.

At her 36 week check up, Dr Vincent felt it would be advisable to arrange for her C-Section to ensure the safety of Rachael and her baby. Although the couple were taken by surprise, they trusted his judgement. Rosario stayed with Rachael whilst Stone went back to the cottage to collect a bag with everything she needed.

After being made comfortable in a private room, Rachael started to feel nervous and excited at the same time. She had almost made it, her baby would soon be in her arms. In a strange way it felt as if she finally had some control over her illness, as if to say, 'yes, the cancer may kill me but I will live on in my child.' It was like having the last laugh and sticking two fingers up at the disease she thought.

When Stone got back, he found Rachael in her room rigged up to a machine which was monitoring the baby's heartbeat.

Dr Vincent came into the room, "Okay guys, I feel we shouldn't waste any more precious time. I have everything arranged in surgery to bring your baby into the world," he said, smiling.

Rachael and Stone were a little in shock as this morning they thought they were just coming in for the usual check on their baby's progress and now their baby would be born. It was a very surreal situation. They agreed time was precious and they understood the prospect of going the full term could be dangerous for Rachael.

Stone was asked to put on a gown, mask and shoe covers as Rachael was given an epidural injection in her lower back. They were then taken to surgery, where Dr Vincent himself was going to deliver the baby.

He greeted the couple and Rachael was prepared for the procedure. Stone was holding her hand whilst the doctor made the incision. It seemed like forever when all the sudden they heard the tiny cries of a baby. The doctor passed the baby to the nurse, "I'm pleased to say you have a healthy baby girl," she said, smiling. Stone and Rachael kissed and started to cry as the baby was handed to them in a blanket. She weighed 8lb 2oz with lots of black hair, the cutest face and the couple could not have been happier.

Rosario was waiting outside and Stone couldn't wait to tell her the great news. He opened the door with tears of joy running down his face.

"Rosario, we have a beautiful baby girl." Rosario came over and hugged him tightly.

"Congratulations! How's Rachael doing?" she asked.

Stone explained she was doing well and that Rosario could see them both when they were back in her room. On his return to theatre, Rachael was being cared for by the nurses.

"Sir, if you'd like to go back to Rachael's room, we will bring her and your daughter to you in a few moments," said one of the nurses.

"Sure, that would be great thank you," said Stone. He kissed Rachael on the cheek and headed to her room with Rosario.

When Rachael and the baby arrived, Rosario walked over to the cot and glanced in at the baby. "Wow, look at you, you little darling. Do you have a name, little lady?" said the lovely Rosario.

"Her name is Maria," said Rachael as she reached out for Stone's hand. Stone was so touched by Rachael's decision to name their daughter after his dear mother.

"That's a beautiful name," said Rosario, smiling.

Rachael was doing incredibly well under the circumstances and it wasn't long before the medical staff were happy to let her go home. It had been almost nine months since Rachael's diagnosis and she had thanked God each day for the precious time spent with Stone and now she had completed her main goal to live through the pregnancy.

Back at the cottage, Rosario and Pedro had been amazing. They'd given the couple Enrique's baby things, including a cot, pram, bedding and some clothes. They'd even stocked up on nappies and formula milk. Rachael had tried breastfeeding for a few weeks but the doctors felt this may not be ideal for a long period as they thought it may be too much for Rachael. This way, Stone could help with the feeds, especially at night.

Stone had wanted to get something for Rachael to mark the birth of their daughter so he had secretly picked up a pendant in Las Casitas and had it engraved with their names on it. He was waiting until Rachael was able to ride on his bike with him so he could give it to her at their special place. That time had come, so he asked Rosario if she would mind looking after baby Maria whilst they went for a quick ride which, of course, she was delighted to do.

Stone told Rachael and she was happy to go out for a while. They headed straight up the mountain road to their Love Tree. Stone had taken a blanket which he laid down for them both. Once they were settled, he pulled out the pendant and gave it to Rachael. She looked at their names engraved on it and smiling, she said, "thank you babe, I love it!" Stone put it around her neck and kissed her softly on the lips. He then pulled out his small knife and proceeded to add their daughters name into the bark of the tree.

"We did it baby, we are now a family, just you, me and baby Maria." He reached out and hugged her tightly. As Stone squeezed her hand, he could feel Rachael's hand trembling in his. He turned to look at her, her eyes were rolling in her head then her whole body started to shake. Stone was beside himself, "Rachael, Rachael, baby, baby what's wrong?" he said, with a trembling voice. He laid her back gently and put his jacket under her head to protect her from injuring herself as her body continued to spasm.

She was unresponsive, poor Stone just didn't know what to do, apart from sit and comfort her. After a short time, her body stopped shaking and she regained some form of consciousness. "Babe, can you hear me? Rachael, can you hear me?" he shouted frantically. In a weak, soft voice she answered.

"Yes, I can hear you, what happened?"

"Darling, you really scared me, I think you had a seizure baby."

Rachael started to breath heavily and she tried to stand up but her legs wouldn't seem to move. "I can't feel my legs Stone," she began to cry.

"Let's get you home and we can speak to Dr Vincent and see what he thinks," Stone was trying to sound positive but deep down he knew this was not a good sign. He picked Rachael up and started heading down the mountain road, leaving his bike by the tree.

Rachael burrowed her face into his neck and shut her eyes. It was a long walk down but eventually he approached the gates of the Fernandez estate. Pedro was washing his jeep and immediately rushed over. "What's happened, are you okay?"

"I think Rachael has had a seizure, erm, we need to get her inside and call a doctor," Stone said nervously. Pedro rushed behind the house to get Rosario who was holding the baby. They all pulled together making Rachael comfortable on the settee in the lounge. She was coherent but her speech seemed slurred. Rosario wasted no time phoning her friend at the medical centre and she had managed to arrange the doctor to come to the house.

It was no time at all before Dr Vincent pulled up in his car. He rushed into the house with his black leather-bound medical bag.

"Thank you for coming so quickly doctor," said Stone. Dr Vincent focused on his patient immediately.

"Rachael, can you hear me? It's Dr Vincent," Rachael opened her eyes.

"Yes I can hear you Dr," brave Rachael responded.

Dr Vincent did a full examination and asked to speak with Stone privately outside.

"Look, I'm going to be straight with you, I've read Rachael's notes fully and to be frank, I'm amazed she has gone this long with no major setbacks, not mentioning the miracle of bearing a child. This seizure appears to have been far more destructive than the first one. Unfortunately, she may not be able to regain her mobility. Slurred speech, dizzy spells and moments of confusion will become more frequent as the tumour increases in size. I should really suggest she comes into my care now, however, she doesn't seem to be in any pain right now and you may even find by tomorrow she has improved slightly but trust me young man when I say I don't think she has long now, so if there are any plans you may have, I'd certainly get moving on them," said Dr Vincent.

Stone took a deep breath and sat down on the edge of the wall by the gates with his hands on his head. "How long does she have Doc?" Dr Vincent put his hand on Stone's shoulder.

"A few weeks, possibly a month but you must inform me if she experiences any pain so we can send someone down with some pain relief. I think she'll be happier here with you and the baby and I know the Fernandez family will look after you, they're good people, I've known them for many years."

He walked over to his car and opened the back doors, pulling out a wheelchair.

"I'll leave this with you, she will need it now," said the doctor.

Stone thanked him and he drove away. Pedro came out to see what was going on, he could see Stone was standing there in a daze with the wheelchair.

"Stone, are you okay my friend?" said Pedro.

"Yes thank you, the doctor has left this for Rachael, he said she will need it now." Stone replied sadly.

Pedro put his arm around Stone and comforted him as they walked back in the house. Rachael was sleeping on the sofa with Rosario sitting in a chair by her side with baby Maria fast asleep in her day cot. Rachael was looking peaceful and in no discomfort at all.

"Look Stone, I think under the circumstances I should have baby Maria overnight for you so it will give you time to see to Rachael and then we can review the situation tomorrow," offered Rosario.

"If you're sure Rosario, thank you!" Rosario and Pedro could see the poor lad was extremely distressed.

"She was so happy when I gave her the pendant, it all happened so fast. I left my bike there, I better get it I suppose," Stone mumbled, he was clearly finding the whole episode a massive strain.

"Look amigo, I will take care of your bike and Rosario will take care of Maria, just take care of Rachael now and we can talk tomorrow," said Pedro. Stone shook Pedro's hand and kissed Rosario on both cheeks.

The Fernandez couple always wanted more children and they would have loved to have a girl, so looking after baby Maria was a task Rosario secretly really enjoyed. The couple made sure Stone and Rachael were settled and they left the house with Maria.

Stone glanced over at Rachael, there was a slight breeze coming through the window, so he closed it slightly and went to get some more blankets from the bedroom. Rachael was still sleeping so Stone decided to call his best friend Jimmy.

There was a phone in the hallway so he could keep an eye on Rachael at the same time. He knew Jimmy would be at the garage, so he called Redwing's. Greg answered the phone.

"Hi Greg, it's Stone, hey man is Jimmy there?"

"Hey buddy, yeah sure, I'll just call him. It's great to hear your voice man," Greg replied.

"You too buddy."

Jimmy took the receiver from Greg. "Stone, what's up bro?" he said with concern in his voice.

"It's happening Jimmy, everything's happening. The baby's here and she's well but poor Rachael has taken a bad turn today. I'm so scared Jimmy, I can't lose her now. I thought we would have longer, I don't know what to do."

"Okay man, calm down, you'll get through this," Jimmy said. Stone told him about how well Rachael had been up to now, all about the baby and how good the Fernandez family had been but his main concern now was the Jenson's. He knew Rachael had been writing the odd letter but he felt that it was only right for them to know that Rachael had suffered another seizure, and there was a chance she may only have weeks left.

"Jimmy, I think they should know where we are now but Rachael doesn't want them to know about the baby because she feels they will take her from me. I can't have that and I've promised her I won't let that happen."

"Look buddy, I'll let them know and if you want them to come to Mexico, I will show them where you are," said Jimmy.

Rachael started to come to, groaning a little. "Jimmy, I gotta go buddy, Rachael needs me. Bye buddy and thanks again," said Stone.

He put the receiver down and went to comfort Rachael. She opened her eyes and looked at Stone. "Where am I? Where's Maria?"

"Stay still baby, just rest now darling, we'll talk in the morning," Stone replied. He then went upstairs to get the mattress from the bedroom and made it up by the sofa. He gently lifted Rachael onto the mattress and he lay beside her stroking her hair until she drifted off again. The couple went right through to the morning, cuddled up together tightly as the cockerel sounded in the distance.

Rachael opened her eyes and looked at Stone. "Morning handsome," she said in a soft voice, as if totally unaware of the previous day's events. Stone was relieved by her reaction but he knew something was not quite right.

"Baby how do you feel? Do you recall what happened yesterday?" he asked quietly. Rachael opened her eyes slightly wider in a state of confusion.

"No, what happened?" she said, slightly slurring.

"Baby, you had another seizure by the Love Tree, just after I gave you the pendant." Rachael lifted her hand to her neck and held the pendant in her fingers.

"Yes, I seem to remember you putting it around my neck and we sat down together but that's all I remember," she said.

Rachael tried to get up but she still had problems with her legs. Stone helped her up but she could not walk properly and got terribly upset. Stone comforted her and explained that due to the seizure this was expected. He carried her to the bathroom and helped her to the toilet and ran her a bath.

Suddenly her mind seemed to clear and in a huge panic asked where Maria was. Stone explained everything and lifted her in the bath. As each hour passed by, she seemed to get some feeling back in her legs and her speech seemed to return to normal. Stone knew that although this was encouraging, he also remembered what Dr Vincent had said and he was not going to tell Rachael as he felt this would be too much for her.

When Rachael was dressed, she tried again to walk and managed to take small steps. She was keen to see Maria so Stone went over to Rosario to collect their baby. He thanked Rosario and Pedro for having her and he asked if he could shoot into town a bit later as he wanted to buy an engagement ring and two wedding rings.

They were both very excited at this news and would comfort Rachael and help with the baby whilst he was gone. Rosario also said she knew a priest that could marry them if they wanted her to arrange something. Stone smiled and said a big yes please.

When Rosario came over, Stone told Rachael he was calling into town to get some nappies and milk, unbeknown to her he was getting ready to propose. Stone could see his bike back under the car port at the side of the house as dear Pedro had collected it for him.

Rosario noticed Rachael was gradually returning to her usual self and this was nice to witness after such a scare the previous day. She could plainly see the love in Rachael's eyes for her child and it was heartbreaking to watch a mother and child having precious last moments together.

Stone was back after a couple of hours. He placed the nappies and milk on the table in the lounge and winked at Rosario, as if to say, 'I have the rings'.

Rosario smiled and as he walked her to the door she said to Stone. "I'll see what I can do and get back to you but in the meantime if you need us, please don't hesitate to shout." said Rosario. She was truly a wonderfully kind lady, Stone thought.

Chapter 24

Jimmy had managed to get Christopher Jenson's telephone number in Connecticut from Katie Goldberg.

At first the Jenson's were angry but then they soon realised Jimmy was just passing on a message. They'd prayed news would come eventually but had hoped Rachael would have defied the doctors and exceeded their expectations of her mortality and perhaps be able to return with them to Connecticut.

Jimmy reassured them his friend was taking good care of her and it was him that had asked for them to be notified.

The Jenson's started planning to travel to Mexico. Jimmy intended to meet them at Benito Juarez in a few days after his call, with a specialist doctor summoned by Rachael's father.

It would be a long ride for Jimmy but he knew this would give his friends time to complete their plans before the Jenson's arrived.

Back at the Fernandez place, Rosario had been terribly busy trying to arrange a quick wedding for the stricken couple. She had dug out her own wedding dress with Rachael in mind. Back when Rosario married Pedro, she was roughly the same size as the soon to be bride and thought as time was of the essence perhaps Rachael may want to try it on. Rosario had spoken to her Priest and he was happy to marry the couple by their special place at the top of the hill, overlooking Las Casitas.

She had also planned for there to be a small reception party on their property and had called on a few friends to arrange flowers and a buffet.

All Stone had to do now was propose to Rachael. Stone had asked Rachael if she would come back to the Love Tree with him so they could relax again in their favourite place. At first Rachael seemed hesitant as the last time they went there on the bike she was taken ill but deep down she knew that they could have been anywhere when this happened.

Pedro had said Stone could take his jeep as the wheelchair would go in the back just in case they needed it. Rosario looked after baby Maria and the couple made their way to Pedro's jeep. Rachael was still finding it difficult to walk, so Stone told her he had the wheelchair in case she felt tired.

The couple drove out the gates and straight back up to their favourite place in the world.

When they got to the top, Stone got the wheelchair out for Rachael and wheeled her over to their tree. He turned the wheelchair a round to face the beautiful views. Rachael stared out to the distant hills with a smile on her face.

Stone reached in his pocket and got down on one knee and presented Rachael with the ring. "Rachael, will you marry me." Rachael's eyes filled up with tears of joy, she looked deep into his eye.

"Yes, yes of course I will, I love you so much," Stone put the ring on her finger, she loved it and it fit her finger perfectly. In white gold with a cluster of small diamonds enthused into both sides with a larger diamond mounted in the centre. "It's a beautiful baby," she said smiling.

He then sprang another surprise and said the wedding was organised for the weekend and that Rosario had been busy organising everything for them. "How would you like to get married here Rach, at our special place?"

"Oh my, really, that would be amazing baby." Deep down in her heart she knew that her time was soon to be over, so marrying the man she loved straight away, seemed simply perfect.

When they got back to the house Rosario was waiting at the door holding little Maria. She was so excited to see Rachael after the news. Stone carried Rachael into the house and Rosario had already brought the dress in for her to look at. She hugged Rachael. "Congratulations, I hear someone is getting married," she laughed.

Stone was asked to wait outside whilst Rachael tried on the dress. He could hear excitement through the window, so he guessed the dress was a success.

"Ok you can come back in now," said Rosario cheerfully.

The wedding was to be at the Love Tree on Saturday afternoon. Pedro had organised an archway of flowers and seating for around 20 guests looking out onto the stunning view.

All those helping with the planning were guests too, so at least there would be witnesses so Rachael and Stone would feel supported. The only person Stone was missing was Jimmy, his best man although he hadn't asked him yet. He was likely to be leaving in the morning, so Stone phoned him to explain everything. Jimmy said, "Look I know you don't have much time but I've arranged to meet the Jenson's and bring them up after you told me to tell them about Rachael's condition."

"I know buddy, it's the right thing to do but I can't have them here Saturday, they will spoil the wedding and Rachael will be really pissed with me. Plus, I would really love you and Billy to come if possible and I wondered if you would be my best man?" Jimmy was lost for words and he was slightly taken back.

"Erm, okay, yes, I'd love to man. Let me speak to Billy, maybe we can fly up Friday evening and be there for the wedding and then I can meet the Jenson's Sunday."

"Oh man, I wish now I hadn't asked you to call them but after that last seizure I got scared and thought I was going to lose her. Let's wait until we're married and then arrange a meeting."

Stone asked Pedro to take a few thousand dollars for all the flowers, food and preparations that Rosario and himself were making. At first Pedro tried to decline his offer but Stone insisted as the couple had been so generous and he didn't want this to hinder them financially in any way.

Friday night came around very quickly and as a surprise for Rachael, Jimmy and Billy had arrived with Katie Goldberg just in time for a few evening celebrations.

The men sat in the courtyard with a few drinks and Rachael, Rosario, Katie and baby Maria stayed in the house. Rachael was so happy to see Katie arrive, it was a very emotional moment. Everyone had a lovely evening and then settled down around midnight, as the big day was approaching fast.

Stone spent the morning with Jimmy, Billy and Pedro, with little Enrique playing football in the yard and the friendly dog just walking around wagging his tail. As the time got close to 1pm the lads all got washed and dressed in their suits. Both Jimmy and Billy had brought along light coloured suits with crisp white shirts. Pedro had a white suit and even little Enrique had a tailored jacket and trousers. Stone had brought along his cream chino style trousers, a light blue blazer style jacket, with a white shirt and white tie. It was a strange combination but it seemed to work and considering everything had been arranged in the last few days, it was the best he could do. The lads then made their way up to the tree where the priest was waiting. It looked beautiful up there. Pedro and a few of the locals had done an amazing job. There was a grand looking archway leading up to the tree and chairs with white covers on and silver balloons swaying in the breeze around the tree. It was simply breathtaking and they had even somehow placed an organ by the tree, powered by a small generator.

Stone stood nervously as the guests arrived. Billy took a seat at the front and Jimmy stood by his friend waiting for the bride. Stone gave Jimmy the rings just as a white Mercedes pulled up to the side. Rachael was helped from the car but she was having problems walking so Billy jumped up and took her arm on the right side and Katie took her left arm. She was determined to walk down the aisle and not be pushed in the wheelchair. The organ started to play the familiar wedding march and Rachael walked towards Stone. She looked stunning in Rosario's dress and as she pulled back her veil to reveal her dark curled hair and tanned skin, she took Stone's breath away.

She stood by his side and he gripped her hand tightly and looked into her eyes. "You look beautiful darling,"

"You don't look so bad either." The priest then introduced himself and the wedding was underway.

When the moment came for the rings, Jimmy stood up and presented them to the Priest. Rachael's face was a picture as Stone slid the ring over her finger, another perfect fit she thought whilst admiring it on her hand. Then Stone's ring was pushed over his finger by Rachael and the couple could not have been happier.

"You may kiss the bride," said the Priest with a huge smile on his face. Everyone cheered and the couple kissed. Rosario and Katie had tears running down their faces as they watched the couple embrace each other. It was such a beautiful moment and so clear to see how much they loved one another.

Little Maria was only a few weeks old and she was sitting on Rosario's lap unaware of the day's events, mostly sleeping through these early days. Stone helped his wife back to the car to head back to the Fernandez house where a party had been laid on. It was a wonderful do, everyone enjoyed it. Jimmy had made an emotional speech where he spoke about his lifelong friend and he spoke affectionately about Rachael's bravery, not forgetting the safe arrival of baby Maria. The married couple even managed a dance to a song called Love Bites by Def Leppard which was one of their favourites. Rachael whispered the first few lines of the song in Stone's ear,

"When you make love, do you look in the mirror," she giggled. Stone was so happy she hadn't lost her sense of humour. Bill and Jimmy got a little choked up watching the couple slowly move around the courtyard. Rachael had both her arms around Stone's neck and he supported her weight with his arms locked around her. It was clear to see her legs were struggling to move but Stone held her tightly.

The wedding was enjoyed by everyone and as the evening drew in, Rachael became incredibly tired, so the couple thanked everyone and went back to the house.

Rosario had baby Maria for the evening, she was so very fond of her and Stone was so grateful.

Jimmy was expecting to meet the Jenson's the following day, he had planned to call them in the morning. Billy had a flight booked to go early the next morning, so he said goodnight to everyone and made his way to one of Rosario's guest rooms.

Chapter 25

Sunday morning was a warm sunny start to the day. Pedro gave Billy Keegan a lift to the airport to catch his early flight home.

Back at the Fernandez estate, the faithful cockerel was in full voice and Jimmy was up, pacing around his room nervously as he knew he'd arranged to meet the Jenson's.

Stone was cuddled up with Rachael in their bed, slightly hungover he kissed the back of Rachael's neck, she was in a deep sleep and did not stir. So, Stone closed his eyes and drifted off again.

Later that morning, around 10am, Rosario knocked on the door to see how the newly weds were doing. Stone heard the door and looked at the clock, he was amazed that it was so late. He jumped up and went to the door to greet Rosario.

"Good morning Rosario, I'm sorry we seem to overslept. Thank you for having Maria," said Stone.

"Oh, that's okay, she's still sleeping actually, I just wondered how Mrs Schiano was doing?" she laughed cheekily.

Stone smiled, "she seems to still be sleeping Rosario, I'll let you know as soon as she's up."

"Okay sure, if you need anything, please let me know."

Stone went back upstairs to see how Rachael was, she was still fast asleep. He walked up closer to the bed, "Rach, darling, Rach," he called but there was no answer.

His heart started to pound as his eyes stared at the covers trying to detect movement or any signs of breathing. He walked even closer to her side of the bed, listening for the sound of her breath.

Thankfully, he detected her quiet breathing so gently called again, "Rach, Rach, baby can you hear me?" Rachael started to stir, she opened her eyes slightly and answered him.

"Hi handsome," she said in an incredibly quiet, timid voice.

Stone was so relieved, he reached over to kiss her on the cheek. "How are you feeling this morning babe."

Rachael had shut her eyes again, clearly not hearing him. This worried Stone as she didn't seem very coherent. He sat on the edge of the bed, wondering if by disturbing her he may cause another seizure or something, so he decided to take a shower, get dressed and then try to wake her again.

As he got dressed, he could see Rachael trying to wake up but it was clear she was struggling. He rushed over to her, kneeling by the side of the bed. Rachael said in a soft voice, "Stone, baby, can you take me to the Love Tree?"

"What's wrong baby?" said Stone.

"I think it's time," she said quietly. The young, frightened Stone ran downstairs and straight over to

Rosario's house. Jimmy was pacing up and down in the courtyard.

"Buddy, what's wrong?" he said. Stone explained that something was wrong and that Jimmy should contact the Jenson's.

"Buddy, please get them on the first available flight here, I don't think we have much time Jimmy."

Rosario came to the door immediately, Stone explained something was seriously wrong with Rachael and that she was asking him to take her to their special place.

He then ran back over to the house and up the stairs as fast as he could. Rachael was still laying in the same position.

"Baby I'm going to take you to our tree." He helped Rachael to sit up and then to stand, with his support. He helped her to the bathroom and she asked if he could help her into her favourite summer dress with the red flowers on. She made a further request which shocked Stone.

"Please baby, take me on the back of your bike to the tree, I can hold on tightly, it's not far." Although this was not ideal, Stone agreed as he knew this may be his beautiful wife's last request.

He carried her downstairs where Rosario was standing in the courtyard holding baby Maria.

Rachael kissed Maria on her head and told her she loved her with all of her heart. She hugged dear Rosario thanking her for everything. Tears filled the beautiful Mexican woman's eyes as she knew Rachael was saying goodbye.

Jimmy helped Rachael onto the back of his friend's bike and Rachael held tightly around Stone's waist with her head resting on his back.

The bike gently pulled out of the courtyard and headed up towards the tree. Rachael held Stone with all her might. She was at peace with her fate now and just wanted their final moments to be special.

Stone pulled the bike over as far under the tree as he could and after placing a blanket under it, he lifted her off, placing her down gently onto the soft fabric. There were still signs of the wedding, loose confetti blowing in the light breeze and some balloons attached to the branches above them.

The couple sat down with their backs to the base of the tree and looked out to the sea in the distance. Rachael leaned her head on Stone's shoulder and the couple just held hands and spoke about the special times they had in Las Casitas and their beautiful daughter. Rachael begged Stone not to let her parents take Maria from him. She had noticed how strong the bond was becoming with Maria and Rosario and wondered if the Fernandez family would continue to help once she had gone.

Stone found it hard to discuss but didn't want her to worry about anything, so he just agreed with everything she said.

It was exactly 1pm when Rachael took her pendant off and put it in Stone's hand. She told him she loved him and that she wanted him to have it, her voice seemed weaker, faded somehow. Stone could feel he was losing her and as she laid her head on his lap, he ran his fingers through her hair to comfort her. Her breathing became laboured and through his silent tears, he talked to her about anything that came into his mind until she took her last breath. Stone knew she had gone, still stroking her hair, the tears streamed down his face. He could hear a car in the distance approaching as he sat with Rachael still laying on his lap.

The car pulled over, with an ambulance behind. Jimmy got out of the car, followed by Christopher and Susan Jenson.

As Rachael's parents, accompanied by a medical team, approached the couple, it soon became clear that Rachael had gone. Utter heartbreak was etched on Stone's tear stained face.

Susan and Christopher stood back a few moments whilst the medical team looked after Rachael. They had to prise open Stone's fingers which were holding Rachael's hand to separate them. After Rachael was assessed by the team, she was confirmed dead at 1.47pm. Christopher fell to his knees crying, whilst Susan rushed over to hold her daughter, kissing her frantically.

Jimmy tried to comfort Stone but he was in complete shock. Christopher looked at Stone, "This is your fault, this is all your damn fault, you took my baby girl!" he shouted.

This was too much for Stone, he ran over to his bike, started the engine and sped off as fast as he could up the mountain road. Jimmy ran after him, as far as his legs would carry him, shouting out Stone's name.

Rachael was taken to the ambulance, Susan got in the back with her, whilst Christopher sat in the hire car that Jimmy had driven, and with his head in his hands, he cried out in pain. The ambulance slowly started to make its way back down the dusty track, past the Fernandez property. Rosario and Pedro watched as both the vehicles passed their gates. They could see Rachael's father was clearly distressed so it didn't take much working out what was likely to have happened. Rosario started to sob; Pedro embraced his wife to comfort her, with tears in his eyes. Baby Maria was resting peacefully in the house, thankfully too young to know anything about the tragic events which were unfolding, totally unaware that her grandparents had just driven past her whilst she lay sleeping.

Stone had reached the top of the mountain, he jumped off the bike and started to pace up and down, holding his head in his hands, shaking it back and forth, refusing to accept what had just happened. The cliff edge was just a few yards away, it was like Spike's Edge, another sudden drop straight over into the sea he thought. For a split-second Stone wondered why his life had led to a cliff edge, was this my destiny, is this how it ends, thought Stone.

The broken hearted young man reached in his pocket to find Rachael's pendant and in a moment of pure heartbreak and sadness he threw the pendant over the edge. It was also a wild sense of anger that had driven him to do this and the moment the pendant slipped away from his fingers, he instantly regretted it. He watched it land on the rocks below, with the waves crashing over it.

He started to curse himself, now pacing up and down anxiously, walking back and forth from the cliff edge. Stone could hear Jimmy screaming his name, getting closer and closer, so he jumped back on his bike and started the engine. Jimmy could hear the bike at full revs as he was getting closer so he was worried he'd be too late. Stone swung the bike round over to the far side of the mountain edge where he could see the ambulance in the far distance. The cruel cold words of Jenson were still ringing in his ears and Rachael's last breath was continuously looping in his brain, it was all getting too overwhelming for him. In a moment of pure pain and madness, Stone screamed Rachael's name, opened the clutch and raced towards the cliff edge as fast as he could, changing up through the gears. Still shouting her name at the top of his voice, he looked at the sky, he could feel the heat on his face burning the salty tears away, he smiled and said quietly to himself, "I love you Rachael, wait for me."

Jimmy was almost there, he could hear the bike getting louder and his distraught friend screaming out Rachael's name. Suddenly the engine revs seem to fade, an eerie silence stopped him in his tracks then suddenly the sickening sound of an almighty explosion could be heard. Jimmy ran over to the edge of the hill and could see the wreckage of Stone's bike smashed into the rocks, just a few feet away from the sea. Jimmy screamed his friend's name, fell to his knees and cried into his hands.

Chapter 26

Mexico, some years later.

Along a dusty track, a motorcycle could be heard heading up through the hills of Las Casitas. A man in his 50's, with a white beard, tanned face and dark glasses, was riding his Harley Davidson up towards the top of the hill, where Rachael and Stone had spent their precious last moments. The man passed the Fernandez property and continued to climb the track where he reached a large tree. He parked his motorcycle underneath and climbed off. The man took his helmet off and reached into his saddle bag, where he pulled out a beautiful bunch of flowers. He walked over to the tree and laid the flowers down, just underneath some carved initials. The man kissed his fingers and pressed them on the tree. He sat down underneath the branches for a while enjoying the view, listening to the birds sing.

Just about an hour had passed when the man lifted himself back onto his feet, brushing the dust off his jeans as he walked over to his motorcycle. He put his helmet back on, started his bike and headed off back down the track.

As the man reached the Fernandez property, he pulled in through the gates and into the courtyard. He could see another Harley Davidson parked by the main house with a guy standing beside it. He was around the same age, with grey hair and white stubble. As he pulled his bike closer, the man called his name. "Stone, buddy, how are you?"

"Hey Jimmy, I'm good thanks," he answered.

"I take it you've already been up to the tree?" asked Jimmy. Stone nodded, feeling a little emotional. He had laid flowers by the tree every year on the anniversary of Rachael's passing.

"I'll never forget that tragic day, I really thought you'd gone over the edge man."

"I know, I'm so sorry you had to witness that Jimmy, I was so close to going over with the bike but realised my daughter needed me and that's what Rachael would have wanted." said Stone.

The door to the main house opened and a beautiful olive-skinned, dark-haired woman appeared. "How'd it go pa?" asked the women.

"Fine thanks darling," answered Stone. He hugged her and they walked towards the house arm in arm.

Jimmy followed behind, "How are you Maria?"

"I'm good thanks uncle Jimmy, Frankie can't wait to see you," she answered. With that, the door burst open and a little boy ran out. "Grandpa, grandpa!" he shouted as he sprinted over to greet Stone.

"Hey champ, how you doing, little man?" asked Stone.

"I'm good grandpa, I missed you!" the little lad shouted. Sadly, Pedro had died a few years back but lived long enough to witness his son Enrique and Maria marry and have gorgeous little Frankie. The couple had been sweethearts from a young age, eventually settling down on the Fernandez estate.

Rosario soon appeared at the door looking rather emotional, she immediately walked over and hugged Stone, with tears in her eyes.

"Are you okay Rosario?"

"Frankie and I were at the beach this morning and by some miracle Frankie found this," she opened her hand to reveal a small pendant. Stone looked at it closely.

"Surely it can't be Rachael's pendant can it?" His eyes filled with tears. Rosario placed it in Stone's hand. "It is her pendant! Frankie, you have no idea what this means to me. You've made grandpa so happy." The little guy was chuffed he had made everyone happy, he danced around the courtyard kicking up dust and singing at the top of his voice.

Stone looked up at the sky, as if staring into the heavens to see Rachael.

"It's a miracle," said Rosario behind him. Stone turned to look at her.

"Yes, it is, my Rachael must have had something to do with this. It truly is a miracle."

Maria could see her father was becoming emotional so she walked over and gave him a huge hug. Jimmy put his arm around Rosario and little Frankie started hugging Stone's legs and they pulled themselves together in one big family hug. Stone looked up at the sky, smiling and said,

"Thank you, Rachael"

The End

Printed in Great Britain
by Amazon